Cooper And The Queen

COOPER AND THE QUEEN

By

Don Hunter

Mirador Publishing
www.miradorpublishing.com

First Published in Great Britain 2011 by Mirador Publishing

Copyright © 2011 by Don Hunter

All rights reserved. No part of this publication may be reproduced or transmitted, in any form or by any means, without permission of the publishers or author. Excepting brief quotes used in reviews.

First edition: 2011

Any reference to real names and places are purely fictional and are constructs of the author. Any offence the references produce is unintentional and in no way reflects the reality of any locations or people involved.

A copy of this work is available through the British Library.

ISBN : 978-1-908200-26-6

Mirador Publishing
Mirador
Wearne Lane
Langport
Somerset
TA10 9HB

Author's Note

I would like to state that the events (other than those already in the public domain) are in no way intended to be anything other than a fictional account. They in no way represent the real or actual events. Neither do they represent the opinions of those public figures represented in this fictional narrative. With that in mind, sit back and enjoy a really good story.

Don Hunter grew up in Cumbria, attended Workington Grammar School and did his national service in the army before training as a teacher at Chester. He taught high school in England and in British Columbia, where he gained his B.Ed, at the University of B.C., before joining the Vancouver Province daily newspaper as a reporter and feature writer and eventually senior columnist. He is the author of three other books and a credited screenwriter. See more at www.donhunter.ca

For June, Susie and Taryn.

Prologue

Today

LONDON (CP)- London newspapers today report that Queen Elizabeth II has decided to abdicate. The reports link the Queen's decision to years of unrest within the Royal Family and claim that she has persuaded the Prince of Wales to step aside, making way for his elder son, Prince William, to become England's next Monarch.

A further report, from a Canadian Press affiliate in Vancouver, claims the Queen intends to spend an extended period in her favourite Commonwealth country, Canada, where she and the Duke of Edinburgh currently are enjoying a private visit.

**Central Vancouver Island,
British Columbia,
Canada.**

The Duke of Edinburgh was not going gently.
No surprise there, Matt Cooper thought. Philip had fought the idea since it was leaked to the London press.
But it's over, Philip. Pink-slip time. When she goes, you go. And she is *going. We're all going. She's had enough. We've all had enough. Let it go, man.* Cooper leaned his rangy frame against the granite wall of the sprawling oceanside mansion and groaned quietly as the Duke rejoined the fray, his patrician nose leading the charge from under a shapeless black baseball cap that Jesse Lee had found for him. A short-sleeved navy golf shirt with an anchor design on the breast pocket was tucked into a pair of smartly pressed Dockers. The Duke's thumbs were hooked into his side pockets, his fingers outside and aimed straight ahead, gun-slinger fashion.

Cooper frowned across the flagstone terrace at Jesse Lee, who either failed or chose not to notice Cooper's no-no look as she braced Philip's glass with another gusher of Tanqueray and waved it past a bottle of tonic water.

Philip had judged the sun to be over the yardarm a couple of hours since. Now he raised a hand, aimed an admonitory bony finger, and said. "I really do wish you would give this a little more thought, my dear."

Cooper winced as Her Royal Highness deliberately lowered both the level in her crystal glass of Okanagan Valley Chardonnay, and the temperature attendant on the conversation. She placed the glass on the artfully-carved, silvered driftwood table, where she sat across from Jesse Lee and the drinks.

She turned to Philip, and Cooper marvelled at the way her skin had remained so unspoiled, resilient. The rest of her, too, he thought, as the lowering sun silhouetted her full, still firm bosom under the simple summer-weight tan blouse. The official royal birthdays had come and gone, the big one the eightieth, but she remained looking a good decade younger. "I have thought about it, Philip. All I'm going to. And don't call me 'my dear.' It's patronising." She removed her gold-wire rimmed glasses, breathed on the lenses, and wiped them on a napkin.

Cooper manufactured a cough from a chuckle, and the Duke shot him a less than chummy look.

More times than Cooper could recall, the Duke had said, "Always taking her side, Sergeant, aren't you?"

And Cooper's response, always, was, "Well, she is the Queen, sir."

They were collected at the home of the forest-industry family who for most of the century had provided a refuge for "retreat time" for members of the Royal Family visiting Canada's West Coast. The diminutive timber baron and his ample wife were present, seated and rocking gently in an oversized patio glider, as were the two policemen, Jim Quinsam and the now-retired Jack Kovich, and the newspaperman, Darshan Dhillon. The latter trio were perched on the terrace's broad stone wall within easy reach of a cooler filled with a selection of beers and ales. Their three wives sat at a red-cedar picnic table, shaded by a canopy umbrella and spellbound by the royal dispute and their role as audience. A flat stretch of sand lay between the low-built mansion and the lazily swelling Strait of Georgia which separated the Island from the mainland of British Columbia and the city of Vancouver, where things had gone to hell in 1983, more than three decades ago.

Near the drinks table, a white-throated black spaniel panted gently in the day's barely diminished heat. Earlier, Cooper had noticed Rajinder Dhillon puzzling as she watched Her Majesty fondling the dog's ears and talking to it. "Sit, Oliver," and the dog stood and offered its right front paw, as if to shake hands. Her Majesty laughed and said to Jesse Lee, "Well done. He's a credit to his ancestry." Cooper couldn't imagine what Rajinder Dhillon must have made of it. Or of anything else that was going on, for that matter. He watched the heads of the four couples shift side to side, like Wimbledon spectators, as the royal debate continued and Philip sailed on, into a stiffening breeze.

"It is such a *critical* moment," the Duke said.

She rolled back her head, worked her shoulders. Like a tired but confident fighter at the end of the ninth of ten rounds, Cooper thought.

It was she who had insisted that they come to the privacy of the mansion, just north of the small town of Qualicum Beach; she who had insisted that Cooper's old friends, the Koviches and the Quinsams and the Dhillons, be included.

"She," Philip had grunted, "who must be obeyed."

In Cooper's years with the household, Philip publicly had always played the dutiful consort. In private, it was a different matter, with the Duke pressing hard to have his way. Today was considered private, and as usual she was giving as good as she was getting.

"It has never been anything *but* critical from the start, Philip," she replied, and Cooper thought that, if he were the Duke, he would let things go about now. And knew there were two chances of that happening—slim, and fat.

"But it's a dreadful time to think of abdicating. So much still up in the air. Charles-" his raised hand briefly stalled a response "-I know, you persuaded him that he should step aside in favour of William, but William *is* still very young-"

She cut the Duke off with a chopping motion which would not have shamed the executioners of certain Windsor forebears.

"That's nonsense. William will be ready, with the right guidance, and with Kate by his side. She will be an excellent partner. And Charles will be there for him—he may be considered a bit odd by many but he does have some sense of what's right—and so will Charles Spencer, William's uncle."

Cooper won a searing glance from the Duke, as she rolled on.

"He may have made an exhibition of poor Diana's grave, but Charles Spencer was absolutely right at the service." She quoted the ninth Earl Spencer, speaking to the dignitaries and celebrities in Westminster Abbey on September 6 1997, with his eyes on his dead sister's two young sons, William and Harry. "'I pledge that we, your blood family, will do all we can do to continue the imaginative, loving way in which you were steering these two young men, so that their souls are not simply immersed by duty and tradition, but can sing openly as you planned.'"

Rajinder Dhillon dabbed a tissue to her eyes. The Duke leaned over and touched Rajinder's hand and whispered something, which evidently comforted the slight, Asian-English woman.

Philip did have some redeeming moments, Cooper thought. There was a little more to him than the clown-prince portrayed by the international news media whenever his foot found its way to his mouth—regrettably often, granted—and he offended one or another ethnic group, occasionally even a whole nation. He never did it intentionally, and never understood the fuss that followed. He was, simply, a man of his time whose time had long passed. He just did not get it. More than once he had said to Cooper, "What did I do that was so wrong?" Cooper would try to explain. "Well, Sir, asking a Maori leader if they still throw spears at each other (following a ceremonial dance display in New Zealand) is considered by some to be offensive." Philip's nose would crinkle and a bemused smile would shape his face. "It was a joke," he would say. "I really do not understand." And he really would mean it. At other times his dry wit was hard to beat. Cooper smiled at the memory of Philip being interviewed by a BBC reporter when the corporation made a documentary on the history of the seven-hundred-year-old Windsor Castle, the family's weekend retreat. Philip remarked, without a hint of a smile, on the number of visitors who wondered why the castle would have been built so close to the noise of Heathrow airport.

Philip had chosen to believe that things would stay the way they were indefinitely, Cooper thought. Philip must have chosen not to listen when she had signalled her intentions during the extensive Jubilee-year Canadian tour, well before the former butler Paul Burrell put the seal on things. In a luncheon speech in Vancouver, she said, "I treasure my place in the life of Canada and my bond with Canadians everywhere, now more than ever." She had glanced at Cooper and Quinsam, seated together near the head table.

Philip had just smiled around at the gathering and nodded his approval.

"She's gonna pull the plug, isn't she?" Quinsam had said.

Philip had not been amused during that tour— some mutterings about dignity—when Cooper had been instrumental in arranging for her to drop the puck in a ceremonial face-off at a season-opening game between the Vancouver Canucks and the San Jose Sharks. She had been escorted along the red carpet to centre ice by hockey legend Wayne Gretzky, whose sporting sobriquet "The King" resulted in a splashing of predictable King of Hockey-Queen of Canada headlines the next day. She had enjoyed them. "He's also known as The Great One," she had informed Philip, who remained unimpressed. The Duke had not shared in the laughter earlier in the day when Cooper described taking a call from an American magazine reporter who had asked what colour and size skates the Queen would wear at the face-off. Nor later, after they had watched the first period of the Vancouver-San Jose game, when she seemed to try lightening the mood by saying, "Did you know, Philip, that in Canada there's a joke that says, 'We went to a fight, and a hockey game broke out.'?" The Duke had turned away and disappeared into the bedroom of the Royal Suite.

"He'll be all right," Cooper had said, "It's just being back here again. Bad memories."

"Conditions are changing, Philip," she said now. "A species must adapt to survive, and the Monarchy is no different. William will become part of his generation, he will be able to speak to them, and they to him. And young Harry will become more of an asset than he was in is formative years. He is a fine soldier and he'll always be there to support his brother. We have to change, Philip. Adapt, or die."

There was a short, charged silence. Cooper tensed as he watched Philip's lips compress and his jaw tighten. He relaxed when Philip finally rattled the ice in his glass and turned away.

She accepted the retreat. "Let's leave that now," she said. "Charles has agreed to step aside-at least he has that much sense. I think he was relieved, if the truth be known. Now he and Camilla can get on with their lives and forget the rest of it."

At the picnic table, Rajinder Dhillon, Helen Kovich, and Maria Quinsam barely breathed. On the glider the chains creaked as the timber baron and his wife turned and smiled triumphantly at each other as visions of their next dinner party danced in their heads: *"Yes. . .right here. . . the patio. . .history in the making. . . and we were there!"*

She finished her wine. "I still cannot help but wonder how things might have worked out if Charles had been given it all to handle from the beginning, when I was uncertain for a while. . . if he'd been allowed to. . . " She shook her head. ". . . you know. . . "

Cooper caught the Duke's eye, and Philip responded.

"That was not an option. You knew that. We made the decision."

Cooper glanced across at Quinsam, who was looking sideways at Dhillon, who was looking mightily puzzled.

She caught the exchange between Cooper and Quinsam, and she retreated graciously.

"You're right, Philip. It was not an option, and we--*I*--made the decision. I take that back."

Cooper heard Dhillon as the journalist turned to Quinsam, the Mountie, and said, *"What* are they talking about?"

Quinsam said, "It's a domestic, Darshan. Best to stay outa them."

#

Cooper recalled Quinsam's account of being summonsed by Queen Elizabeth, the day after Quinsam had first put Maggie Grant up in place of the Queen, in full dress, in public before thousands at Vancouver's B.C. Place Stadium.

Quinsam described standing frozen to attention in her drawing room on board the *Britannia* while she gave him what he said later was the worst verbal shit-kicking he'd ever experienced.

She had done everything short of ripping off his corporal's stripes and personally drumming him out of the Royal Canadian Mounted Police.

"The very ugliest drill sergeant I ever had was like a fucking dance teacher compared with that."

She had concluded: "Don't you even *think* of repeating that performance again, Corporal. Remember-I must be seen to be believed. I *will* be seen!"

That had been 1983.

#

Philip nodded and accepted the retreat.

"But understand me," she continued. "I am finished with it. I have been on the throne long enough. We will return to London to put things in place, and then we will formally announce the abdication."

Philip muttered. "Damned Burrell. . . arsehole. . ." He looked at Cooper, who shook his head slowly side to side and glanced at the guests. Philip fumed, started to say something, stopped, stamped back to the bar and held out his glass for Jesse Lee to replenish.

Cooper's thoughts again slipped back to the start of it all, at his cottage further south in the Gulf, on Galiano Island, with Jack Kovich on the phone from Vancouver, telling Cooper his vacation was being cut short: "Your Queen needs you."

Cooper smiled. Maybe he would remind Jack that he still had some of those vacation days owing.

February 13, 1983

LONDON (CP) - Queen Elizabeth and the Duke of Edinburgh left Southampton today aboard the Royal Yacht *Britannia* to begin the most extensive royal tour ever of the Western Hemisphere.

The month-long tour, taking in the Caribbean, Mexico, and California, will end in Vancouver.

"It will end on the day that I kill her."
— Sean Dooley

CHAPTER 1

Ottawa, February 1983

The Prime Minister of Canada would have preferred telling the wiry little Irishman to get his grubby ass out of his office and return to whatever Belfast back alley had spawned him.

McGuire reminded Jacques Therrien of types he had seen thirty years ago when he had travelled the British Isles in his youth. He recalled the shabby collar-less shirts of the men walking gaunt greyhounds and hawking gobs of phlegm onto Belfast's grimy back streets. The young Quebec intellectual had found the people of Ulster disagreeable then, and his visitor offered no evidence that things had improved.

As soon as McGuire was seated in the spacious study on Parliament Hill, he had dug a half-smoked, squashed cigarette from his pocket and held a plastic lighter flame at it. He would have dropped his ash on the plush Tibetan carpet if an executive assistant hadn't sprung forward to catch it on a copy of the *Globe and Mail*.

"Find him an ashtray," Therrien said. The Cambridge-educated Quebecer had always privately voiced sympathy for the bloody cause that McGuire represented-in that Therrien claimed an intellectual affiliation with the goals of the committed revolutionary and anti-colonialist everywhere But this was his first contact with the reality--an active member of the Provisional wing of the Irish Republican Army, parked in his office--and the experience was not enriching his day.

Therrien had first examined the slight, bramble-haired Ulsterman on a security-camera monitor from an outer office. "Talk to him? I'll be damned if I will," he'd advised the deputy commissioner of the Royal Canadian Mounted

Police who had made the suggestion.

The Prime Minister's reluctance was linked in no small way to the fact that he was already late for a guaranteed coupling with a popular young network television reporter cherished particularly by male viewers, though considerably less for her journalistic insight than for the relentlessly unbuttoned top four buttons on her Ralph Lauren shirts and the scrap of lace she wore beneath as an excuse for a brassiere.

Deputy Commissioner Martin O'Connell convinced the Prime Minister that the flint-eyed little man in the navy polyester slacks, lumpy tweed sports jacket and scuffed Clark's Wallabies was indeed who he said he was--the Commanding Officer of the Belfast Brigade of Provisional IRA--and that what he had to say needed to be listened to.

"Christ! If I'm going to accommodate every lunatic with a story of a threat against the Queen I might as well shut the House down-let them line up and take numbers!" He made a display of checking his wafer-thin gold Bulova.

The deputy commissioner, who knew both the prime minister's precise destination and his general objective, kept his face straight, and persisted.

"McGuire is not some street thug, sir. He *is* the IRA in Ulster, and he's deadly serious."

The Prime Minister checked his watch.

"He says if you're not prepared to listen, then you had better be prepared to-ah, 'take all the fallout and shit when she gets topped,' was how he actually put it."

The Prime Minister rolled his eyes.

"With respect, sir, I believe you must see him."

Now O'Connell sat with the Prime Minister and a glum minister of external affairs, Charles Garrett, who had been sinking comfortably into his second vodka martini in the National Press Club when he was summonsed. The Prime Minister shifted in his chair as McGuire talked in the harsh, almost impenetrable accent of the streets of Belfast's Andersonstown area where he had been birthed and schooled. McGuire's message was simple. And presented in the manner it was--quietly and matter-of-fact--it had their attention.

"His name is Dooley. Sean Dooley. He was a soldier-one of ours, that is."

He blew into the cup of coffee that had been slid onto the polished maple side table at his elbow, and sipped it. He lowered the cup into its saucer and wiped the back of his hand across his mouth.

"You'll remember the blowin' up of Mountbatten, I would think. The Earl?"

O'Connell's head lifted.

"And at Warrenpoint the same day-18 paratroopers done? August 27, 1979, it was."

They waited.

"Dooley did them both. Oh, others were arrested and one man was convicted. But it was Dooley ran the show."

O'Connell grunted. The tall, jowelly external affairs minister sat slowly upright, and the Prime Minister sighed.

"A soldier's acts. Acts of war against a declared enemy. I believe it was Lord Carrington back in the Seventies who said 'We are at war with the IRA'? He would be speaking for Queen and country then, I imagine?"

McGuire picked up his cup. He sipped, and put it back.

"Anyway, those actions. The man who designed them was Sean Dooley."

O'Connell said, "I suppose you can *design* atrocities. . ."

"Ah, well, violent death is always an atrocious thing, to be sure."

"Especially when the violence is premeditated and innocents such as women and children are murdered. Two fourteen-year-old boys were killed with Mountbatten, as I recall, and one helpless old woman."

McGuire's lips pursed.

O'Connell had reluctantly agreed to a "without prejudice" meeting when the call came in to the RCMP's Ottawa headquarters and after his staff, in quick communion with the computers of the Canadian Security Intelligence Service (CSIS), concluded that the man on the other end very likely was who he claimed to be.

"He gave us three addresses," an intrigued inspector reported. "Two in Toronto and one in Vancouver that we've had surveillance on for months for guns and plastic explosives. He said we should stop wasting our time. The guy knows everything; how many people we've got working, which watches-"

"Where is he?"

"Ottawa International. He told us not to bother locking-on to the phone number--which we already had done--and gave us the location of the pay phone he was using. Then, he asked which bus, for Chrissakes, he should take into the city."

A sergeant and the inspector took an unmarked car and found McGuire waiting patiently where they'd told him to.

McGuire's eyes were on the Mountie now.

"Children, is it? Interesting you would raise that."

He sipped coffee, removed the expiring cigarette from the corner of his mouth and used it to light another one.

The Prime Minister glared as McGuire confirmed that the cigarette was burning by puffing it into a serious glow and then exhaling streamers of smoke, first from his nose and then his mouth.

"Does the name Shannon McBride mean a thing to you?"

McGuire's question was aimed at the Mountie.

O'Connell shook his head. "Not off-hand, no."

"Not off-hand, no" McGuire mimicked. "Christ." He spat a tobacco shred onto the carpet and rubbed it in with his shoe.

Therrien closed his eyes, and sighed.

McGuire turned to Garrett, the Minister of External Affairs, whose face had drooped into tired bloodhound lines as he sought a clue, and then to the Prime Minister.

"Either of you?"

Garrett looked mournful, and shook his head. The Prime Minister shot his cuff and looked pointedly at his watch.

McGuire told them about Sean Dooley's niece.

#

The arrival in early December of a squad from the Parachute Regiment's Second Battalion was nothing unusual for the Armagh border village that lived with the routine ambushes and executions conducted by both sides in the civil war for the Six Counties of Northern Ireland.

Nor was it any more welcome than at other times. The troops were met with stony faces from the adult population and a barrage of rocks and insults from the village youth, many of whom had family members locked up, maimed, or dead as the price of soldiering for the Republican movement. A good number of the deaths had come from the muzzles of the self-loading rifles and Sterling SMGs carried by the tough young soldiers wearing maroon berets, and blue-and-white-winged parachute badges on the right arm of their camouflage Denison smocks; others from the more silent weapons of the less visible but equally deadly troopers of the 22nd Regiment, Special Air Service. The villagers drew little distinction between the two airborne regiments, though possibly fearing more the latter. To them, each represented a terrorist arm of the British occupation forces.

The paras were there three days, on edge, prowling and patrolling black-faced in threes and fours at all hours. Taut, watchful young men from the turbulent inner-city slums of London and Liverpool and Glasgow, and from Belfast. From villages in the gentle English West Country, from hamlets and bleak fell-side farms in Cumbria, and from the industrial back streets of Tyneside. All heavily armed, prudently apprehensive, and highly skilled at their deadly craft.

Shortly after dusk on the third day, a Royal Army Signals Corps corporal lifted his hand and flagged the young first-lieutenant in charge of the platoon.

"They've spotted the lorry, Mr. Shaw."

The lieutenant took the field phone unit, identified himself in a biting Geordie accent, and listened. The three days of preparations had been invested on the strength of an informer's tip. A flat-bed lorry loaded with bales of hay would be crossing the border. The hay was a cover for a major movement of explosives and ammunition into the Six Counties - more fodder for the cause.

The lorry was two miles down the road in the Republic, heading in.

The young Parachute Regiment officer nodded. "Harvest One, over and out."

His sergeant slipped away and deployed his men.

They waited until the vehicle was negotiating a tight turn in the narrow street in front of the stone-built, four-room school.

If Shannon McBride had not stayed late in school that day, what took place in the next few seconds would have been reported on the evening news as nothing more than a major haul for the British forces and the shooting of a badly-wanted IRA killer.

The slight thirteen-year-old with raven hair and green eyes put on her black Macintosh and her woolen gloves and left the classroom and the big upright piano where she'd been practicing the three pieces she was to play in the school Christmas concert in two weeks time. She had finally worked out the trying left-hand repetitions in "Deck The Halls", and Mrs. Byrne had beamed at her and told her to get along home.

Out on the street in the growing dark she stopped and watched as the lorry, its gears grinding, struggled around the tight turn just a few yards away. The lorry hit the kerb and jumped. She put a hand to her mouth and caught a small breath as the stacks of baled hay rocked, swayed, and seemed ready to topple.

The small movement of Shannon McBride's young hand to her mouth in the near-dark registered in the peripheral vision of lance-corporal Danny Coates. The Liverpool lad had completed three four-month tours in Northern Ireland and was having serious doubts about the wisdom of having chosen a fourth, which had still two months to run. Too many more moments of loose-gut fear; too much time in the shadows of the council houses in the Falls and Ballymurphy, where the next half-brick tossed by a jeering riot-haired punker might not be a half-brick at all, but a "busy bomb" - a pack of gelignite studded with nails, with a detonator and a fuse. The package would leave you shredded and dead, or blinded and maimed.

All of this shifted at survival speed through Danny Coates's mind when he saw the feather of movement against the school wall.

That's how it happened. The fuckers suddenly appeared, from around a corner, behind a wall, dropped their deadly message, spilled your guts like dog shit on the pavement, and disappeared.

Despite his dread, Danny Coates was not inclined to reckless action. He was, first, a soldier in the Parachute Regiment, a thoroughly trained member of the British Army's meticulously and gruellingly-selected elite Airborne Forces, and a proven leader among them. He expected to be promoted to full corporal before the month was out. And he was a veteran of the Ulster campaign. He had never yet shot at shadows.

He kept his eyes on the patch of wall where the movement had been, and he signalled his concerns to the sergeant. The sergeant slid up beside him, crouched and hard-faced and dangerous.

Inside the lorry's cab, Paidrick Hannah, sweating and slightly stoked from a half-bottle of Powers to calm his twitching gut, lifted his hand from the steering wheel and carefully slipped the awkward big farm vehicle into neutral. At the age of thirty-three, he had already endured three separate stretches inside the Long Kesh prison camp, otherwise known as the Maze. He had experienced the waking nightmares of sensory-deprivation sessions under SAS specialists at Castlereagh interrogation centre. He had escaped from the last stretch, butchering two prison officers with a home-made axe as he did so, and vowed that he would never do another minute inside. This was the thought hammering his mind when he saw the silhouette of the military beret thirty yards away from his cab and moving towards him. He reached to the seat at his left for the Chinese-made Kalashnikov assault rifle. He raised the weapon and aimed through the rolled-down window at the first soldier he saw coming in a crouching, zig-zag run toward the driver's door.

Shannon McBride knew something was terribly wrong. From an angled view through the rear window in the driver's cab, she saw that the driver had given up guiding the lorry. He was leaning out and seemed to be pointing at something across the street. At the same moment, she saw two British soldiers rise from the tarmac surface of the road, their guns snouted at the driver's cab. She did what her uncle Sean had always said to do.

"Get out of their way. Get away from them, whatever you do. Don't call out. Get to the house and inside."

The house was halfway down Church Street, the next turning. Her nylon carry-all with her music and books had slipped the length of its straps in her hands. She slung it up now and took a side step away, keeping her back to the wall.

The super-primed mind of L/Cpl. Danny Coates deciphered the dark, sharp movement of the school bag as the first stage of an over-arm throw, and he yelled as he dropped to one knee and depressed the trigger on his Sterling SMG.

"Bomber! Bomber!"

The hard-faced sergeant alongside him started shooting, too.

The slanting rain of slugs lifted and drove Shannon McBride back against the old brick and stone building. It stitched her slim form from her coltish knees to her delicate blue-veined jaw line with a hideous design of symmetrical red-black holes and splashed parts of her remains against the door and over the front windows of the school. The slugs carried on and chewed chunks out of the granite wall and exploded them among the paratroopers and into the stacked bales of hay, where they clattered and danced and struck sparks from the contraband cargo that had gone as far as it was going in the Republican cause.

Paidrick Hannah died in bloody denims on the suddenly slippery and stinking driver's seat of the flat-bed lorry, forever safe from the cells of Her Majesty's Prison, Maze.

An inquiry cleared Danny Coates of any wrongdoing, while lamenting the death of Shannon McBride. The report noted that an IRA conspiracy had provoked the incident. Danny Coates requested and received a posting back to the battalion's home barracks at Aldershot.

#

McGuire sat back, picked up his cup, and sipped on the now cool coffee.

The two politicians looked at each other, and at Deputy Commissioner O'Connell.

"Really," the Prime Minister started, "I don't-"

"That's his reason," McGuire said.

"What?"

"It's Dooley's reason-it's why he's going to take out the Queen."

The Prime Minister winced.

"The girl was Dooley's niece, his young sister's bairn."

The Mountie grunted, his hands coming together in his lap.

"Siobahn," McGuire said. "Her with the Abbey, you know? But no, you wouldn't know, likely. Her own man was killed by the Brits, as well. Another of ours. Siobahn worshipped the little one, she did that. Lived for her. And so did Sean. They were the only family he had left, Siobahn and the girl. Bonnie girl, she was, the wain. She would have been coming up fourteen. Sean was her da, just about, since her own da was killed, you see?"

McGuire waited for a response.

O'Connell nodded his head, seeing all too well. The

Prime Minister polished a fingernail on his sleeve, and raised an eyebrow at Garrett.

The external affairs minister cleared his throat, straightened his vest.

"Mr. McGuire. That's a terrible thing you describe, a child's death. But I'm still not clear on what exactly your point is to us."

McGuire puffed life back into a moribund cigarette.

"The point is, Mr. Garrett, that at some place along the royal tour, Dooley is planning to assassinate the Queen, and that's his reason. And knowing the man's history, I would not want to bet against him."

He waved smoke away and it drifted across the gap between himself and the Prime Minister. Therrien coughed, and scowled.

"We don't know when, we don't know where. Dooley is a shadow-man. He's been one of us since he was a lad, but he's always operated alone. Nobody meets him, nobody sees him. I don't know what he looks like, and I don't know anybody that does. He leaves instructions, things get done. I don't know where he'll go for her. Maybe the Caribbean, maybe California. If it's either of those, it's not your problem. At least not that part of it, as long as you've passed on the information. If it's in Canada, though, it is your problem, isn't it?"

The question hung in the silence that followed it.

McGuire flicked a finger and freckled the polished table top with cigarette ash.

He said, "Wherever it happens, they'll likely be leaving together."

The Prime Minister glanced at the external affairs minister, who looked at O'Connell.

O'Connell said, "What do you mean, 'leaving together'?"

McGuire removed another tobacco thread from his bottom lip with his tongue and spat it onto the carpet.

"Dooley's badly. We hear he has cancer. He's on his way out, running out of time. This tour's his only chance.

He has nothing to lose."

Garrett stirred in his chair and the lines on his long face deepened. He said, "There's one thing I still don't understand, Mr. McGuire."

The Irishman smiled. "And what's that?"

"Why on earth are you telling us all this? I mean, one of your own people is planning to assassinate the Queen, and you waltz in here large as life and want to inform on him? What are you looking for, some sort of immunity for yourself? A deal? It doesn't make any sense."

McGuire shook his head. "I'm not after any 'deal.'"

He frowned at Garrett. "I thought it would be obvious." He took a long drag on the damp end of his cigarette and breathed the smoke down and out of his nostrils. "*We* cannot afford to have her killed."

O'Connell nodded his understanding, and said to Therrien and Garrett. "It would spoil their game." And to McGuire, "Wouldn't it? You'd be finished."

McGuire studied the career policeman a moment before he replied.

"A poor way of putting it, Mr. O'Connell. It's a queer sort of 'game' you're talking about, a people's legitimate fight for their own country."

He turned to the politicians.

"But he's right, in his way. It could finish us. But worse, I fear it would finish Ireland. Let me tell you, we were never closer to a campaign of genocide by the British than when Mountbatten was killed in '79. I called it a soldier's act, didn't I? And it was. But it was also a renegade act. It was not an action sanctioned by us. Dooley had no mandate for that one. Blowing up the eighteen paras at Warrenpoint right after it was a brilliant move. Magic, that was. But the Mountbatten thing was very poor judgement. For one thing, it's the killing of an old man. That's never going to be popular. The Irish respect their old people. It's part of our ways."

"Jesus," O'Connell said. "Popular!"

McGuire ignored him.

"You have to keep the people with you. A lot of it's PR, like it or not."

O'Connell said, "Oh, spare me."

"And the other thing was that a lot of our lads had served with Mountbatten in the war. They liked him, respected him."

"And murdered him."

"*Dooley* assassinated him," McGuire corrected the Mountie. "He organised it. It was a rogue act and all it did was generate sympathy for the whole feckin' royal gang and their pack of parasites. It set us back years. There were those of us who wanted to find Dooley and take sanctions- the man is brilliant but he does not recognise limits. But we were overruled."

He stubbed his cigarette out in the ashtray.

"We have a similar problem now. Some on the Army Council say if Dooley wants the Queen, good luck to him, and we'll live with the results. I think they're wrong. I think that if he does what he's planning to do, it will be the excuse that the hard-men in Westminster are looking for, to start the blood bath they want-and they're there, those hard-men are there, believe me. It would be their final solution to the Irish problem. I think they would put the country to the torch. That's why I'm telling you," he finished, looking in turn to each of the three faces.

The two politicians were in no hurry to respond.

O'Connell said, "But why did you choose us? I mean, why Canada? Surely this could happen anywhere on the tour? Why not go to the Americans, warn them? Why not the Caribbean part of the tour?"

"It could happen anywhere, you're right. And yes, I could have gone to the Americans-and within five minutes of me advising them, my name, my photo and my address would be painted on every brick wall in Belfast as the tout who tried to shop an IRA legend. We have a lot of supporters in America; a lot of people with roots in the old country and long memories of families ruined and forced out of their country by the British. They might not see it my way."

O'Connell nodded, conceding the Irishman's point.

McGuire went on, "I would bet on it not being the Caribbean. This is Dooley's last, and his biggest. He has to do it right. He'll want to be close to her when it happens and his choice of handgun is a bigger one than most would use. He'll need to have it concealed. The clothing they'll wear in the Caribbean wouldn't be right. He will not take that risk."

O'Connell nodded a professional's understanding of the simple but likely very accurate reasoning. "Makes sense."

McGuire stood.

"I'll leave it with you." He smiled. "What with you Mountie fellas always gettin' your man and that."

He glanced back at the Prime Minister. "You'll have your own reasons for wanting to stop him, no doubt."

The Prime Minister looked gloomily at him over steepled fingers.

#

"I want it cancelled."

The Prime Minister paced his office, hands bunched in front of him.

The British High Commissioner to Canada shook his head. "I wish it were that easy, Mr. Prime Minister. It isn't."

Therrien had sent for David Llewellyn after McGuire had left. Llewellyn was the resourceful son of a collier, raised in the South Wales mining town of Tonypandy, a former Oxford rugby Blue and Welsh international. He had astutely handled Britain's diplomatic concerns in such sensitive outposts as Tehran, Budapest, and Moscow before being handed his current, cushy Ottawa job which, barring surprises, would lead to a comfortable retirement complete with fertile company directorships, and most likely a "K"- a knighthood.

Barring surprises.

Llewellyn had sat grim-faced as a video tape of

McGuire's visit was played. When it was done, he said, "Christ Almighty."

He accepted a glass of Cognac poured by the Prime Minister.

"There's no doubt that the man's serious. Remarkable bloody thing, him coming here like that."

He sipped the Cognac and drummed on the arm of his chair with his free fingers.

"And he's right about what could happen."

He stood and began pacing.

"First, the British people would demand exactly what McGuire called it-the final solution to Ireland. They would absolutely *demand* it. They'd be in the streets demanding it. They're sick of the Irish mess. Sick of those psychopaths and thugs masquerading as martyrs and freedom fighters. Sick of their bombs and brutality, sick of women and kiddies losing their arms and legs and lives! Did you see that thing yesterday?"

He didn't wait for a reply, and the usually submerged rhythms of the Rhondda Valley surfaced in his voice and shaped his phrases as his anger swelled.

"A sixteen-year-old girl in Londonderry dragged from her classroom in the middle of a history lesson. The little bastards shaved her head, painted it with tar, and then they broke her kneecaps with hockey sticks. Do you know how old they were-the ones who did it? They were fourteen and fifteen! Do you know why they did it? Because she stopped to talk to an eighteen-year-old British soldier on the way to school!

"You can bet your life the British people have had enough."

The Prime Minister freshened the three glasses as the senior British diplomat continued.

"The people would demand the final solution, all right. And the Prime Minister would give it to them. First, because she's like that--hard as iron--but also, she would *have* to, gentlemen. The people would put her out on her arse if she didn't. And she would do anything to prevent that. Anything."

The two politicians, whose party recent polls suggested was running several lengths short of being first to the wire in the next federal election, examined their shoes.

"But there is more than that."

Llewellyn walked towards the window and looked out onto the snowed-on and slushy lawns and streets of Parliament Hill. He tapped his glass with a fingernail, turned and faced them.

"I said the British people are sick of the Irish mess. The public mood really is there for what McGuire suggested, if this Dooley creature were to succeed. But also, McGuire knows something when he refers to the hard-men of Westminster. There are certain people wholly ready and willing-- no, make that, *anxious*--to exploit that mood for their own use. There always have been those kinds of people, always will be."

He sipped his cognac.

"There's a ...call it a faction, a clique--whatever you like--of extremely influential people, military and civilian, who are itching to take the Irish thing into their own hands. Their actions would be 'for the good of the nation,' of course.

"They've been wanting to make their move ever since Mountbatten was murdered. To them, that was a knife in the very heart of everything Britain stands for. They see the current government policy of non-retaliation as simply an invitation to more IRA mayhem, with no one paying the price. If the Queen were assassinated, there would be no stopping them."

Therrien said, "Oh, really, Mr. Llewellyn, isn't that somewhat- "

Llewellyn carried straight on. "They would simply take over, Mr. Prime Minister, as outrageous as that might seem to you, from this distance. They would declare a state of national emergency--they would force the Prime Minister to declare it--all the time waving the flags of patriotism, British duty, and bloody revenge. They are fully prepared for it, believe me. They consider the country to be a floundering mess and the politicians running it, ineffective. They have immense influence in the popular press, and they would put out an emotional call to arms the like of which you've never imagined. The script would have been written for them. It cannot be allowed to happen."

He emptied his glass.

"I might remind you, Prime Minister, of a not-dissimilar situation in this country a few years back. Nineteen seventy, I believe? Quebec separatists killed LaPorte, a politician as important as they come. And kidnapped Cross, the British Trade Commissioner. The Canadian government reacted by invoking the War Measures Act, bringing in the army, allowing arrests and detentions without charges, among other things."

The Prime Minister protested, "That was an internal political matter involving a few radicals. It was handled expeditiously and the situation was very quickly back to normal."

Llewellyn smiled. "That's an interesting retrospective, Prime Minister. Nevertheless, the fact is that this country was faced with what its leaders perceived to be a desperate situation, and desperate measures were taken to correct it. The power in that instance, the control, stayed in the right hands, as it happened. It might not have. A kidnapping and a murder by a rag-tag group of Quebec separatists in 1970 was a Sunday stroll compared to the pressures the assassination of Her Majesty would create. There's martial law, and then there's martial law. The Irish question in my country is an internal matter also-but it's a lot more bloody, a *lot* more dangerous. It must at some point be resolved."

He paused.

"If the Queen is killed by this man, there is no guarantee as to who would be doing the resolving."

He consulted his empty glass for a few moments before continuing.

"I know it is popular in some circles to debate the continuing usefulness of the monarchy, to recommend replacing it with a republic."

The Prime Minister shifted uneasily in his chair.

"But, I assure you, the importance of the British monarchy as the steward of political stability can never be overestimated. Never."

He put his glass down.

Garrett cleared his throat and ventured, "And cancelling the visit?"

"The Queen simply wouldn't permit it."

Therrien glared, but Llewellyn continued.

"She is of that stuff that says when adversity calls, you meet it at the front door. You do not hide, you do not run."

The Prime Minister sighed. Llewellyn carried on.

"But also, to cancel would be seen by these same people I'm talking about, this faction, as capitulation by the British government to terrorists. They would drum up and present the image of a British nation captive in its own home. 'The Queen of England as an IRA prisoner in her own palace.' They would engineer a war on--and *in*--Ireland. That I can guarantee."

He looked from one to the other, at their shared frowns.

"Consider the consequences, gentlemen, for the Commonwealth, and yourselves especially: a gang of military thugs--and that's all they'd be--running Mother England, and not just policing but invading Northern Ireland. And just as important-consider the reaction of your neighbour to the south, if that were to happen. By all reports, the man in the White House wanders about singing *Did Your Mother Come From Ireland*? And consider that the IRA acquires most of its financial support in donated American dollars. The popular image in the United States of the IRA is one of Robin Hood and his merry bloody men. If Northern Ireland were to be occupied full-scale by the British Army, Ireland would feel compelled to go to the political wall against Britain in every international forum imaginable. That man in Washington would be as likely to side with Ireland as with Britain however chummy he may be with our Iron Lady. Christ, he might even be capable of sending the Marines to Ireland.

He let them consider the thought.

Garrett murmured, "He might at that."

"And you," Llewellyn said, "might have to decide which side you're on."

Garrett looked at the Prime Minister.

"Cancellation is not an option we would want to explore, gentlemen," Llewellyn said. "Nor one, I suggest, you would want to insist on?"

He put on his coat, neither expecting nor receiving a reply. He shook hands with each of them, and left.

Therrien picked up a phone.

"Find O'Connell."

CHAPTER 2

Galiano Island, British Columbia.

February 1983

Someone was nailing Matt Cooper's eyeballs to the inside of his skull. Four Aspirins and two bottles of cold Labatt's Blue were hunting the culprit.

The sight of the otter kitten in the crab trap wasn't helping the hangover. Sandi would have raised absolute hell over that.

He looked up as the phone started ringing again up at the cottage. Four...six... ten rings...silence. He turned back to the crab trap. He had to do something about the kitten.

He had guessed at first that the dark mass was simply a chunk of kelp caught on the wire frame, as he hauled the trap up from the bay's sandy floor. Then the trap broke surface, and the kitten's head, jammed between the wire squares, was scraping and banging against the rocks. Something had already nibbled at one of the eyes.

He imagined the kitten splashing around, wrinkling its tiny nose at the nectar drifting from the crushed soft-shell clams in the bait pot, and swimming down to investigate, then nosing around, slipping through the circular hole in the top of the trap, nuzzling the pot. Then it would have started running out of air. Begun circling, panicked, before desperately pushing its head through the space between two of the wire bars. Wedged there, and drowned. The white teeth were bared in protest. The webbed front monkey-paws gripped a cross-piece, as if in prayer. The once-lithe body was fixed and stiff.

Sandi would have killed him.

She never left his thoughts. He still turned to speak to her, ask a question, wait for an answer.

He watched the waves lick the rocks, listened to the wharf creaking and the aging Boston whaler bumping and stroking on the car-tire buffers.

Sandi was the first to see the otters when they arrived in the bay, what was it, two years ago? A little more. A few months before Cooper's sun had slipped from the sky.

In his mind he saw her racing up the beach, the sunlight burnishing her cloud of chestnut hair, her shirt--one of his faded old denim jobs--half unbuttoned and sexy as hell, a pair of raggedy-ass jeans stuffed into short, red rubber boots.

He heard her calling.

"Matt! Coop! Come here, come on! Come and see!"

Like a kid, her face glowing, green eyes dancing.

The two of them and Sheena watched the otters every day for a week, laughed at them as they capered on the rocks like summer children, juggling pebbles on their black noses, smarter than circus seals, sliding down rock chutes and torpedoing into the gently swelling bay. Sensing watchers, the otters balanced on their sturdy tails and stared back at the shore. Cooper and Sandi and Sheena sat still as paintings, and the otters resumed play.

In the spring, Cooper saw the female floating on her back. A kitten lay on her chest, between her front paws. Sandi's bold charcoal sketch of the moment hung on the wall in the Cottage's breakfast nook.

Sandi. Jesus.

A tide of memories.

Sheena, raging, "It's not fair!" after the first surge of tears. A young version of her mother. The same bronze hair and green eyes. Standing in her Air Canada flight attendant uniform in the harshly-lit corridor of Vancouver General Hospital. Like a school kid in the navy-blue suit and white shirt, and the ascot in red white and blue. Just in from a London flight and driven straight to the hospital, and into Cooper's arms.

Sandi had been at a stoplight in her blue-and-rust Honda Civic. A Vancouver city police patrol car had ricocheted off a stolen Oldsmobile it was chasing, slewed across the intersection and rammed the Civic head on. The impact broke Sandi's neck. The coroner's report said she died instantly.

"She wouldn't have felt anything," Cooper told his daughter, as he folded her into his arms. "She wouldn't have known anything."

But they both knew Sandi would have known. Just a flash, a split second, just enough to say, "Oh, God, no-" before. . . nothing.

How many times had Cooper, as a beat-cop, rung a doorbell in the dark hours, listened for the footsteps and the apprehensive "Who is it?", and stood in the block of light in an open doorway and said, "I'm afraid there's been an accident. . . "

Jack Kovich gave Cooper the news, "Matt-there's been an accident."

Sheena had damned the young constable driving the squad car. A hot-pursuit cowboy, she said. He must have run a light.

Cooper said, "No, it wasn't like that. He chased the stolen Olds through a green light. The two in the car had knocked over a Chinese corner store for $48 and change. They beat the seventy-year-old wife of the owner half to death with a tire iron. The kid was doing what any patrol officer would have done-what I would have done."

"Why Mom?" Sheena wept. "What did she ever do to anyone?"

Cooper hugged her and held her.

The memorial service for Sandi Cooper drew every city cop who wasn't on duty, and many who should have been. They stood shoulder to shoulder with members of the Royal Canadian Mounted Police, separate forces from the municipalities around Vancouver, and an honour guard of deputy sheriffs and Highway Patrol officers from Washington State, supporting one of their own.

The young constable from the pursuit car, Steve Hammond, walked up to Sheena and Cooper when the eulogies were over.

He said, "I'm sorry. I'm so sorry."

He had been on leave since the incident, and Sheena could have destroyed him. Cooper thought she might. She had raged at her mother's death. It meant the end of laughing, kitchen-table, mother-and-daughter conferences that would tail off into mysterious silences when Cooper entered the room. The end of a sharing of secrets and dreams, of walks along Spanish Banks' windy beaches with her arm in her mother's, the two of them trailed by a dim but devoted spaniel that Sheena had rescued from the pound and named Cromwell.

Sheena could have let the kid have all of that, all of her hurt. But she didn't. Sheena did what she knew a cop's kid had to do. She took the young officer's hand in her hands.

"There was nothing you could have done differently," she said. "Nobody blames you." And she had hugged him, and held him for a moment. Cooper thought he had never loved her more than at that moment.

Cooper took three weeks off from the Major Crimes squad, a combination of compassionate leave and vacation. He spent the first few days mostly alone at the old house in the city's Kitsilano district. He waited to hear the screen door bang shut and for Sandi to thump loaded grocery bags down on the kitchen table. For her to shout and ask if he was there, because if he was, there were more bags in the car.

Sheena returned to work a week after the funeral, doing what she said her mother would have insisted on: have your weep and get it over with, and cherish the memories of the good times. Cooper drove her up Granville Street and over the Laing Bridge to the airport and her pre-flight briefings.

"You going to be all right, Dad?" as he got her bag from the blue Volare station wagon.

"I'll be all right, sweetheart. I'm going to the island for a few days, me and Cromwell, and we'll be fine. You enjoy your flight and call me as soon as you get back."

Cooper kissed her on the cheek, and Sheena gave him a quick, fierce hug. He watched her until she walked through the automatic-opening doors and fell into step with another woman in identical uniform. Her companion placed an arm around Sheena's shoulder and leaned her face close in and talked to her as they walked on through the terminal.

Cooper took the ferry to Galiano the next morning, bundling the spaniel into the wagon with a pile of shirts and socks and several bottles of Ballentine's Scotch whisky, with which he kept close company for the next two weeks.

It had been almost eighteen months now. Sheena was coming out of it, much better than he was. Put it down to youth, and the indomitable resilience inherited from her mother.

"Mom would have said to get on with it, dad."

She dragged him out to dinner, and twice to the movies. And the last time she'd come to the island she rolled comical eyes as one of several resident widows went to transparent lengths to engage Cooper in gossip at the line-up at the Saturday farmers' market. Sheena mentioned the woman later, and when Cooper refused the bait, she said, "You can't live in Mom's shadow forever, Dad. And you know she wouldn't want you to."

She was right. Sandi's wish would have been for him to make a new life. But knowing that and doing it doing were walks down two different streets.

Sheena loved her work, thrived on the travel. And there was something developing with the young pilot she'd brought home a couple of times, Paul Grainger. Well, she was twenty-three, the same age as Sandi had been when she and Cooper had tied the knot. Sheena would be fine.

He wasn't quite so sure about himself.

He looked back up at the cottage. The phone was ringing again.

CHAPTER 3.

Sean Dooley slid his right foot out into the aisle and stretched his leg. He swapped a grin with the stewardess as she deftly stepped over his scuffed, suede boot.

He turned his head to admire her trim bottom as she made her way to the back of the Boeing 747. There had been a time he might have had his hands on those neat cheeks before the day was out. Little chat, boyish smile, maybe dinner that night, to start with. *Had* been a time.

He had shoved the folded copy of the *Sunday Times*, with the royal tour announcement on its front page, into the pouch on the seatback in front of him. The brief statement was keyed to an inside page. There, the newspaper's Royal Family correspondent had rambled on for a good thirty column inches about the importance of the tour, the value of the Queen as an example of stability to the Commonwealth and the rest of the world in these uncertain times. And anything else he could shove in to justify the inflated expense accounts that he would be filing from stops along the route, Dooley deduced, not without a degree of admiration. It now should be clear to the most parsimonious publisher that any tour as grand as this man made the upcoming tour sound would cost an arm and a leg to cover properly. Dooley smiled as he recalled the familiar reporters' ditty: *You cannot hope to bribe or twist, / thank God, the British journalist. / But seeing what the man will do, / unbribed, there's no occasion to.*

The captain commandeered the sound system and announced that they were approaching Greenland, which would be visible from the right side windows.

Dooley eased out of the tourist class seat and stepped into the aisle, giving way to a harassed-looking woman with a crying baby in her arms. He walked back to the galley area, went to the bulbous window and leaned down to gaze at the world of ice and snow and frigid water 30,000 feet below. Icebergs sat, like dabs of sculpted, jagged sherbet, seemingly immobile, their shadowy greater bulks suspended in the vivid emerald and indigo depths of the north Atlantic. So benign, from up here.

The Greenland coast crept into view at 600 miles an hour. Great fjords knifing back into a white wasteland, and vast glaciers of white-turning-to-aquamarine frozen rivers poised to slip imperceptibly into an icy sea.

Dooley had described this picture often to a wide-eyed young girl. He had delighted in the excitement that had flashed from her laughing green eyes when he had promised her, cross his heart, that he would take her on the trip where she would see the same sights for herself.

"Honest, Uncle Sean?"
"Honest, my sweet."
"For sure, now?"
"For sure."
"And cross your heart?"
"Cross my heart, for sure."
"Oh, won't that be the thing, though!"

And she had danced away, laughing and calling to her mother, "Mammy! Mammy! Guess what Uncle Sean says? Guess what he says! We're going on the plane and we're going to see Greenland where there's nothing but ice, and Iceland where there's not half as much, and all of it from the windows on the plane! Do you know how high we will be, mammy?"

Dooley pressed his face against the window and closed his eyes. The fresh cut inscription in the white marble gravestone was a snapshot in his mind.

Shannon McBride, beloved daughter of James and Siobahn.
Lighted our life on 10/3/69; taken from us 5/12/82.
At rest with her loving father James,
also murdered by the British, 1972.

Our time will come.

Jimmy's own bomb had gone off with him in the car when the patrol from the King's Own Scottish Borderers had challenged him. That was a hard one, with the little lass just three and asking why her da wasn't coming home. But it was also the death of a volunteer who knew it could come any time, and was prepared to meet it.

The bairn was different, though. That should never have been. And it would be accounted for.

Behind him the stewardess manoeuvred the drinks cart for a pre-dinner run down the aisle. Dooley left the window and stepped ahead of the cart and returned to his seat, fingering chair backs for balance as the plane touched a pocket of turbulence.

His seat companion, stiff in a suit with a waistcoat and tightly knotted tie, was immersed in the pile of business magazines that had engrossed him since the plane left Heathrow. Dooley never understood why so many people dressed up for travelling as if they were going to church. Dooley wore a red-and-black plaid sports shirt with well-worn cord slacks and comfortable suede ankle boots. His safari jacket was stuffed into the overhead storage compartment. He had greeted the business type when he'd sat down, received a nod in return, and that had been the sum of their conversation.

"Could I get you something to drink, sir?"

Dooley ordered Scotch, and the stewardess scrabbled a handful of ice cubes into a plastic glass and slid the glass and two miniatures of Johnny Walker Red onto the fold-down tray in front of him.

"Ah, and a beer?"

She arched an eyebrow but smiled as she reached into the heart of the drinks cabinet and produced a can of Heineken and placed it beside the Scotch.

Dooley's seat companion awarded Dooley's selection a mild frown as he ordered Perrier with a lime slice for himself.

Dooley dumped the contents of both miniatures over the ice, swirled the mixture, then sipped, enjoying the bite and the peaty flavour.

Dooley leaned back. His eyes drifted to the *Sunday Times* in the seat-back pouch.

The story said that the royal tour would end in Vancouver.

He smiled.

If it got that far.

The pain lanced his gut. He breathed slow, deep breaths until the thing began to recede. He checked his watch. The bastard was early.

He reached into the seat pouch beside the newspaper and fished out the small vial of Leritine pills. He uncapped it, dabbed one pill out with his fingertip. He shuddered as he swilled it down with the rest of the Scotch.

He leaned back and eased up the tab on the Heineken.

tiocfaidh ár lá

Our time will come.

A Queen, for our princess.

Dooley raised the beer can to his lips.

"Cross my heart."

The man in the suit and waistcoat looked at Dooley, then returned to his magazines.

CHAPTER 4

Galiano Island, British Columbia.

Cooper worked the otter kitten's head back through the wire squares and eased the bedraggled corpse through the hinged gate at the bottom of the trap.

The trap had been down since he arrived at the cottage on Friday night. He hadn't checked it yesterday, rather had jumped at the mild sunny day and played three rounds at the little nine-hole golf course with Dale Mitchell. Two years ago Dale had taken his pension after twenty-five years as a beat cop. He cushioned the pension with the income from six cabins he rented out on his five evergreen-studded acres on low bluffs that looked down into Active Pass. Cooper and Dale Mitchell had left the club-house bar long after normal closing.

Cooper had searched for the otters earlier as he stood on the sun deck gratefully gulping the cold beer and wolfing a sandwich of crisp bacon and two fried eggs.

He'd scanned the bay, searching the usual rock crannies and play pools, watching for a head to break the surface and periscope the day. There was no sign.

Then he'd gone to check the crab trap, a dozen feet down.

Sandi would have cried, first. Then she would have held a goddamn funeral. She'd have wrapped the body in something soft, found a shoe box for a coffin, and taken it up behind the cottage and buried it with a bunch of flowers and a cross.

Cooper decided instead on a decent burial at sea. He slipped a yellow oilskin jacket over his grey cotton work shirt and old jeans. He chased a disappointed Cromwell off the wharf and commanded the dog to stay on the beach. When on board, Cromwell had a habit of leaning over the side to inspect the ocean, and falling in. Cooper laid the kitten in the bottom of the Boston whaler and fired up the forty-horse Johnson. He ran a for a good ten minutes out into Georgia Strait with the boat planing most of the way, before he killed the motor and let the boat bump to a stop among the swells. He slipped the kitten over the side and let it go and he watched the waves collect it and take it on. He turned the boat for home and jammed the throttle down.

It was only the last few years the otters had returned to the coast, having been decimated in the last century by fur-pirate entrepreneurs. Nice going, if he had driven them out of the bay again, with his goddamn crab trap.

He swung the boat in neatly and tied up and climbed out onto the wharf. He searched the waters, squinting across the grey-green strait to Vancouver, the southern mainland of British Columbia, and on to northern Washington State. The frosted cone and jagged flanks of Mount Baker shimmered under the sun.

They were going to have had all of this, every day, when he quit the force. Now. . .

The phone was ringing again and apparently was not going to stop. The spaniel bounced and danced around Cooper's legs as he took his time climbing the sloping rock beach and the low grassy bank up to the steps leading to the cedar-plank sun deck. Daffodil tips were starting to show. Sandi had planted hundreds of bulbs on the bank and under alder and scrub-willow trees. Soon there would be a mass of fluttering yellow, a surge of new life.

Cooper ducked through the open sliding glass doors. He crossed the living room, past the airtight wood stove and the low coffee table with the jumble of beer empties on it, and picked up the phone.

"What?"

"'What?' Not even, 'Good morning inspector, or Jack, and how in hell are you'?"

Cooper sighed, loudly, deliberately. "I might have known. Jack, I'm on holiday. You know, golf, a few brews."

Jack Kovich laughed down the line. "A few brews, I'll bet. And how is the golf?"

"Come and find out."

"Tempting."

"Ask Helen for a kitchen pass. Explain that you'll be with me."

"She'd have me locked up. . . Ah, listen, Matt. . . "

Alarm bells. Jack Kovich was nothing if never subtle. Whatever was coming was not designed to improve Matt Cooper's day.

"I'm on *holiday*, Jack."

A long moment's silence.

"Yeah, I know. But, listen, you're due back, what, Thursday?"

"Exactly right. Thursday. *Late* Thursday. *Next week* Thursday. Several days from now."

Jack Kovich laughed again.

"Yeah, well, that's fine, but-how does tonight sound, instead? There's a ferry, isn't there?"

Cooper said, "Okay, which would you like answered first? 'How does tonight sound?' The answer to which is, that dog don't hunt. Or, 'Is there a ferry tonight?' Which is of no concern, because it does not impinge on any of my immediate plans."

A pause while Jack considered 'impinge.'

Cooper reached across the phone to a lonely half-full beer and inhaled most of it before clarifying the situation for his boss.

"I've been here three days. Out of seven, total. That means I have four left-three from seven leaves four."

He chugged the remaining beer.

"I am heavily booked for those four days. I've got a broken window to fix that a goddamn flicker flew into. The local deer have penetrated my guaranteed-deer-proof fence and chewed the apple and plum trees to ratshit, and-"

"Matt. Listen to me."

"-I'm still working on last year's vacation days that I never got to take."

"Matt, I will make all of this up to you. I will come and personally install new glass in your windows, double-glazed, even. And I will rebuild your deer fence. In fact, why don't I just sign out a really big gun and come and shoot Bambi and all her little buddies and end the problem?" A pause. Then, "Either way, right now we need you back here."

"You need me? *Who* needs me? Jesus, Jack!"

"*We* need you, Matt. Your country needs you." A beat. "Your *Queen* needs you, Sergeant."

'Sergeant'. Getting prickly.

Try a petition to reason. Though no successful precedent jumped to mind.

"Jack, the Royal visit is weeks away. We have worked and re-worked every possible detail. I know it, all my guys know it, inside out. The Emergency Response Team is prepared, and we start full rehearsal runs when I get back."

"It's changed, Matt."

"What has changed, Jack? The visit? The timing? What?"

A couple of seconds.

"Your detail, Matt. Your assignment for the visit. That's been changed."

Jack Kovich sounded uncomfortable.

"What are you saying? How can it have changed?"

"I can't explain it on the phone."

"Shit, what-you worried about security?"

Silence.

"For Chrissakes, Jack, my party-line is an eighty-nine-year-old great-grandma who flies the Maple Leaf on two corners of her sun deck and a Union Jack on the chimney-"

"Matt-"

"- her son is a senator, her grandson's a member of parliament, and she's a life-member of the Conservative Party. You couldn't get a secret out of her with truth drugs and a fucking blow torch."

"Matt-"

"And she's stone deaf."

"Something's come up, Matt."

Don't ask.

"I've had Queen's Cowboys hanging from the walls here. The Ottawa kind, with brass up to their eyeballs. Deputy-commissioner types."

Shit.

"I'd like you back, Matt."

Before I have to say get your ass back now, Sergeant.

What could change? The ER Team was primed, ready for anything. What the hell's going on?

He wasn't going to find out on his side of the water.

They compromised, but not by much. Cooper would catch the first ferry in the morning.

He was up before dawn. He had replaced the cracked windowpane and done a crude patching of the deer fence.

He stood on the porch and stared out into the bay. A movement in the water caught his eye. He squinted. It was a deadhead --a half-sunk log--moving sluggishly with the tide.

On the way to the ferry, Cooper stopped at the garbage dump. He swung the crab trap over his head and tossed it as far over the bank of rubbish as he could and heard it land among the mounds of rotting matter and rusting stoves.

CHAPTER 5

Vancouver

Black-bellied rain clouds sat above the city like a bad mood. Flurries rode on sharp gusts of a West Coast lazy wind–the kind that can't be bothered to go around you, so goes straight through. The underground police parking lot was full, as usual. Cooper cruised two blocks and won a tight race with a young Asian woman at the wheel of a crimson Mercedes 380 SL for a space on Hastings Street, where he stuck the station wagon against the curb. The wagon smelled sweetly of the split alder and fir he'd tossed into the back before he left the island, as well as of the residual spiders, sawdust and bark chips from a dozen earlier loads that he intended to sweep out sometime.

Cooper locked the door. He turned to the sound of a honking horn. The woman in the glistening Mercedes was giving him the finger, and her lips, painted to match her car, moved distinctly in the two syllables of "ass-hole."

Cooper tossed her a kiss. He walked around the corner and entered through the brass-handled glass doors of 312 Main Street. He waved to the duty desk sergeant and winked at the russet-haired woman corporal trying to get sense out of a wasted-looking young aboriginal woman who was weaving around at the counter, drunk, drugged, or both. From his street experience, Cooper guessed she was from a reserve up north, or in the interior. He wondered again why girls like her left home-or didn't quickly return when they saw what was available to them in downtown Vancouver. At the elevator he punched the button for the third floor.

Jack Kovich was behind his desk, his two hundred and sixty-five pounds challenging the integrity of both his high-backed chair and the seams and buttons of his midnight-blue uniform. Silver rank badges studded Kovich's epaulets.

Cooper did not miss the quick but thorough scrutiny by his long-time friend. He returned it with a manufactured scowl on his long-jawed face.

Kovich grinned. "I'm delighted to see you, too, buddy. And I owe you one when this is over, okay?"

"Four days holiday is what you'll owe me when this is over. Whatever it is."

Cooper pulled a rail-backed wooden chair away from the wall and sat, legs crossed, facing Kovich.

"So tell me, Inspector, why I'm in downtown Vancouver being told to fuck off by Chinese chicks on $50,000 training wheels, instead of sitting in the clubhouse describing how I birdied the par-three fourth. You remember the fourth, the one where you stand in the woods on a hill and pop a wedge, maybe a nine iron, over the creek, past two maples and a yellow cedar into a banked green?"

Kovich laughed, and swung round to a coffeemaker on a shelf behind his desk. "And the truth is, what did you really take on the fourth?"

"I took a seven but I marked it down as a bogey four. That's what it should have been."

"Shoulda, woulda. You cheated."

"I rationalized."

Remind me not to play any more money matches. What an asshole."

"You're only the second person to tell me that today."

"Yeah, well, it's still early."

Kovich poured coffee into two plastic cups and Cooper took one and sipped. He pulled a face, and reached for a tricorner packet of cream. He tore the tab cover off. Approximately a third of the cream spurted out and ran down his hand, some splashing the sleeve of his navy blue sports coat and dribbling in under his shirt cuff. The rest plopped onto the new charcoal-grey wool slacks that he'd worn only once before.

"Shit," Cooper tossed the container into a waste bin beside Kovich's desk, "You ever open these things without spilling them?"

"All the time." Kovich's shrewd grey eyes, in a broad face below the familiar sandy buzz-cut, measured him.

"Of course you do. That's why you're the Inspector. I knew I'd learn the reason eventually."

Kovich barked out a laugh, and Cooper brushed droplets of cream from his clothing.

Cooper grinned at Kovich. He could read Jack like a large-print book.

He's thinking that maybe I could do with a hair cut, but he won't say so. He'll leave that to the Chief to say, if the Chief chooses to, which is unlikely.

Cooper had once overheard Jack in conversation with the Chief, discussing Sgt. Matt Cooper. He was outside Jack's office door, about to enter. He stopped at hearing his name.

"No, Matt is not what you would call a perfect company man," said Kovich. The Chief's concurrence was a grunt.

"Not a systems man-'fuck 'em if they can't take a joke' is his style."

"Say that again," the Chief growled. He had once overheard Cooper liken the departmental management style to that of a lance-corporal from Cooper's army days: "When in danger, when in doubt, run in circles, scream and shout." Another time, he heard Cooper advise a young constable, "Don't ever make the mistake of thinking that the people in charge know what they're doing." Cooper had smiled broadly at the Chief each time, like he was just joking.

"But he's one hell of a cop," Kovich continued. "Good as they come. Better than most."

"Hmmmn," from the Chief, but no dissent.

Jack reminded the Chief of the night that Matt Cooper had saved Jack Kovich's life.

They had been partners, Cooper a rookie constable, Jack with two years seniority, when they answered the dispatcher's call to the drug store on East Broadway. A hype, a chronic criminal, armed with a shotgun, was holding the pharmacist and his wife. When they showed up, the gunman came screaming through the doors like death with its dick out and blew their windshield away on the dead run.

"Matt saw it all coming," Kovich said. "Dragged me flat onto the seat and dropped out the driver's door while the glass was still flying. And then while the asshole was trying to reload, Matt came up on one knee and put three slugs in the fucker's belly and one right in the toy box."

The Chief said, "I remember."

"For the rest of his life that fucker was going to be shitting into a bag, and trying to remember what a hard-on felt like."

There was a soft laugh from the Chief.

Cooper had got to his feet and looked in through the exploded windshield and shuddered at the sight of both front seat-backs in ribbons. He leaned against the black-and-white, shaking like a drunk and said the last time he'd been that close was in Korea. Kovich crawled out and shook the glass fragments from his uniform and out of his hair. He shoved a gauze pad into where most of the blood seemed to be coming from the hype who moaned that he was 'fucken dyin', man.'

They had stress teams today, for what they called post-critical-incident trauma. On that night, the sergeant sat them down and helped with the incident report. He poured half a pint of Ballentine's into them, and sent them home for the rest of the shift. In the space on the report form for justification for use of a firearm, Cooper wrote: "See patrol car."

They paraded the next day and Cooper climbed in behind the wheel in the black-and-white, his knuckles tight on the wheel, and waited for Kovich. Kovich arrived in two minds as to whether to hand in his badge and start looking for a day job. Instead, he slid in beside Cooper and they spent the next three years together in the same cars and the same bars, before Jack started his systematically-plotted rise up the police department's management ladder.

That was, shit, twenty-eight years ago. And all things considered, he didn't feel a whole lot different now than he did then-or look it, the last time he checked. No more than five or six pounds heavier than the one-ninety he'd played at wide receiver at the University of British Columbia. That lasted the one short year that he had endured the dry dismembering of English Literature that passed for teaching, before going out and finding his calling as a cop. Still a good weight for his six-foot frame. Hair, yeah, showing grey streaks in the black, but that was to be expected. And there were lines around the corners of the eyes, and shallow clefts running from his nose to the sides of his mouth. But everybody got lines, and Sheena said lines just added character. But definitely rougher around the edges since Sandi died. The hands a little less steady-the extra couple or three shots of Scotch at night, when things got too quiet in the rambling old house in Kitsilano and he sat listening for her. Should have forgotten about the cream packet, drunk Eddie's fucking awful coffee black.

Cooper flicked the last cream gobs on to the floor, dusted his pants off, and looked at Kovich.

"So, what we got?"

Kovich said nothing, just removed a large brown envelope from his slide-out centre drawer. He opened the envelope, removed six eight-by-ten glossy coloured photographs and slid them onto his desk top.

"This," he said.

He laid the prints face up in two rows of three.

Cooper crossed to the desk and looked at the familiar face, repeated six times.

An identical picture, framed, hung on the wall behind Kovich's desk. Same tiara, the Order of Canada and the Canadian Order of Military Merit pinned to the Star and Garter. Sequined off-the shoulder-dress, string of pearls and earrings. Queen Elizabeth II. Elizabeth Alexandra Mary of the House of Windsor. Age fifty-six on this day, mother of four grown children, grandmother of a bunch of others, and well preserved. Most Excellent Majesty of The United Kingdom of Great Britain and Northern Ireland and of her other Realms and Territories, and Defender of The Faith. Queen of Canada, if you didn't count some hard feelings in Quebec.

Cooper scanned the pictures.

"What?"

"Find the lady."

"What?"

"Find the lady. Find the Queen."

Cooper studied the pictures, across, and up and down. They all looked like copies of an original.

Finally, "You crafty bugger. And you thought you could fool Sergeant Cooper. It's the new staff-sergeant exam, right? Six pictures of the Queen, you pick one without stepping on your dick, you're promoted. Right? Jesus, Jack, that is brilliant. That is how you will maintain the quality of management in this department that we all love and admire."

Kovich smiled.

Cooper continued. "That's almost as smart as the one they use in the *Express* news room that young Dhillon told me about. It's for the guys who want to be assistant city editors. They line them up in the john with their cocks out, and the ones who can keep one or more shoes dry get on the short list. He says if they get their *socks* wet they make them editorial writers."

"Hah!" Kovich laughed and thumped the desk top with his meaty fist. "Love it!"

The *Express* editorial page recently had run a three-day campaign against police brutality after a skid-road wino claimed a constable-jailer had beaten him unconscious for throwing up on the jailer's pants and shoes. The jailer insisted that the man had fallen downstairs. He was cleared after an internal investigation, which the *Express* described as a whitewash.

Kovich said, "What do they do about the women?"

Cooper said, "According to Dhillon, some of them have bigger dicks than the guys. Maybe we could use that for the inspector exam. What d'you think?"

"Yeah-except, how many tries do the candidates get to find their weenies?"

Cooper laughed. That was vintage Jack Kovich, mostly

extinct now, replaced by a calculatedly sensitised and sanitised version that expressed "thank you" on occasions where the earlier Jack would have found "fuck you" more than adequate.

Cooper recalled how Jack Kovich reached a career decision one filthy Friday night as they neared the end of a four-to-midnight foot-patrol shift among the human wreckage and pissing rain along the festering streets of Vancouver's skid road. Cooper had called for the wagon to meet them at Hastings and Carrall where half a dozen local citizens were vigorously engaged in a snot-and-vomit-splashed contest for the soliciting rights to the intersection's Southeast corner, with the contenders being the two established genders and several undecideds. By the time the bodies were dragged from the scrum and assisted into the wagon, the two cops' uniforms were decorated with a rich gravy of blood and excreta from the full range of bodily apertures. It was not the first time it had happened, but it was the worst they'd experienced. And for Kovich, it was the last.

"Fuck this, Matt," he said, as they marched, with their tunics stripped off in the downpour and held out at arm's length, the two blocks back to the Public Safety Building. "I'm going for an inside job. If they don't give me one, I'm fuckin' history."

Jack had repeatedly told Cooper that he had no great interest in being a street cop. Having grown up in the industrial east-end of Vancouver, a block from the docks, Jack had had all the street he needed.

"I want *off* the fuckin' streets, Matt."

Whereas Cooper enjoyed the streets. He wanted to clean them up, get the bad guys. But also, he had a fascination with the transient people of the sidewalks and alleys, with why they'd become what they had. How the fortyish--looking sixtyish--"Slack Sally" had slid from a prestigious position as a senior nurse at St. Paul's Hospital to a drab working the skids for a fix. How the golf pro at one of Vancouver's exclusive private clubs had finished up fishing for his supper in restaurant dumpsters.

The questions never bothered Kovich. For him the answers were simple.

"They're fuck-ups," he said, after briefly considering one of Cooper's observations on the drifting skid-road souls and addicts. "They fucked themselves up and they don't want to get un-fucked. It's no big mystery."

Jack applied for assignment to the vice squad, told Cooper he enjoyed the desk work that went with it, and vowed never to walk another beat. He also explained how this determination coincided with a realisation that most of those officers senior in rank to him in the department were at best about half as bright as he was-and nowhere near as cunning.

"I'm going for the top," he told Cooper, on one of their R&R nights rating the strippers at the Cecil Hotel. He added his belief that the key to advancement on the force was to demonstrate respect for senior ranks.

"I mean, like, *show* it. You don't have to feel it, you know?"

"Seem to be obsequious, you mean," Matt said, and, at Jack's frown, "Kiss ass."

Jack's brow cleared. "Yeah. Well, *seem* to. Hell, I can be the chief constable. You just have to watch how they do it. Some of those guys couldn't pour piss off a plate with instructions on it, but they know promotion is basically a blow-job contest. Some a' them would suck the shine off a brass door knob."

Whatever Jack had done, it had worked. And their friendship had survived his deliberate manoeuvring, and his ascent through the ranks.

Kovich waved a hand over the six pictures.

"Anyway, this one isn't that easy." He tapped one of the pictures. "Four of these are Queen Elizabeth. Two of them are somebody else."

Cooper studied the pictures again. They looked the same. Unless, the eyes, there-no, that nose-*What the hell was going on?*

"So?" Kovich said.

"Christ, Jack, I don't know. So somebody's doctored

some pictures, what-?"

Kovich tapped two of the prints.

"Nobody doctored nothing. That one, and that one."

He had the pictures in two horizontal rows of threes and had tapped the top left and the lower middle prints.

Cooper studied, compared, shrugged. "So? What?"

Kovich shuffled the pictures and laid them out in two rows again.

"Now find them."

Cooper picked two, was wrong on one.

"Amazing. I give up. I guess I'm not gonna make staff-sergeant. What are we playing at here, Jack?"

Kovich told him.

Cooper stared at him.

"Tell me you are joking."

Kovich shook his head, no.

"You're *not* joking. Well hell, if it's that serious, call the thing off-cancel the damn tour."

"The tour goes ahead. She does not cancel because of threats. If she did, they'd never get started. That's the line, Matt. And ours is to die or do."

Cooper couldn't help grinning at another Jack Kovich excursion into the world of familiar phrases. Only once, in the early years, had Cooper advanced a correction, when Jack had claimed that there was more than one way to skin a horse. "Cat," Cooper said. "Cat. More than one way to skin a cat." Jack had puzzled for a second, then said, "What sick bastard would want to skin a cat?"

"So I'd like us to get at it," Kovich said.

Cooper took his time digesting the information and calculating the implications, which were not in his favour.

"The decoy idea," he said. "I mean that's what this woman's going to be, isn't it, a decoy? And that came from our fearless leaders in Ottawa? Jesus, Jack, what if she gets shot? What if she gets killed? What do these fucking people use for brains?"

He paced in front of Kovich's desk.

"They can't be serious."

"They are serious. *We* are serious. But for Christ's sake, we're not putting her up as a target!"

Cooper stopped pacing. "You're not?"

"Nobody's getting killed!"

"Well, that is good to hear. And maybe I missed something-but I don't think so. Let's run it again." He ticked the elements off on his fingers.

"First, we got a red alert that an IRA hit man with some very serious stuff on his sheet is going to blow away the Queen of England-"

"And of Canada."

"Right. Let's not short-change her. And he could nail her anywhere on the tour, including Vancouver if he doesn't get her before that."

"That's about it."

"And we would like to prevent that," Cooper continued, and he waved down an attempt to interrupt by Kovich.

"No, let me run the rest of the movie, Jack."

Kovich rolled his eyes, but he nodded, carry on.

"Some thinker in Ottawa, who I have to guess did not get there on a scholarship, says we have a woman in Vancouver who likes to dress up, and looks like Her Majesty. So, assuming the Queen makes it to Vancouver, why don't we dangle this woman in public in place of the Queen and see if this guy really is a shooter. And that doesn't make the woman a target? Who's shittin' who, Jack?"

Kovich waited a moment. "You finished?"

Cooper nodded. "For now."

"Okay, listen to me-to the end, that is. Okay?"

"You're the boss."

Kovich shifted his bulk. His chair groaned.

He doesn't like this, Cooper decided. Which meant that Cooper wasn't going to enjoy it much either.

"First," Kovich said. "Don't start flying to conclusions-what?"

Cooper lost the grin. "Nothing. Carry on."

Kovich cleared his throat, slurped some coffee.

"Okay, let's get this clear. First: no specific order has

come from Ottawa about the woman. All I said was that we had Ottawa brass here, right? They've been told about it, and they're shittin' their pants, but that's all. They're bureaucrats-if you don't make a decision, you won't make a mistake, you know?"

Kovich sought more from the coffee dregs, grimaced. He crushed the plastic cup and flipped it into the waste bin.

"So they kept their heads up their asses, and just went along with this," pointing to the six photos.

" I still don't-"

"I was going to finish, remember?"

Cooper faked a contrite salaam. "Sorry, carry on."

Kovich snorted. "Sorry, my ass. Anyhow, the point I'm making is that this, the other woman business, did not come from Ottawa. This is coming from-this is strictly local."

Cooper's head lifted. Jack had a gift for triggering alarms, and another one was clattering.

"Local? What? The Chief? What does he- ?"

Kovich's hand rose, big enough to eclipse a small sun.

"Just listen 'til I'm through, just listen, sergeant. I'm not exactly hilarious about this myself-and now what's so fuckin' funny?"

"Sorry, Jack. Go on, I'm listening."

"That's it. I've told you everything they've told me, which admittedly is not a whole hell of a lot."

"You're right."

"That and the fact that Quinsam is going to be running his own show."

"Quinsam?" Cooper sat up. "What the hell-?"

"- and no questions asked. And Quinsam says he wants my best man to run it for him. I mean, that's where it is. So I'm askin' you, okay?"

I'm tellin' you, okay?

"Quinsam is running this? The original noble savage?"

"The same. She--the Queen--asks for him anyway, you know that. Ever since they ran into him that other time."

"Yeah, yeah, I know. Full-blooded Native Indian Mountie and isn't he cute as a bear cub in his cherry coat and cowboy hat? Major hit with her and Philip and they want to see him every time they visit Canada. It's a wonder they haven't taken the big prick back with them. Stick him in a soldier box outside Buckingham Palace and let the Limeys see a real aboriginal."

Kovich's face creased. "I thought aboriginals were from Australia."

"Just the Australian ones."

The creases relaxed. "Yeah. Makes sense."

Which is more than everything else is doing.

Kovich said, "Quinsam gets to be her personal bodyguard, apart from the assorted special teams, which right now we are up to our asses in, let me tell you, and this is what he wants. And Ottawa says what Quinsam wants, Quinsam gets. No questions. And he wants you. Do we understand this?"

Kovich was flushing up, the rolls of neck that overflowed his crisp white collar flashing a sanguine signal of unease.

Cooper sat forward on the wooden chair.

"Let me get this clear, Jack: Quinsam says jump, and you say, 'How high, sir?' Without any protest, without any attempt at rational discussion, you let Quinsam--*Corporal* Quinsam--you let him pick me to, what, baby-sit this woman? And for this you're gonna take me off Emergency Response? Is that it?"

Kovich was silent.

Cooper felt walls closing in on him. "I don't believe this. I've been ten years running Emergency Response. We've trained six months for just this one. And suddenly you want me to play hide-and-seek with an old lady that looks like the Queen?"

Kovich met his gaze, but said nothing.

That's exactly what he wants.

"Jack, you *can't* take me off ERT, man. Don't *do* this to me."

Kovich raised his hands, dropped them. It's done.

"Jack?"

Cooper felt sick. The Emergency Response Team had given him a needed focus since Sandi's death. And he'd been effective, hadn't he? Had directed a dozen call-outs, all with a potential for deadly force and all resolved with no casualties to the team. So what the fuck was the problem? This bullshit about Quinsam wanting Kovich's best man was just that, bullshit. They could have assigned this minder's job to a rookie, or to some lifer beat-cop hanging on for his pension. Plenty of each around. The rookie would bask in the perceived status, and the lifer would get to rest his aching feet. So what the fuck was going down?

And then, a glimmer. Some recent department individual evaluations showed Cooper with lag-times in a couple of areas, responses not quite as sharp as they could have been. Cooper had dismissed the last assessment, attributing the results to a bout of flu.

"Not the old twenty-six-ounce flu, was it?" Kovich had joked.

Or not joked. Was Jack really wondering if Dr. Ballentine's and a few brews--"*A few brews, I'll bet.*"--was behind Cooper's sliding evaluations? And hadn't wanted to say so to his face, instead had come up with this trumped up assignment with Quinsam? And a flash, a wisp of a thought, that maybe Jack has a point. And the thought as quickly banished.

It took Cooper a moment to register Kovich's limp response: "She's not an old lady."

There was a loud rap on the door. It opened and Jim Quinsam filled the space. A smile split the Haida Indian's dark-honey-toned face. The narrow, white-ridged scar that extended from the right corner of Quinsam's lip to the bottom of his chin only slightly marred the smile. The scar was the bequest of a hockey stick from his late-teen years when he had been a marginal National Hockey League prospect and still living in the Queen Charlotte Islands, the Haida nation's homeland across the wild Hecate Strait from the B.C mainland.

Cooper was on his feet. "You asshole."

"You recognised me!" He laughed and grabbed Cooper in a bear hug, lifted him off his feet and put him down.

Cooper stepped back and they shook hands warmly.

"Man, they really beat the bushes this time." Cooper examined the big Indian, fifteen years his junior. Glowing-gold skin. Thick raven hair brushing his collar. The latter was a dress-code concession to the frequent assignments that took Quinsam into the down-scale urban scene in under-cover drug operations. Cooper had worked many of them with him. Quinsam wore a RCMP parka over a green down-filled vest, plaid shirt, worn jeans, and stained, rubber-soled work boots. Without the Mountie crest on the parka, he could have been a native logger hitting the city for a festive weekend.

Cooper saw Quinsam shoot a glance past him at Jack Kovich, a query to which he seemed to get an answer.

Cooper said, "Where the hell did they find you? I thought you were back in Regina at the Academy, teaching, what, surviving on moccasin soup, wasn't it?"

Quinsam laughed. "That, and how to stay on a horse. But the institution life ain't for me. I'd forgotten about the spit an' polish bullshit. I got a posting back up the coast. Old stompin' grounds. Where the heart is."

"Where all the familiar nookie is, you mean. Prince Rupert?"

"And across to the Charlottes sometimes. Downtown Massett, fun spots like that."

Kovich poured another coffee and handed it to the Mountie corporal. "Okay, we can bullshit later, maybe have a beer. Why don't you run it all down for Matt right now, Jim?"

"And then I can tell you what to do with it," Cooper laughed.

He was the only one to do so.

Quinsam took a chair so that he sat obliquely to Cooper and half-facing Kovich, who had returned behind his desk.

Kovich's expression told Cooper that, for Jack, the fat lady had sung. His part was over. And over to Quinsam.

Quinsam said. "How much have you told him?"

"Just the basics. There's a look-a-like woman involved, and it's your show. Matt has some concerns about the double. Figures we might be setting her up.

The Mountie looked at Cooper.

"Okay, I can see your thinking. So, here's my take on it. It's a precaution, a bit of smoke and mirrors is all. We're gonna have the Queen covered, like fur on a bear, in California and here. Anybody in a crowd who looks even mildly unhappy will be invited in for a chat-a long one. We got hundreds of military, and police in civvies as well as all the uniforms. We got some hard-ass airborne types coming in from England as further backup, and we'll have all the help from the States that we could want-down there, and here.

Cooper said, "Good. It sounds like you've got it locked. So, what's the point of using the double? I mean, what's the point?"

Quinsam's eyes stayed on Cooper.

"The point is that I want her as an option. That's the point."

And what Quinsam wants, Quinsam gets.

Cooper looked at Kovich, who was busy suddenly dusting off the edge of his immaculately maintained desk.

Quinsam punched Cooper lightly on the arm, a buddy-shot. "Ah, shit, Matt. Come on, I don't want to sound like a prick, eh?"

"But?"

"Well, yeah, 'but.' Look, the point is, I *am,* as usual, her personal security, and we *do* have a potential big problem. And I am going to make sure I have every bit of edge I can possibly get. All right?"

Cooper shrugged.

"Chances are the other woman will stay on the bench. Chances are, she won't even dress."

"'Chances are,'" Cooper said. "Who was it used to sing that? Sinatra? Peggy Lee? I forget."

Quinsam gave him a patient smile.

Cooper said, "'Smoke Gets In Your Eyes,' That was another one."

Good sense told Cooper that maybe about now would be a good time to shut up. He said, "But if you have to dress her, you will, is that what you're saying?"

Quinsam nodded slow confirmation. "Bottom line-if I have to, yes, I will."

"And Ottawa agrees?"

"Jesus!" Quinsam's slapped a closed fist into his opposite palm, lifted his head back in a give-me-patience-Lord pose. Then he spelled it out.

"Matt. Listen. My instructions are to do what I have to do to keep the Queen from being harmed. This--the double, the impersonator, call her what you want-"

"Target?"

Quinsam ignored the interruption. "... is one of the things I'm doing. I've told them what my options are, and nobody argued."

That was the line, and it was going to be toed.

"I don't expect anybody to get hurt. But I repeat-I will do whatever it takes to ensure the Queen's safety."

Kovich sealed it. "It's been decided, Matt. It's how it has to be."

Well, that bit's been decided, anyway.

Cooper stood. He paced as he spoke.

"All right, so it's a lock. I accept that part of it. You're gonna use a double, a decoy. Personally I don't see it, but that's not my call."

Kovich smiled his approval.

"But, the next bit. Me. Why *me*, especially? Why do I come off Emergency Response and get the goddamn dummy to look after? I mean, how can you take me off the team, Jack? Who decided that?"

"I told you!" Kovich's face flamed. "Jim asked for you, and I approved it. It was a mutual thing."

Cooper turned on Quinsam.

"That so, Jim? You picked me out of all the shit-hot shooters to keep an eye on Miss Runner Up?"

Kovich was half out of his chair.

"You're outta line, Matt!"

Quinsam said, "I asked for you, Matt, yes."

Cooper eyed Quinsam. Then he looked at Kovich.

"Wait a minute, now. It couldn't be, old buddy, that you're believing those assessment reports? Ol' Matt's losing it?"

Kovich's gaze wavered.

"You don't trust me to look after the Queen-so you give me Mrs. Dress-up instead?"

Kovich said, "You're taking it the wrong way, Matt. We need the best man we've got for this job."

"Sure." He paced across to the window. He leaned a hand against the window frame and looked down onto the human clutter and busy traffic of Main Street. At a bus stop across the street, two mottle-faced drunks punched the air in lieu of each other. A bus slid into the stop zone and the driver left his seat and stood on the step as the pair tried to stagger aboard. He pushed them away. One of the two spat a stream of stringy phlegm at the door as the driver shut it on them.

Cooper spoke while still staring out the window.

"And what if I say no? What if I ask to be re-assigned?"

Kovich answered. "I hope you won't do that, Matt." He waited a second. "You would not be a happy camper doing jail duty, or running the front desk."

Cooper turned his head.

Kovich looked miserable.

Cooper recalled advice Jack had given him years before. Cooper and Sandi had engaged in one of those difference of opinions where the adversaries push themselves so far into a corner that the jaws of life couldn't get them out. In that case it was Jack's wholly better half, Helen Kovich, with considerable personal experience to draw on, who had done the retrieving and refereed the outcome. Cooper couldn't remember what the fight had been about. But he remembered Jack's advice: "If you are going to fight, Matt--women, the department, whatever--know one of two things: know either that you're gonna win, guaranteed, or, that a loss will be worth whatever it could cost you. Otherwise, forget it."

The formula had always been too black-and-white--too *Jack*--for Cooper, whose contests were waged on his gut feeling of right and wrong.

But this time it was clear he wasn't on a winner. And the options--jailer, or desk jockey--were non-starters.

He said, "What I should do is tell you to stick your decoy idea where there's no sunshine, and follow it with the Vancouver City Police Department." He glared at Kovich. "If I could think of anything else to make a living at, I would."

Sandi: *"Coop, you must be the only cop in Vancouver who doesn't know he's not having a good time."*

"But nothing comes to mind."

The decision was made. And Cooper knew, despite his protests, that Kovich likely was justified. He had lost a step or two. He also knew that it was nothing he couldn't fix, and would, once this was over. Maybe it had needed something like this to make him pay attention to the story he'd been seeing in the mirror lately.

"Who would get the team?"

"The guy you trained for it," Kovich said. "Chursky."

Cooper nodded, then looked at Quinsam. "Has anybody talked to this woman yet?"

Kovich released a quiet sigh of relief.

Quinsam grinned at Cooper. "More or less. We had the idea put to her on a 'what-if' basis. Mrs. Grant said, 'Where do I sign up?'"

"Mrs. Grant? Sounds like somebody's cleaning lady. Where do I find her?"

Kovich told him.

"Great, I could use some entertainment."

He turned and walked to the door and closed it firmly behind him.

The sound of Cooper whistling "There's No Business Like Show Business", to a beat that resembled a funeral march, accompanied that of his footsteps receding along the linoleum-tiled corridor.

Kovich said, "I'm glad I didn't have to spell it out. He knows, though." He shoved the six glossy photographs into his desk drawer. "Main thing is, we're not taking any chances-and he'll be out of harm's way." He looked up at Quinsam. "I hope you're right about keeping her on the bench."

Quinsam said, "I hope so, too."

CHAPTER 6

Vancouver.

Dooley took a Leretine pill from the pharmacy container and swallowed it with orange juice. He was up to double the dose he had started on, now using one gram of the stuff every six hours to still the carving pain.

He turned on the television set and watched a young woman with a manufactured smile prattling about a low-pressure system that might bring more rain to the Lower Mainland of British Columbia. Station T-VAN, she assured her audience, took absolutely no responsibility. Silly cow. Dooley wondered if her kind talked like that at home.

He walked over to the hotel room window and looked down three stories onto Beach Avenue and across to the sloping strip of trodden sand that ran into a slate-grey English Bay. Eight bulky grain freighters tugged restlessly at their anchor chains in the morning drizzle, waiting their turn to nose under the Lions Gate Bridge to the loading wharves on the north shore of Burrard Inlet.

Dooley followed the progress of a softly rounded young woman jogging south on the sidewalk opposite. Smooth thighs and muscular buttocks competed for space in her brief, yellow satin shorts. Under a faded red sweatshirt, ripe breasts thrust against the three white initials of the University of British Columbia.

Dooley loved this city. Yesterday he'd ridden the Grouse Mountain ski lift. The tram was stuffed. School escapees, bouncing to get at the snow. Couples, some in their sixties at least, glowing, and laughing as the car lurched to a stop and they fought for balance. Back home, people their age would be content to park in front of the fire in their slippers and cardigans and watch the telly until someone came in to check their pulse. He'd savoured two pints of local ale in the Grouse Nest bar and strolled out onto the deck and absorbed the sweeping view across the city and into the flat farmland suburbs near the airport. He could handle this kind of living. Could have.

He gazed across the beaches and ocean to Point Grey, where the university residence towers shouldered through the mist. Further to the west a wedge of lightening sky above the spines of the Gulf Islands promised a day that would only get better.

A splash of scarlet and turquoise shifted his gaze to the beach on the Kitsilano south-side of the bay, where two wind surfers raised their sails. A gust caught them and they scudded out from shore, brilliant painted water bugs racing the wind, skidding and sliding, one of them suddenly slapped by an errant wave and knocked sideways into the trough.

At the crosswalk below Dooley's window a uniformed constable of the Vancouver city police mounted squad appeared riding a tall dark bay. The cop crossed when the pedestrian light flashed. The horse flicked its tail when its hoofs touched the sand and it broke into a canter along the open beach.

Dooley's first trip to Vancouver had been right after Mountbatten and Warrenpoint. He had returned to the city for extended stays three times since and if life's plans had permitted, he might have made it his final home.

If they hadn't murdered the child. If the doctors had found something minor when he'd started shitting blood, and not cancer of the colon advanced to the point where surgery would have been pointless.

And like the kids say-if your granny had wheels she could be a double-decker bus.

When he'd walked through Canada Customs at Vancouver International Airport a week ago, they'd told him to have a nice stay, and one of the young women officers had asked if he was here for the Royal Visit.

"Wouldn't miss it for the world," Dooley said, and the woman laughed, "Lucky you," and waved him through.

Dooley's cover was as a journalist, a roving freelancer with credentials from a news features service in the north of England. He had carefully chosen the guise more than two decades ago, when he had dedicated himself to the cause of Irish independence. Not that there had ever been a question about his future. In the Dooley home, on each new year's calendar, the date of April 24 was marked in black and printed in the square for that day, the single word "Remember." On that date in 1916, Easter Monday, Dooley's maternal grandfather, Daniel Cunningham, had stood on the steps of Dublin's General Post Office on O'Connell Street beside Padraic Pearse as Pearse read the Proclamation of the Republic on behalf of the Provisional Government. Daniel Cunningham was severely wounded during the gun battle that followed and, when a month later the British executed him as a leader of the uprising, they did so with him strapped into a chair. There had never been a doubt about the path that his grandson would take.

Sean Dooley's best friend in school had been Joseph Sheehy, also from a rabidly republican family. After leaving school Joseph became a trainee reporter with the *Irish Times,* and often Dooley would string along with him on assignments. It soon registered with Dooley that the simple act of flashing a press card was an "Open, Sesame." No one seemed to question the right of reporters--or anyone looking as if he were a reporter--to be just about wherever they chose to be. To test this, Dooley had a copy of Joseph's press card made up, with his own name printed on it. The card--usually a casual wave of it--and a notebook or tape recorder in his hand, had taken him unhindered past Garda and barriers at any number of events. He had never been asked who he was.

Dooley carried identification from "World News Features", with an address and telephone number in Manchester. The likelihood of anyone ever checking was negligible. If anyone did, however, he would have received either a recorded message that all World News Features staff were busy just then, or if he were home, the live voice of Joseph

Sheehy, saying, "World News Features. . ." Joseph Sheehy actually was the Managing Editor of the Manchester bureau for the massive Time-Mail Newspapers chain. The World News Features telephone was in his two-room flat in Worsley. Sheehy knew only Dooley's cover-name, to verify if necessary, which had never happened. He and Dooley had not met for many years and Sheehy knew nothing of Dooley's activities, though he may have guessed at their nature. This was best for both of them.

At the hotel check-in a smiling young woman receptionist had handed Dooley the small wooden box marked "camera equipment" that the supporter somewhere in the Canadian post office had finessed through customs. Always there would be someone willing to smooth the path for Sean Dooley.

In his room he unpacked the guns.

The likelihood of these particular weapons being used in Vancouver was slight; he would reach her in California. But Dooley had not achieved his bloody successes by accident. He planned with the care of a brain surgeon. The room was rented until three days after the scheduled end of the tour in Vancouver.

The weather woman had stopped blathering, and the early news anchorman's baritone filled the room as the television picture switched to a sun-stroked dusty road in Jamaica's Montego Bay.

"The Queen received a joyous and noisy welcome from thousands of Jamaicans today as she and the Duke of Edinburgh continued what is to be the most extensive royal tour of the western hemisphere ever taken. . ."

The authoritative voice accompanied scenes of smiling black faces and an even happier-looking Elizabeth Windsor. She was trailed by the usual gang of inflated local politicians, fretting security people, and hungry news media flock, God bless them.

". . . today the Queen moves on to Acapulco. . ."

Dooley stepped over to the wall closet, reached into the deep right-hand pocket of his sand-coloured safari jacket, and brought out the Colt.

At first glance the weapon was nothing more than a regular tried and true semiautomatic Colt Government .45 ACP, better known throughout its history as the Colt .45.

A professional would have noted Dooley's refinements.

The corners of the custom-installed combat-competition rear sights were carefully rounded to prevent any snagging on pocket or holster. Every moving part was polished and de-burred, and the trigger-pull reduced to a smooth 4 1/4 pounds. The barrel was throated and the feed ramp polished to prevent jamming. The ejector port was enlarged and flared. The Pachmayer custom neoprene grips felt moulded for his hands. The deep pockets in Dooley's safari and pea jackets were lined with slick tight-weave nylon as further insurance and as a deterrent to any accumulation of fluff and dirt.

He took the jacket off its hanger and slipped his arms into the sleeves. He dropped the Colt, cocked and locked, into the right hand pocket, and moved into the drill. She was walking towards him. He was as close as the press hounds were allowed, which was often just steps away. Smooth fast draw, gun raised to eye-height in a two handed combat grip. Both arms extended and the left thumb smoothly dropping the safety catch.

At anything inside ten yards he could invariably put a double tap--two quick shots--inside an inch circle. Everything in a maximum of two seconds, from the draw to the shots fired. And she would be closer than ten yards.

He checked the other weapon. Whatever else the Krauts had cocked-up, they had always known how to make guns. The twenty-four ounces was light as he hefted it, after the solid weight of the Colt. As deadly if needed, though.

He jumped as the phone rang, and he checked his watch. On the button, nine a.m.; tea-time back home.

"Hello. Siobahn? How are you, love? Yes, yes, of course I am. Yes, regular meals, pills, the lot. Don't you worry."

He listened. "Right, well, you take care. I'll call you from down there. God Bless.

"A kiss for sweet Shannon," he added softly.

He put the phone down and went back to the window.

A sudden shower pattered on the glass.

A sweet and deadly kiss.

The newsreader said that from Acapulco the Queen would move on to southern California.

Dooley checked the phone book and called Air Canada reservations.

"I'd like to book a flight to Los Angeles."

CHAPTER 7

Grand Cayman Island.

The Queen read the transcript of the BBC early morning news and the digest prepared for her of the London newspapers. Two of the tabloids had decided she was "furious" over a report that Andrew had sneaked off to Mystique with that saucy little film actress, Koo Stark. She clucked her tongue. Personally, she had quite liked the Ferguson girl the couple of times she'd met her. A bit hefty, perhaps, and certainly not straight out of the convent. But how many of them were these days?

She sipped cautiously on her second cup of blended Chinese tea. Her stomach was still queasy and she had foregone her usual Harrod's breakfast sausages, managing instead only a slice of honeydew melon, four strawberries, and one slice of dry toast along with the tea.

The royal yacht *Britannia* had docked at Grand Cayman the night before, following a roisterous start to the tour in Kingston. Thousands of Jamaicans had danced in rainbow Conga lines in the city streets. They had stamped their feet and roared their approval when she smilingly announced herself as the Queen of Jamaica. She seemed oblivious to a circle of sober black republican faces.

She emptied one of the red boxes on to the desk top. The prime minister was becoming an absolute bugger for work. There was a stack of cabinet memoranda inches high, as well as petitions, letters and invitations. And that was only the first box. Two more hours work at least.

There was a tentative knock at the door.

"Yes?"

Simon Shaw-Guilliard, her private secretary, peered round the opened door.

"What is it, Simon? I'm very busy."

She looked just slightly shaky, he thought, which was testimony to her remarkable stamina and resilience. Shaw-Guilliard was wise enough to withhold any comment that might have sounded remotely like "I told you so." He had reminded her of her own standing rules the previous day, just before she disregarded the one of never eating shell fish away from home. A beaming Kingston chef had offered her a taste of conch chowder, and she had cheerfully accepted.

Consequently, both Shaw-Guilliard and the Queen's personal physician, Dr. Amelia French, spent most of the night standing-by as Queen Elizabeth coped with a severe case of the Caribbean trots. Once, Shaw-Guilliard heard her remonstrate with the Duke, who apparently *had* said I told you so.

"Oh, bugger off, Philip!" she'd snapped, while making another dash for the loo.

Now, Shaw-Guilliard said, "There's a bit of a flap on with the Canadians, I'm afraid."

She put on what the staff referred to as her "Miss Piggy face."

"What now?"

"A threat; they seem particularly concerned." He coughed. "The Prime Minister suggested cancelling."

Her eyes flashed. "Over my dead body!"

Shaw-Guilliard winced. He touched the edge of the rosewood desk. "Ma'am, please."

"Well, really, that man!"

"Mr. Garrett, the external affairs minister, is due at Owen Roberts Airport in about an hour, ma'am. He insists on seeing you."

The Queen glared at the imperative, but Shaw-Guilliard soldiered on.

"This was arranged overnight, Your Majesty, while you-"

Her eyes narrowed and he altered tack.

"-were sleeping. We saw no reason to interrupt your rest; you have a full day ahead."

She glanced at the papers piled in front of her. She sighed.

"Very well, Simon. Have him join us for lunch."

#

Garrett sipped on a dark rum punch onboard a glistening white launch on a sapphire bay, and listened to the Duke of Edinburgh.

"I'm sure you understand, Mr. Garrett, if we chose to hide from every threat on our lives, we would never leave Buckingham Palace."

Garrett sweltered in a dove-grey worsted three-piece suit. He sat in a deck chair facing the royal couple. The Queen was bare-legged, her feet in a pair of light straw sandals. A loose, shoulder-less cotton dress suggested a firmness of flesh uncommon in a woman in her mid-fifties. Garrett banished an unworthy thought and paid attention to the Duke. Philip seemed comfortable in deck shoes, knee socks and Bermuda shorts and short-sleeved khaki shirt. A floppy white hat guarded his scalp from the sub-tropical sun.

"Of course, sir, and that was Mr. Therrien's initial response. He said that both Her Majesty and he had more to concern themselves with than some crackpot."

"Quite so," the Queen said.

"However," Garrett went on, "after listening to this man McGuire, the Prime Minister changed his mind. His first inclination was to cancel the Canadian tour."

The Queen glared.

"Mr. Llewellyn though was rather firm about that."

"I should think so," the Queen said. "I have said it a hundred times and I shall repeat it, Mr. Garrett: I have to be seen to be believed. Please understand that. And make sure the Prime Minister understands it."

She sipped on a glass of iced Malvern water and studied Garrett and his streaming face.

"Indeed, ma-am," he said.

He took a long swallow of rum punch, and continued.

"We have discussed some possible, ah, arrangements," he said. "Some contingencies, you might say, Your Majesty."

The Queen set her glass down and folded her hands in her lap. The Duke of Edinburgh cocked his head slightly, politely, waiting.

Garrett wiped his face and beavered on.

"There is a, well, a rather unusual suggestion, from Corporal Quinsam."

"*Corporal* Quinsam! Of course, he was promoted! How is he? He sent us the most delightful Christmas card, didn't he, Philip? Wonderful totem poles!"

"Very nice," Prince Philip agreed.

"And what is Corporal Quinsam's suggestion?" the Queen asked.

Garrett told her.

"Good God!" she said.

"Bloody Hell!" the Duke said.

"Not if I lived for a thousand years, Mr. Garrett!"

Later, wishing Garrett farewell, the Queen said, "Corporal Quinsam is an ingenious young man, Mr. Garrett, and he means well. My husband and I are greatly looking forward to meeting him again. I must say though that judgement seems to have fallen to enthusiasm in this case. There will be only one Queen Elizabeth on the streets of Vancouver."

Garrett nodded glumly.

"However, that does not have to be an issue at this stage."

"No, ma'am."

"I suggest that you advise the Prime Minister simply that my husband and I have been fully apprised of Corporal Quinsam's proposal. I would think that should satisfy him?"

"I'll tell him exactly that, Ma'am."

"Splendid."

CHAPTER 8

Vancouver.

The curtain rose and a softly lit Queen Elizabeth II shifted in a chintz-covered high-backed mahogany chair. She was in full regalia; sequins, Star and Garter, pearls and tiara. On her lap was a copy of the *Illustrated London News.* A spindly side table held a Royal Worcester set of teapot, cup and saucer, milk jug, sugar bowl, and silver tongs and spoon.

The audience applauded, and she smiled across the lights. She placed a book marker carefully on a page. She laid the magazine on the table and stood.

"I don't always dress up in the evenings."

Laughter and more applause. She could have been in a Buckingham Palace drawing room.

"Just when we're going out. State balls and such."

They waited.

"It's a dinner tonight." She shaped a Miss Piggy face. "Your Prime Minister." She frowned. "What'shisname."

The audience howled.

She offered a smile at the same time properly regal and decidedly saucy, and the audience rumbled expectantly.

Cooper stretched in his aisle seat. He pressed the light-button on his Timex. Just after eight. The Emergency Response Team would be warming up for a workout. Checking weapons, swapping jokes. Bloody Kovich. Maybe it *was* time to get out. Take the pension. Fuck 'em.

His attention flicked back to the stage.

She frowned. "I do get fed up with always smiling, you know."

The voice, Cooper realised, was the real thing. The cosy theatre on Southwest Marine Drive crackled with audience pleasure.

"I said to my husband, I said," and she tilted her face, braced her shoulders and faced an imaginary Duke of Edinburgh, "'Philip, why can't I be miserable sometimes?'"

The audience waited.

"And he said, 'Oh, you can, my dear, you can!'"

A great belly-laugh erupted from a large shape two rows in front of Cooper, prompting a spreading of guffaws around it, like ripples in a pond.

She slipped her happy face back on, and Cooper caught himself smiling.

"Dear Philip," she sighed. "He's the only man I've ever really loved you know."

They revelled in it, laughter giving way to applause and then to sputtering laughter again as she added coyly, "Well, there was a stable boy once. . .nothing serious of course. Nothing like Philip." She reached over and picked up the poppy-patterned translucent cup from the table and raised it, her little finger extended extravagantly.

She sipped delicately, and replaced the cup.

"People always ask, and the answer is that yes, we do have separate bedrooms." She smiled and her eyes twinkled. "With a through-door."

She waited until the laughter tapered.

"At our age, you know, things tend to-well, actually I asked Philip. I said, 'Philip, my dear, which is supposed to go first in the ageing process-the ah, natural urge, or the memory?'"

She picked up the cup and sipped again while they waited.

"He said, 'Actually, I don't recall.'"

Despite the predictable punch line, Cooper chuckled spontaneously at the image she evoked of the puzzling, gangling Duke of Edinburgh, brow furrowed in search of the answer.

Cooper had an aisle seat in the tenth row.

Kovich had handed him an envelope. Inside was a ticket to Queen Elizabeth impersonator Maggie Grant's one-woman show, and reviews of the show clipped from the two city dailies.

He'd read them over a double Scotch and water at the lounge in the Fraser Arms Hotel up the block from the theatre.

The *Express* had a colour picture on the front page of the Entertainment section, keyed to the review inside. The picture could have been the Queen, except for the cheeky smile the photographer had coaxed from the Grant woman, and to which Cooper kept returning. The headline declared, simply, "Queen Maggie", and the review enthused about the remarkable physical similarity, and Maggie Grant's skills as a mimic. A short profile said she was a single mother who had started a modest stage career after a friend sent pictures of her in her Queen get-up to a theatre company.

Hers was the final act of a program that had relied heavily on British tits-and-bum and bathroom humour interspersed with a bagpipe act, a woman who sang Vera Lynn favourites, and rousing sing-along choruses of songs from the two world wars, none of which Cooper joined in. Only an ingrained courtesy, and an uncertainty about theatre protocol, had kept him there through the preliminaries.

Cooper had left a note with the woman at the ticket window asking the Grant woman if they could have a chat after the show. The woman assured him it would be delivered backstage.

"She'll be in the Green Room."

"Green room?"

"Upstairs. The bar."

Small mercies.

The show continued with a description of life at the palace, from the garden parties and receiving lines that threatened to leave her with paralysed lips and hands, to the rigid 4:30 p.m. daily feeding time of the royal herd of Welsh Corgis. And the dinner parties, where not a bone is left in any meat for fear of unsightly plates, and where even tomatoes are de-seeded in deference to senior citizens who might otherwise get the seeds stuck under their dentures.

"I've had to watch pensioners digging them out." She

shuddered. "Not pretty." The laughter rolled like a small thunder.

She told the story of her mother and the kitchen staff.

"A lot of the, ah, boys at Buckingham Palace are, well, they're-"

"Pansies," came a prompt from the centre of the audience.

"Thank you," she said. "My mother phoned down to the kitchen one night--she'd already had a couple--and said, 'I don't know what you lot of old queens are doing down there, but this old Queen up here would love another gin and tonic.'!"

She waited until they'd stopped falling out of their seats, and she finished the act with a story about the time that King George V was lying at death's door with bronchitis.

"A favourite family story this one," she said leaning forward, lowering her voice. Many in the audience leaned forward in response.

She was as good as the clippings said, Cooper decided. She had them captive.

"My great aunt Victoria, his sister, called his number at Sandringham, and when the receiver was lifted she shouted, 'Is that you, you old fool?' And the switchboard operator said, 'No your Royal Highness, His Majesty is not yet on the line.'!"

She made a gracious exit on a wave of applause that climbed and swelled until she returned twice for curtain calls and bouquets of yellow and red roses.

Cooper edged out among the departing crush.

He was in the lobby and turning towards the stairs when a hand nudged his elbow.

"Matt Cooper. What's this, a warm up?"

Cooper turned into the smiling face of Darshan Dhillon, the *Express* police reporter.

"Oh, God, the press. Do you never sleep? How you doing, Darshan?" as they shook hands. "I thought the Canucks game would be more your style tonight."

A young, attractive Asian woman left the coat check

counter and joined them.

"Matt Cooper. Sergeant Matt Cooper." Dhillon made the introductions. "My wife, Rajinder-Raj. She brought me. She's a Brit. Dead loyal, as they say."

"A pleasure." She took Cooper's hand lightly.

Dhillon said, "What about you Matt? A practice run for the visit, right?"

Cooper laughed. "We just can't keep a thing from you guys. Okay, Darshan. It's yours, and it's exclusive." He looked around, and leaned closer to Dhillon. "You can report on good authority that Sgt. Matt Cooper is desperately afraid for the Queen's safety during the tour, and is going to get Mrs. Grant to take her place. We plan to just slide her in there when nobody's looking. And then if anything happens we'll say, 'Gotcha!' and we'll get the bad guys. And then I'll be a hero and get promoted to Chief."

Dhillon's wife was laughing.

Dhillon shook his head, disgusted. "Jesus, you get worse, you know that?"

Cooper appealed to Dhillon's wife. "What? I give the guy the scoop of the century, and he mocks me. Darshan, how are you going to get ahead if you ignore breaks like this? How are you going to crack those exclusive interviews for assistant city editor?"

Heads turned in the lobby as laughter erupted from both Dhillon and his wife.

"He's promised to wear Wellingtons," she said, and the three of them laughed louder.

"Okay," Dhillon said, "Okay, so let's try this-how's the Emergency Response Team working out?"

Raj Dhillon groaned. "Oh, God, shop talk. Give the man a break, Darsh." She looked apologetically at Cooper. "He doesn't know when to quit."

"He does carry the job with him," Cooper agreed. "The lid's on, my boy. As usual. Anything on the tour, they got a spokesman. All official, you know the drill."

"Yeah, right. Anyway, I am going to be putting a piece together on the security angle. You know: 'City police and all special security forces are at razor pitch as the royal tour date approaches. . .'"

Dhillon's fingers danced across an imaginary keyboard.

"Razor pitch. That's good," Cooper said. "That anything like fever edge?"

Raj Dhillon laughed, a light musical laugh, and Dhillon said, "Hey, first draft, man-uh, you on your own?" He looked around the lobby.

"Mind your own business!" His wife said.

"I told you. I have a major undercover operation with theatrical overtones to organise. You can quote me."

"Oh, sure," Dhillon laughed. "And then you'll help me find another job."

Cooper gave Dhillon a friendly punch on the shoulder.

Dhillon's wife took her husband by the arm. "Come on, the baby sitter, remember?"

She nudged him towards the double glass doors fronting the street and they waved good night.

A nice young couple. A happy young couple. Let it last for them.

He watched them duck their heads against a sudden squall of rain and make a dash for their car.

Cooper re-ran his moment of madness. Quinsam would have him locked up if he knew. Dhillon likely was still laughing about it, though. *Sure, Matt. Thanks a lot. I'll write that. And by the way, I have this very nice piece of south-exposed property in the Northwest Territories. . .*

At the top of the stairs Cooper found himself behind a line forming at the bar on his right. The small, softly lit lounge was filling with couples and groups laughing and mimicking Mrs. Grant mimicking the Queen, in an assortment of British accents. Cooper picked out the northern English ones, having been raised by a mother whose broad vowels, formed in a coal- mining village in the county of Cumberland, remained uncorrupted by almost sixty years of life in North America.

A woman standing alone caught Cooper's glance; a willowy fortyish with a cloud of teased and dyed coppery hair and chartreuse eye shadow. She wore a pink cotton shift with a zippered front open to approximately her navel. Under the shift she appeared to be wearing a Maui tan and little else. Nothing else, Cooper corrected, as she raised a crimson-finger-tipped hand to adjust a gold hoop ear ring, and the shift front opened.

The woman smiled as the line moved and Cooper squeezed by her. Cooper was acutely aware of a subtle perfume wedded to the damp, inviting scents of a woman's warm body.

He ordered a Ballentine's and water and wondered if there might not be more to little theatre than he had imagined.

When he turned, the pink shift was talking to a plump young man poised with the back of one bent hand on his hip, the other hand flouncily adjusting his few remaining strands of corn-silk hair. Maybe one of the guys from the Queen Mother's kitchens.

The pink shift caught Cooper's scrutiny, and she rolled her eyes.

At the top of the stairs, a slight, trim woman with short blonde hair scanned the lounge. She stopped when her eyes reached Cooper, and she nudged the taller, rangy woman with short coal-black hair standing on the stair beside her.

Cooper saw the gesture, the clear interest from both women as they worked their eyes over him and then shared what could have been an approving glance.

The place is a meat market. Quinsam should be here.

To his right he watched the pink shift pat the corn-silk hair and turn towards the bar. She held her empty glass fetchingly high as she slid past people and came abreast of Cooper. "I think just one more," she said to no one in particular. She brushed against Cooper. "Sorry," she lied.

At the top of the stairs, the blonde said, "That has to be him."

Her friend agreed. "Yeah, tall, dark and pissed off. Although he looks like he's about to get cheered up," she added, as the breasts inside the pink shift made contact with

Cooper's arm.

Cooper stepped back to let the pink shift slip by. He caught a long look at tanned slopes and the suggestion of pointed brown nipples. "No problem."

"Mr. Cooper? Sergeant Cooper?"

The blonde from the stairs was at his elbow, looking up.

Cooper looked down into a pair of green-flecked hazel eyes that were at once openly curious and somehow guarded. Apprehensive, Cooper thought. Someone from a case that he couldn't quite remember? It happened a lot, people stopping him and asking if he remembered the time he caught the burglar in their parents' house, or the time he arrested them and thanks to him they were on the straight and narrow, and so on.

He couldn't place this one.

The blonde hair was laced lightly with silver. A faint dusting of freckles across the bridge of her nose and planes of her cheeks made a girl of her, while fine lines at the eyes and the corners of the mouth spoke the reality. A pleasing reality. He took in a neat figure accented by full breasts under a fine wool, maroon sweater. She wore a dark blue denim skirt that stopped just above her knees.

"Yes?"

Her smile wavered.

She said, "I'm Maggie Grant."

Cooper stared.

"I'll be damned."

"I wear a wig on stage. And colored contacts. They're a nuisance. And I darken my eyebrows."

She chuckled at his surprise.

"And I say stuff like, 'My husband and I. . .'" and the unmistakable voice of Queen Elizabeth II sailed out and they were suddenly enveloped in a clatter of laughter and applause as drinkers turned and recognised the star of the show.

Close your eyes, Cooper thought, imagine the wig and glasses back on. Her Majesty.

"This is my friend Jesse Lee." She indicated the taller,

Cooper And The Queen

slender woman with her, who was dressed in all black; patent leather high-heels, black tights under stirrup pants, and sleeveless blouse.

"Hi." Jesse Lee acknowledged Cooper and her examination of him put Jack Kovich's scrutiny to shame.

The pink shift shrugged and drifted to the far end of the bar.

Cooper recalled his words to Kovich-some little old lady that looks like the Queen. She smiled at him.

Her tall friend said, "She's wondering if we're going to stand here until the bar closes, or what?"

Maggie Grant laughed, "Well done, Jesse-sitting on the fence as always. Why don't you just say what's on your mind?"

Cooper said, "No, no, she's right, and we're blocking the way. Let's find a seat. What can I get you?"

Maggie Grant ordered pear-cider, Jesse Lee a bourbon.

Half an hour and two drinks later, Jesse Lee excused herself and stood up to go to the rest room.

Cooper stood to let her pass, and waited until she was out of their hearing. He said, "I assume she's gone to get the brass knuckles and the rubber hose pipe?"

Maggie Grant laughed, an infectious, unguarded sound.

Earlier Cooper had brought the drinks to the table and set them down. He sat in one of the springy armchairs, facing Jesse Lee, with Maggie Grant in a wing-back chair at his left.

"Cheers." Jesse Lee's eyes had fixed on Cooper over the rim of the glass.

"All the best." He raised his glass.

"You look like you lost a dollar and found a dime."

Maggie Grant groaned.

"Well, he does. Look at him. Christ!"

Cooper let her continue.

"They said you might be less than thrilled." She tossed her short black hair.

Cooper caught the look flashed by Maggie Grant, which said she wished her friend would zip her lips.

Cooper said, "You refer, I assume, to my former good friends, Corporal Quinsam of the Queen's Cowboys, and Inspector Jack Kovich of my very own department."

He smiled along with the barb, caught the smile mirrored in Maggie Grant's eyes. He sipped his whisky.

"And what else did they say, those two fine peace officers?" He stretched his legs and sat back in the soft chair. "Did they tell you, for example, that I think this is one of the dumbest stunts I've heard of in nearly thirty years as a cop? Did they tell you that I suggested that if they insisted on going through with this and if they wanted to keep close tabs on Mrs. Grant, we have a handy little device called a beeper that they could give her, and have her call in now and again, as opposed to having a senior officer's time taken up baby-sitting her?"

Cooper hadn't thought of the beeper until just now, but he liked the sound of it.

Maggie Grant seemed disappointed by his tone, and she shot her friend another look, which this time appeared to work; Jesse Lee struck a note meant to be more conciliatory.

"They said, actually, that there wasn't anyone else they would have asked--trusted--to do this. They spoke very highly of you, in fact." She nodded affirmation of the regard in which he was held.

Cooper grinned. "I'm sure they did. But just to keep the record good and clear -they didn't, actually, *ask*."

Jesse Lee's eyebrows arced.

"They made me an offer I couldn't refuse."

Maggie Grant buried a laugh.

Jesse Lee affected a sweet smile and said, "Charming. Who said chivalry was dead?"

Since the three of them sat down she had interrogated Cooper, to the point that, when it seemed she might be finished, Cooper had said, "Would you like me to cough, now?" and she'd had the grace to join in Maggie Grant's burst of laughter.

Now Jesse Lee returned from the rest room. She sat, and

asked, "So, what is it, exactly, that you propose to do with Maggie?"

Cooper said, "*I* have no plans to do anything with her. If anybody has plans, it's Quinsam. And frankly I think the corporal's stripes are not quite tightly stitched on in this case."

Jesse Lee shot Maggie Grant a quick, arch look.

"I think," Cooper continued, "and I have told him, that he could be putting this charming lady here at considerable risk."

Jesse Lee nodded *I told you so* at her friend, who responded, "Oh, for Heaven's sake! How? I mean, I'm just going to be standing in the wings."

Cooper chewed on a sliver of ice. He set his glass down.

"It's fairly simple. Bad guy with a gun shows up, planning to kill the Queen. You for whatever reason happen to be just where he expects the Queen to be, dressed in Queen get-up, looking exactly like the Queen, and talking like the Queen-which you do amazingly well-"

"Thank you." A surprisingly shy smile.

"-then, in my opinion, he is not going to ask you for your ID, but would start shooting-and you could be dead."

"That's what I've been telling her, and she won't listen! It's crazy!" Jesse Lee glared at her friend.

Maggie Grant said, "*Is* someone planning to kill the Queen?"

"It's always possible," Cooper said.

"All things are possible, of course." She smiled. Behind the smile, some steel. "Anyway, I have agreed to help, and I'm going to help. If they ask me to dress the part, and play the part, that's what I'm going to do. My God, Jess, can you see it? I could *be* the Queen. If they want me to do it, I'm going to."

"And she is unanimous on that," Jesse Lee said.

Maggie Grant laughed. She reached over and touched Cooper's hand with hers, a friendly gesture.

"I'm sorry if it's putting you out , but that's truly how I feel. And I didn't ask for an escort. That wasn't my idea at all."

She was not going to be dissuaded.

And certainly Quinsam wasn't going to change his mind.

"It's all right. I know it wasn't your idea, and I don't hold it against you."

"Lancelot du Lac," Jesse Lee said, but with a smile, which Cooper returned.

He said, "And in truth, I'm not anxious to work the jail detail."

Both women looked at him, querying.

"That was the offer they made me: Take this assignment, or take charge of the jail cells. I don't imagine you've seen the drunk tank on a weekend, or on Mardi Gras-welfare Wednesdays?"

They shook their heads.

"You need a fire hose, hip-waders and a gas mask."

"Very evocative," Jesse Lee said. "Thanks for sharing that."

"Any time."

He glanced around the now almost empty lounge.

"Anyway, I'm here."

Maggie Grant seemed more at ease now.

She said, "So, when does it start? The, ah, you and me thing?"

"Cooper and the Queen," Jesse Lee interjected. "I like it."

Cooper smiled. "It just started. I'll follow you home tonight if you're driving, or I'll drive you home if you're not, which ever you prefer. We need to set up a schedule. I'll want to know where you are every minute of the day between now and the end of the royal tour. That's my assignment."

Maggie Grant finished her drink, wiped the bottom of her glass and a small circle of moisture on the table with a tissue, and put the glass down. She looked at Jesse Lee, who said, "Go ahead."

"I'll take the ride home, if that's all right?"

Cooper said, "Whenever you're ready."

"I'll get my coat." She stood, stepping around Cooper's chair with an actor's supple, balanced movements.

Cooper led the way as they went down the stairs and out the theatre's front door.

CHAPTER 9

Long Beach, California

"Sir, I'd like to help, but you're not on the official press list." The young Hispanic woman smiled, sorry.

Dooley knew he wasn't on the official list. The procedure for getting onto the official list was for news organisations to submit a list of reporters and photographers for whom they wanted accreditation. World News Features was not about to raise its head that way-and had no need to. Murphy's Law recognised no boundaries, including royal tours, as Dooley well knew. And people always allowed for Murphy's Law, especially with reporters. At events the size of a royal tour, cock-ups happened, and Dooley had joined a line-up of late-comers pleading their cases.

Dooley was well into his appeal in his well-practiced, broad-vowelled northern England accent--"They've done it to me again; it's marvellous, isn't it? The buggers'll spend hundreds of quid to get you here and put you up, and then they don't tell anybody you're coming! I mean, bloody 'ell!"--when his recent past conveniently caught up with him.

"Pat!" One of a gang of English reporters heading for the lounge bar broke off from the group and strode across the lobby.

Dooley turned, and his thin face cracked into a smile above the sparse goatee.

"Donald! Good to see you again!"

The reporter wore his laminated photo-ID clipped to his suit jacket lapel.

"You too, what's it been-seven, eight months?"

"Aye, summat like that," Dooley replied.

He assumed a martyr's face and indicated the accreditation desk. "Let me get this lot sorted, and you can buy me a pint."

"You're on, mate. This one beats that other rubbish, eh?"

"Say that again," Dooley said.

The last time he'd met Donald Parker had been July of the previous year when both appeared with their notebooks at the "other rubbish"-the aftermath of a two-bomb explosion in London that killed eleven soldiers of the Household Cavalry and the Band of the Royal Marines, as well as several horses. Before that had been October of 1981, when the Royal Marines Commandant General Sir Stewart Pringle lost a leg when a bomb exploded in his car. Dooley was the architect of both events.

He was aware of the big Mountie watching and listening. Dooley knew who Quinsam was. Everybody knew who Quinsam was. Since the Queen's special Mountie arrived in California, the tabloid packs had feasted on his aboriginal background and served-up their own versions of it in the guise of news stories.

Quinsam had been flirting with the girl when Dooley arrived at the convention centre media accreditation desk. The royal-blue name-badge on the grey silk blouse over her sweetly curved left breast identified her as Maria Sanchez.

Dooley continued his lament.

"They've done the same to me in Africa, Australia, Hong Kong-"

"It must make it difficult," she said.

Dooley noted Quinsam's amused smile as the Sanchez girl sympathized with his ode to misfortune.

Finally she nodded at the departing Donald Parker. "You know him, then."

"Donald? Oh, aye, we've crossed paths. We certainly have." Casual; one of the boys.

The pain caressed Dooley, and fled. He shuddered, and recovered.

Maria Sanchez was looking at Quinsam now, the question in her wide dark eyes.

Quinsam's gaze lingered on Dooley, looked into his eyes, seeing those of a drawn, tired man. He examined the

World News identification card that Dooley had produced. He nodded. "Sure, he seems to be one of the pack. They know him. He's here to do a job, and somebody screwed up."

Dooley relaxed, nodded his gratitude.

Maria Sanchez reached into a drawer, brought out a Polaroid camera, and pointed it at him.

"Say Mozzarella."

"Mozzarella?"

The flash popped.

"Thank you. I'll make up your pass."

Dooley turned, examined Quinsam.

"Thanks for the help."

"No sweat," Quinsam said. "Another Limey, eh?"

"Yeah. Frank Patterson. Pat, if you like."

"Fine. I'll remember." Quinsam frowned. "You okay? You look a bit-"

"Rough, I know. Not enough sleep, too much duty-free. I'll manage."

He redirected the conversation. "You're the Red Indian."

Quinsam feigned admiration. "I can see why you're a reporter."

Dooley grinned. "I read about you on the plane. *The World Examiner.* You're related back to Sitting Bull, aren't you?"

"Apparently. And Geronimo, I understand."

"And General Custer, a bit, wasn't it?"

"Seems so."

"Your people got around quite a lot."

"Is that your style?"

"What?"

"*The Examiner.*"

Dooley's face crinkled in concentration.

"Not really-they're a bit subdued for my liking."

Quinsam's laughter lifted heads all around the media centre.

Dooley was in. He had never doubted that he would be, but it had eased matters when Donald Parker showed up.

That was the second time Parker had unwittingly smoothed Dooley's career path.

CHAPTER 10

Vancouver

"Thanks, Dale, I'll get over there." Cooper put the phone down.

Shit.

He poured two inches of Ballentine's into a stubby glass, took the ice tray from the fridge, and dropped two cubes into the whisky. He swirled the whisky and ice mix and swallowed half the drink. He improved it by another inch of whisky.

Vandals had paid a visit to the Galiano cottage.

"The front door's off its hinges and one window's shot," Dale Mitchell had reported. "I've nailed a couple sheets of plywood up for now. They got inside and made a mess but I figured I'd better leave that for you."

"Fair enough."

"I phoned the Saltspring detachment and they'll get a constable over in the morning. I told them maybe you could make it over. Hey, it probably looks worse than it is," he finished, a bit lamely.

It would be hit-and-run city punks. Roar off the ferry, get wasted in the pub, find a target. Then back to the city on the night ferry, with the knowledge of a job well done. Bastards. And with one constable in and out a couple of days a week, the chance of finding them was nil. The incidents had increased in the last half-year and Cooper realized he'd been lucky up to now. The place stood empty so much of the time. He wondered, as he had increasingly lately, if it was decision time. Sell the cottage, if he was going to stay with the force and in the city; or take his pension, sell the Kitsilano house, and move to the island as he and Sandi had planned. Fishing, golf-and what, now, without her? Time on his hands. Empty nights-and empty bottles, most likely.

Cooper had no illusions about how easily he could slide from daily social drinker to card-carrying lush.

He left the thoughts. He would discuss the cottage with Sheena when she was back.

He reviewed Dale Mitchell's call. The plywood would be, as much as anything, a signal to other thugs on the prowl. And he didn't like Dale's last line. It sounded more like the place had had a real trashing.

He would catch the first ferry in the morning.

Which raised the problem of Maggie Grant.

"All you have to do," Kovich had said, "is stay close. Just so that we know that you know where she is and that Quinsam or I can get to her, and you, whenever we need to."

He was staying close. Cooper and Maggie Grant had agreed on a routine during the first week of his assignment to her, which was the last week of her run at Metro Theatre.

Each morning he called her around ten o'clock.

"Good morning, sergeant."

"'Matt', please."

"Good morning, Matt. Yes, everything's fine."

About noon every day they met for lunch, usually at a White Spot, but occasionally extending the police department's benevolence to Chinatown and dim sum.

Jesse Lee had joined them twice.

"You're not as grouchy as you were," she conceded, while grabbing another basket of shrimp rolls from a passing cart. "I imagine it has a lot to do with the kind of company you're keeping."

Maggie shrugged helplessly at Cooper.

"Pass the plum sauce, please Jesse," Cooper said.

Once they had bumped into Sheena, outside Maggie's local Safeway. Cooper had introduced them: "My daughter, Sheena. Sheena, this is Mrs. Grant-"

"Maggie," Maggie had interjected.

"Maggie," Cooper confirmed. "She's, ah, she's-"

"I'm his assignment," Maggie said, and she rolled her eyes.

Sheena laughed out loud.

"She's really nice, Dad," she told Cooper later. "For an assignment, I mean," and she'd gone off chuckling. Cooper had explained only that Maggie was on a job for the department, and he was helping out. Sheena never delved into the details of Cooper's work, and her taste in theatre, since she had started frequenting London's West End, was far removed from little-theatre revues. She would never have made the connection.

Each evening at six o'clock Cooper picked Maggie up and drove her to the theatre. At ten-thirty he returned to meet her in the Green Room where they had a drink before Cooper drove her the fifteen-minute run home. Twice he stayed and took in her show again. She wondered aloud if that wasn't stretching things above and beyond.

"No, I don't feel that I have to," Cooper assured her. "I just wanted to see if it was as good as I thought it was the first time."

On the night when he was watching for the third time, she added to her script.

"They usually give me a policeman of my own when I travel." The audience chuckled.

She pouted. "But I always have to give him back," and as they roared she aimed her smile at the aisle seat where Cooper sat.

"Well, was it?" she asked afterwards.

"Was it what?"

"As good."

"Oh, yeah, sure."

"Don't excite yourself," she murmured.

"What?"

"Nothing."

"I liked the line about the cop."

She laughed. "Good. I'll keep it in."

They spent several afternoons like tourists. They shopped at Granville Island Market for fresh produce brought in from farms in the Fraser Valley. Once they went to an early movie, "The Man from Snowy River", with Kirk

Douglas. It was the first time Cooper had been inside a cinema in two years. When they came out, into a cold but unusually bright Vancouver afternoon, Maggie asked, "Are you enjoying yourself? I mean trekking around with me like this?"

Cooper nodded. "Sure. . ."

"Right. Better than the drunk tank, I know," she said, and she snapped her umbrella open. Cooper looked at the cloudless sky. She muttered, "habit." She rattled the umbrella and closed it.

Cooper reported to Quinsam, "She has, ah, spirit. Little quick on the draw sometimes."

"Spirit is good, "Quinsam said.

Cooper learned her personal history.

"I was born in England, near Chester. I remember the old Roman walls around the city; they have shops right in the walls and you can walk along the tops."

The family emigrated when she was twelve, surviving one savage winter in Toronto before discovering the civility and sanctuary of the West Coast. Both her parents had since died.

At a youthful fifty-one she was a year younger than Cooper.

"Which makes me five years younger than the Queen, so I have to add a few age lines during the makeup. Not many, though, she's a wonder, how she maintains her looks."

Maggie had married Nathan Grant, a criminal defence lawyer whom Cooper well remembered. Grant's career was noted no less for the heights to which it soared with several dramatic acquittals of major felons, than for the plummeting rate of its descent when he discovered the joys of proscribed substances and began accepting his fees in kind from some of his regular clients. The Grants had one child, a daughter, Michelle.

"He started drinking a lot, lawyers' conventions and things, then at home, white rum and Russian Vodka at all hours. The drugs made him crazy. Everything started to go wrong, losing cases, getting suspended once. And he blamed me. I was the closest. He got physical, slapping me at first, then using his fists . . ."

She paused, remembering, then continued.

"I stuck it for a while, until I got enough away from him for a down payment, then I took Michelle and bought my house and took whatever jobs I could find when she was in school."

A year later Nathan Grant launched his two-seater Jaguar rag-top off the Upper Levels Highway in West Vancouver and dropped and bounced down three hundred feet of rocks to his death. The one witness to the accident, the driver of a semi-trailer rig hauling a load of fruit from California, said the Jag driver was wild-eyed and laughing as he accelerated across the highway centre line and took flight. Fortunately for Maggie, her husband had not entirely depleted his bank accounts before he died, and he had never changed the will that Maggie had persuaded him to have drawn in happier, sober times.

"So I got enough to pay off the house and have a small income."

Her daughter left with a friend to see Europe after graduating from high school.

"She went looking for her family history. She met a young man who lived two streets away from the house where I grew up. She made one trip home to tell me, than returned and married him. She has a Cheshire accent and two kids under the age of three. I've visited them once. I'm delighted for her. Funny old world, isn't it?"

And she'd asked about him.

"I know about your wife. . .that was terrible."

Cooper told her in a few short sentences.

"My folks were from England as well, from up north, Cumbria, the Lake District. I was born here-well, in Victoria. My dad was a dreamer. He bought a fishing boat and never did learn how to handle the thing. He went down with it, in Hecate Strait. My mother brought me and my brother up. David. We were twins."

She read the loss, and waited.

"We both went to Korea. I was in the airborne. He was going to be a doctor; he was in the medical corps. He didn't make it back."

"I'm sorry."

Cooper nodded.

"Yeah, that one was hard. It was hard on my mother. She still lives in Victoria. Great lady."

Maggie Grant smiled at the affection in the words.

Cooper asked her how she came to be impersonating the Queen.

"I bumped into Jesse, whom I'd known in high school. You know what she's like - she took me on as a project. She got me involved in a little-theatre group, which I realize now was her sort of therapy. I was never much for going out, after my marriage failed. In fact, although I didn't realize it, I was pretty much of a mess. Avoiding people, afraid to answer the door, even. I think I'd just had all the confidence knocked out of me. I didn't feel worth anything."

Cooper felt a rush of anger against the man who had abused this wholly decent woman.

"I've never really talked to anyone other than Jesse about this, you know."

"Well, I'm a policeman, so it's okay."

She laughed, a bright, genuine burst of laughter, and Cooper joined in.

"It just grew from there. I'd do the act for a few of the theatre group, at parties, get-togethers. Then Derek, the show's producer, turned up at one of the parties and afterwards he offered me the spot."

She chuckled. "I thought he was just being polite and I said, oh, sure, of course, and the next thing I know he's on my doorstep with a contract: They want to *pay* me! Can you imagine that?"

Cooper had stopped the car in front of Maggie's house, a trim 1960's bungalow surrounded by fir and oak trees on a deep lot on West Fourteenth Avenue. She caught him off guard when she said, tentatively, "Would you like to come in for a coffee, or something?"

He hesitated. A flutter of vaguely appealing reasons urged him to accept. But these reasons were conflicting with what was still--though unreasonable, he knew--a smoldering resentment against Quinsam and Kovich for his being here and not with his Emergency Response Team. And there was the lifetime instinct of a cop on a job to remain detached, objective, uninvolved.

"I better not," he said finally. "It's getting kinda late."

Maggie nodded, said a crisp, "Good night, then," and was quickly out of the car and inside her house with the door closed behind her.

Cooper regretted his response before Maggie was fully out of the car.

"It's getting kinda late," he mimicked himself as he drove home. *You got a curfew suddenly?* And, Christ, the woman was just being sociable. And shouldn't he be putting her at ease, not on edge, as he seemed to have done, given the loud crack the door had made as she slammed it shut? He would accept the next time she asked him in.

Maggie didn't repeat the invitation.

"I was just being sociable," she told Jesse Lee, describing what she considered had been Cooper's snub.

"I invited him in for coffee and he just froze. He sat there for ages looking for an excuse and then said it was too late, for heaven's sake! I think he stopped just short of reminding me that I'm his assignment. I mean, Good Lord!"

Jesse said, "He's just pissed off because they've stopped him practicing killing people. I thought he was starting to act like a human being, but obviously he's just an asshole."

"He most certainly is *not.*"

"Oh? Hello?"

"Oh, shut up, Jessica!"

"'Jessica' is it? Well, well."

Maggie turned away, blushing.

#

On the night the show closed, they left the cast party around midnight. They drove along Southwest Marine Drive, past a stretch of millionaires' mansions. Cooper pointed out the ones built from fortunes made running bootleg liquor to the States during Prohibition. "Today their grand-kids do it on the Vancouver Stock Exchange," he said. The homes boasted tennis courts and swimming pools, and servant quarters that were bigger than either of Cooper's or Maggie's own places.

On the north slope of Dunbar Street, Cooper slowed the car and they admired the night sight ahead. Beyond English Bay and the First Narrows, the lights of West and North Vancouver glittered at the feet of the North Shore Mountains. Under a pale full moon, a necklace of lights trailed across the ski slopes of Cypress Bowl and Grouse Mountain and Mount Seymour. The twin peaks of the Lions towered over all, like two white-cloaked watchers.

Maggie sighed and stretched as Cooper stopped at the traffic light at Sixteenth Ave. He swung left, and she picked up her gloves as he drove slowly west before making a right turn and then a left on to West Fourteenth, where he pulled up in front of her house.

Maggie said, "Thanks, Matt." She climbed out and stood, hugging her coat around her.

"That's okay. You're welcome."

Cooper sat with both hands on the wheel, waiting for her to shut the door. He wondered if she might ask him in again.

Maggie shivered under her coat.

Cooper waited. *If she did ask, he would accept.* He looked straight ahead, both hands on the wheel, as if he was already driving.

Maggie sighed, and a puff of breath clouded around her face. "Well, good night, and thanks again for staying for the party."

Cooper said, "I enjoyed it. It was. . .fun"

It sounded as if he might have just found the word among some old socks and wasn't sure what to do with it.

Maggie said, "I'm glad." She shivered. "Good night, then."

She's freezing, thought Cooper, and being polite while I keep her standing there. What an asshole.

"Good night, Maggie. I'll talk to you tomorrow." He reached over and pulled the door shut.

She waved as the car moved away. Cooper lifted his hand in return and watched the picture she made in the rear-view mirror. She looked like a lost kid, shivering, her coat collar turned up around her ears, and still waving as the car turned the corner.

She's a nice person, Cooper thought, a decent person. But not a very happy one.

But who was?

#

That had been last night. He dialed her number and told her about Dale Mitchell's call.

"I have to go to the island. I'll call Jack Kovich; see if they want to put somebody else on you for the day."

Maybe he could have phrased that better.

There was a fertile silence, then, "I don't *need* anybody *on* me. You think I'm about to run away?"

"Ahh, right. But Quinsam says you need somebody. And it's Quinsam's-"

"Yes, yes, I know. It's Quinsam's show and there's a chain of command and you're not going to break it."

A little touchy.

"Where is he? I'll call him."

"Quinsam? He's in California."

"Oh, that's useful."

Silence. Soft breathing.

"Well, that's where the real Queen is."

"Yes." A hint of a chuckle? Less pissed off, anyway.

She said, "I know. I've been watching the TV. They're

having terrible weather. Storms. I'll come with you."

"What?"

"Could I come with you?"

"With me-"

"To Galiano."

Cooper hadn't even considered it.

"I've never been to Galiano."

"Well-"

"When does the ferry leave?"

"It leaves Tsawwassen at nine-twenty, so I have to leave here by eight-thirty, latest. Get back about seven thirty, eight, at night. But I don't think it would be a whole lot of fun; they're forecasting rain-"

"I'll be ready at eight. What do you want me to bring?"

He could tell her flat out, no, I don't want you along, which would do wonders for their professional relationship. He could try explaining that he had had no woman at the place since Sandi died, and that that thought was bothering him right now--although he had only just recognized it--and she would likely accept that. But that was not something he wanted to get into. On the other hand, it was going to be a quick trip there, assess the damage and arrange for some repairs, and get straight back.

He said, "Okay," and he heard a soft laugh of pleasure.

"You don't need to bring anything. Just wear boots, stuff like that. You got boots?"

#

They were pink Wellington's into which she had tucked a pair of faded black denim jeans. Above them she wore a loose white wool sweater and an old maroon parka.

"This all right?" she asked, as she opened the passenger door. The smile under the blue eyes was a fraction apprehensive. Like a schoolgirl worried about wearing the wrong outfit, Cooper thought. She smelled like fresh flowers.

"That's just fine."

Her smile switched to high beam, and she swung a canvas tote bag in with her.

"I packed some lunch. In case you hadn't had time."

"You're right, I didn't think about it."

Cromwell sniffed towards the bag. He had jumped onto the back seat from the floor as Maggie opened the car door, and he sat examining her, his head tilted in inquiry, ears cocked.

"Cromwell," Cooper introduced them. Maggie leaned over and carefully offered a hand to the dog. "He's beautiful."

The spaniel nuzzled her fingers.

"It usually takes him longer than that. He's picky about people. Okay, Cromwell, sit." The dog stood and offered Maggie its right forepaw. "Good boy. Ask him to shake a paw. Say, 'Gimme four.'"

Looking mystified, she did. The dog lay flat on the seat, chin resting on its front feet, looking for approval.

Cooper said, "Attaboy," and laughed at Maggie Grant's puzzled face.

He pulled on to the road. "It was Sheena. She was about fourteen when we got him from the pound. She said that dogs should be individuals, not a bunch of sheep. So she taught him all these backward commands."

Maggie Grant laughed. "And the name?"

He described how Sheena had first explored the Stuart royal family context, given the pup's alleged breeding as a King Charles Spaniel. The obvious names were considered--Charlie, Chuck, and Stu--and Gwyn, for Nell. Nothing was decided before they went to bed. Sheena covered the tiled kitchen floor with newspapers, except for about one square yard in front of the refrigerator. The dog chose that space to do what nature required.

"Sheena said that obviously there was not a royal bone in the dog's body. She was studying English history at the time. She named him Cromwell."

Maggie Grant's laughter filled the car.

Cooper turned the radio on and they listened to airborne traffic reports and made small talk during the thirty-five minute run to the ferry terminal. In the Massey Tunnel, under a backwater of the mighty Fraser River, she flinched and pressed towards Cooper as a flatbed truck stacked high with pallets of four-by-four cedar fence posts overtook them in the outside lane. The truck's thundering air-wash almost lifted the station wagon off its wheels.

"Bastard," Cooper muttered.

Maggie said, "I hate the tunnel. I always think that just as I hit the middle, this crack in the roof that has been developing for the longest time will finally break open and the river will come in and all the cars in the tunnel . . ."

Cooper feigned great alarm and craned his neck, searching the tunnel roof ahead of them. Maggie grinned and changed the topic.

"Did you know that the Queen opened the tunnel?"

"I seem to remember that."

"July 15, 1959. She was wearing-"

She stopped and laughed as she caught Cooper's widening smile.

"Sorry. I can get carried away with the trivia. The audiences like it."

"I've noticed."

"I'm going to shut up about it now."

"Good." Cooper laughed, and she punched him lightly on the shoulder.

They drove out the south end into bright sunlight and Cooper stayed in the right lane for the ferry turnoff and took Highway Seventeen towards the ocean, across the flat and now flooded farmlands of the Fraser River delta.

Four vehicles were ahead of them at the ticket booth for the Gulf Islands ferry. They pulled up behind a decrepit black Ford pickup. A yellow-eyed, belligerent-looking Billy goat stared at them from where it stood in the truck's box. It was tethered to rickety sideboards and protected by four bales of hay.

"They can do that? Just stick a goat on a truck and take it on the ferry?"

Cooper said, "Couple of weeks ago the same guy walked two of them on as foot passengers. Tied them up beside the dogs on the car deck. As long as nobody complains, nobody bothers. One guy brought a car trailer full of chicken manure on before Christmas. Uncovered. That was pushing it."

He raised a hand and returned the wave of the goat-truck driver who had signaled after seeing Cooper in the side mirror.

"A friend?"

"You get to know people on the islands run, especially when you've been doing it for fifteen years. We got the place when Sheena was, oh, about seven, I guess." He held a thought for a moment. "We were going to retire here."

They edged up to the ticket booth and Cooper paid the fares. The booth attendant stuck the yellow Sturdies Bay destination ticket under the windshield wiper.

As Cooper pulled in behind the goat in the loading lineup and switched the motor off, Maggie said, "And what now?"

Cooper looked at her, then turned his face and gazed out through the windshield.

"Right now? How about a hot chocolate."

Maggie nodded and Cooper climbed out of the car.

He strode towards the cafeteria and waiting area. She watched him pull his black police department parka closed against the bite of a northwest wind that rode in up the ferry slips off the Strait of Georgia.

So stay out of it, Maggie. 'What now?' is none of your concern, is what he just said, because you meant what now about his plans for the island, and he doesn't think it's any of your damned business.

I was just being sociable.

Sure, like when you invited him in for coffee. He is not interested. You are his assignment. Got it?

Cooper returned with two cardboard cups.

The windows steamed up as they sipped the watery,

sweet chocolate powder mix. Cooper started the motor and turned on the fan until the glass cleared.

Cooper exchanged waves with several drivers when the tubby *Queen of Sidney* elbowed into the dock and unloaded. A bulky bearded young man wearing a tattered black toque pulled down over his ears rolled a window down and yelled, "Let me know if you need anything, Matt!" Cooper acknowledged with a thumbs up sign.

"That's nice."

"Yeah, it is. The island's like that. Everybody'll know what's happened. If you need something, you'll get it. On the other hand, if you want to be left alone, you needn't see anybody from one month to the next."

The ferry emptied, and a crew member directed the Gulf Islands-bound traffic up the sloping ramp and then down into lanes on the car deck. Cooper tied Cromwell to a low iron rail near a cream-painted steel door leading to a set of stairs. He dropped a ragged blanket for the dog to sit on. He gave Maggie a handful of biscuits and she made a fuss of laying them down before the spaniel and petting it. She and Cooper headed up the two short flights of steel stairs to the cafeteria deck.

Cooper chatted with a couple of the crew, asking about kids and wives, and he exchanged casual greetings with several more passengers.

"You want breakfast?"

Maggie nodded. "Sure." She was chuckling.

"What?"

"Nothing. I just, well, I like this. So far we've passed I think eleven people and you've talked to nine of them. What's the matter with the other two?"

She means it, too, he thought. She is enjoying herself.

They slipped their parkas off in the warmth of the cafeteria. They joined the friendly, gossiping line-up. They ate bacon and scrambled eggs and hash browns, and drank coffee that Cooper said ranked right alongside that brewed by Jack Kovich as being suitable for removing rust.

They were halfway across the strait when the skipper's

voice crackled out of the public address system.

"Attention passengers-killer whales off the starboard side of the ferry. That's to your right as you face the pointy end."

"Oh!" Maggie's cup went over, followed by a stream of coffee across the Formica table top as she jumped to her feet and rushed to the windows.

A pod of orcas romped northward through the grey-green swells, within a hundred yards of the ferry.

"Look!" Maggie cried, as one of the killer whales shot out of the water like some great black-on-white torpedo. It climbed, and made a shimmering, curving descent and a gigantic belly flop re-entry that raised a cloud of spray and brought shouts of pleasure and spontaneous applause from the passengers crowding the windows.

The whales ploughed northward, swooping into and through the waves at an angle away from the ferry. People pushed closer to the windows as the distance between the orcas and the boat increased. The scything dorsal fins slipped under the surface, and seconds later rose from the depths like triangular sails, cutting through the swells' rolling bellies, and submerging. Soon the whales were just occasional black shadows against the heaving ocean, and then there was only the water.

The cafeteria buzzed with voices rejoicing in the moment.

"Oh, my goodness," Maggie said. "I've never seen them before, not like that. Isn't that incredible? I've lived almost my whole life here and I've only ever seen them in the aquarium. Oh, my goodness, wait 'til I tell Jesse!"

She was almost dancing. Cooper smiled at her brightened eyes and radiant face.

Twice during the whales' brief performance, unaware she was doing it, she had grabbed Cooper's arm and squeezed, transmitting her pleasure. When the ferry rolled, they had come close together as they worked to keep their balance. Each time, Cooper had been stirringly aware of her body warmth through her sweater and the thin cotton shirt under it, and of her full breast pressing against his arm.

They returned to their seats. Cooper said, "They must have known you were coming."

She smiled at his suggestion of a command performance.

"Even travelling regularly, every weekend, we used to see them maybe twice, three times a year," he said.

He looked away from her and gazed out the window. Ragged streams of a thin rain crawled across the outside glass.

She said, "You don't come regularly now?"

The ferry was heeling, beginning a sweeping right turn past a low headland towards a bay where the waves lapped against a wharf that jutted out from a flat rock shore.

Cooper crumpled his empty coffee cup.

"No, not as much," he said, mostly to himself. He broke away from the thought. "We're just about there."

A voice on the address system broke in. "We are now arriving at Sturdies Bay on Galiano Island. All passengers disembarking here please return to the car deck."

They followed a line of families and backpackers down the stairs and Maggie untied a tail-thumping Cromwell and loaded him into the wagon.

They drove off the car deck and onto the wharf and Cooper felt the palpable change as he always did.

He said, "We are now in a different world. In the city, you can shut your door, but you're still in the city. Once I drive off that ferry, it's-well, a renewal is the best way I can describe it." He shrugged. "You have to feel it, I guess."

Cottages sat on low bluffs to the right of the wharf, each with a staggered, rickety-looking set of steps leading down the cliff face to the sloping rock beach. To the left, round orange and yellow floats dotted Sturdies Bay, marking crab traps lying on the ocean floor. A grey painted launch with a Maple Leaf flag and the Royal Canadian Mounted Police crest bobbed beside a gill-netter and two cabin cruisers at the government dock. The bay's grey-green waves swirled and broke onto a sandstone beach where properties ran back to houses of a variety of shapes and styles. Most of them favoured cedar siding, chunky shake roofs, and expansive windows.

"I feel it," Maggie said. She rolled her window down, and sea smells and those of the coast forest filled the car. She inhaled deeply. "That's gorgeous."

They turned left from the wharf approach onto the island's main road and started down a short hill that curved to the right into a blind bend at the bottom. An approaching red pickup truck blasted past them on the bend and Maggie flinched and ducked away as the vehicle rocketed back to its own side of the road. The driver raised a hand as he flashed by, and Cooper returned the greeting casually.

"The local inhabitants use the yellow centre line as a loose navigational guide," Cooper explained. "Usually they line it up with their hood ornament, so that one front wheel is on each side of the line. If they can maintain that relationship they figure it will keep them from driving into the ditches."

Maggie laughed, a girlish, joyous laugh.

"I'm serious. There's a Gulf Islands driver, a species. It doesn't matter who you are or what you were before you arrived here. We've got retired judges and cops, plumbers, professors and vicars and I don't know what else, and they all become the same. They reach a determination, for reasons known only to them, that at any given time they are the only ones remotely likely to be driving on the island roads. Having decided that, they then take the quite logical position that there's nothing to avoid, and therefore no reason not to drive in the middle or on either or both sides of the road, whichever takes their fancy-"

"Lookout!" Maggie yelled, as Cooper drifted across the yellow line on the next bend and faced a fully loaded, mud-spattered logging truck thundering straight at them.

"Shit!"

Cooper swung the Plymouth back and hugged the ditch. Overhanging brambles and scrub willow branches clattered like small-arms fire against the windshield and side windows as the logging truck roared past. The driver laughed down at them from behind his wheel and waved.

Cooper raised a hand and steered back onto the road.

Maggie was recovered, and laughing. "I see what you mean."

Cooper's grin was sheepish.

CHAPTER 11

Long Beach
California

Dooley knew enough about the business to understand the delicate dance that comprises the cop-reporter relationship. Each digs up facts. The reporter shouts his findings from the housetops. The cop develops lockjaw. At the same time, they need each other. And they use each other. A reporter agrees to hold back certain details that if released could jeopardize an investigation; a cop provides not-for-attribution details that put the reporter ahead of the pack. Sometimes a closeness develops.

Dooley was intent on getting close to Quinsam. The Mountie was the one he would have to go through to get to the Queen when the moment came. He jumped straight in and asked for a one-on-one chat with Quinsam that afternoon. "As much of it off the record as you want," he assured the Mountie. "Just want to get my bearings, you know? Me being late and that. Maybe I can do a piece on you."

Quinsam snorted. "A number, you mean? You're a bit late for that."

Dooley chuckled. He knew that Quinsam's arrival had been serendipity to a press crowd wearying of reporting the daily train of official events and exchanges of mutual goodwill between the U.S. and the U.K. Reporters had filed their features about the Royal Yacht, cheerfully observing that it contained only single beds and describing how the red-blooded Charles, Prince of Wales, had at least had the good sense to haul a double aboard for his honeymoon with Princess Di, while older sister Anne and her husband Capt. Mark Phillips, in an earlier movie, had actually conducted their nuptials on two singles lashed together.

Along with the *World Examiner's* extravagant version of Quinsam's family tree, there had been no shortage of excess from the members of the fourth estate as they strove to satisfy editors and outdo their colleagues.

Newspapers and magazines exploded with features about the big, watchful member of the legendary Haida tribe from the remote Queen Charlotte islands in the stormy Pacific northwest. They painted occasionally accurate images of Quinsam's raven-haired ancestors, paddles flashing, sweeping down the misty Pacific Coast intent on plunder and pillage. Tossing village maids into their dugout cedar war canoes, and driving terror into the hearts of every tribe from the Alaska Panhandle to Baja California. The British Sunday papers had updated that scene. They splashed stories suggesting the big Red Indian Mountie had only recently abandoned weekend activities that included restocking his home village with ravishing lovelies from remote native settlements along Canada's wild west coast. The British papers arrived a day later and the American reporters passed them around and marvelled at them. In the bar, working his way down a glass of draft, Dooley had listened to an Associated Press reporter chiding the British tabloid crowd.

"Apart from the fact that I don't know how the fuck you get away with stuff like this, nobody calls Native Indians 'Red Indians.'"

"We do," A London *Sun* man said. "If we just said 'Indians', everybody back home would think they were all Pakis-with turbans, like. We have to distinguish, see."

The AP reporter said, "Yes, I should have considered that. One of those fine British cultural differences. Forgive me."

The *Sun* man laughed tolerantly. "Fucking Yanks."

Quinsam nodded as Dooley reported that exchange. "I know. I told that *Sun* guy that they left out the bit about me harpooning whales and eating them raw. He told me he was holding that for next week!"

Dooley felt Quinsam growing a little more comfortable with him. He asked Quinsam how he had come to be the

Queen's personal tour bodyguard.

Quinsam at first waved it away. "That's an old story."

Dooley waited. People like to talk about themselves. Even cops. Including Quinsam.

"Okay. I was fresh out of the academy, my first posting, Vancouver, and a royal tour came up. I was on crowd-control duty, dozens of us, on the streets. The cars were approaching, her and Philip in an open Caddie, and this little girl, about five, ran out of the crowd, under everybody's arms. I mean, this kid was *going to see the Queen*. The driver didn't see her, and he'd just received the signal to speed up the motorcade. The Caddie shot away, and the kid was headed straight into the front wheels of an escort patrol car behind it. You don't think, at a time like that. I just grabbed her up, and that was that. Not a scratch on her."

"And you?"

"Ah, a bump, coupla bruises, you know."

"Separated shoulder and cracked ribs," Dooley supplied.

"Hey, if you know all that-"

"I didn't know it like you told it; that's good copy. And what happened next?"

"Well, that was the good part. The Queen realized what had happened. She ordered the limo driver to stop, and she got out of the car--the plainclothes security guys were freaking--and went straight to the kid and picked her up and dusted her off and made sure she was okay. Then she checked me out and waited, held up the whole parade, until an ambulance was brought and took me for X-rays. Next day, she sent for me. Two inspectors went with me to the hotel-goddam brass, as if I couldn't find it on my own. She invited me into the suite and told them they could go back down to the lobby and wait." He grinned. "Pissed them off."

"She poured me a couple of Scotches and we talked about things, family, ordinary stuff. And the next time they visited Canada, she asked for me as special personal staff. So, here we are again."

"With you staying close to her."

"When she's in public, like a second skin. You just

never know."

"No, that's right, you don't."

"And that bit's not for quoting."

"No problem. You've been to the yacht since you got here?"

#

"Jim!"

The Queen's pleasure was transparent as Quinsam appeared in the entrance to the drawing room of the Royal Yacht *Britannia,* docked at Long Beach.

She stood up from the settee and went to Quinsam, touching his arms and squeezing them in welcome. She stepped back and admired his ceremonial-dress turnout, the traditional cherry serge tunic over yellow-striped blue breeches, polished riding boots and jack spurs, and the gleaming full Sam Browne harness with the white parachute-line lanyard running from the butt of his holstered revolver and up and around his collar. Above the corporal's rank chevrons on his right sleeve, the roughrider spurs badge signalled his term as a riding instructor at the RCMP Academy in Regina. A crossed-rifles badge and, above that, crossed revolvers, occupied the lower right sleeve. Above each weapons badge a miniature crown indicated he was a Distinguished Marksman. Higher on the sleeve sat two gold five-year service stars.

She claimed his tan Stetson from under his left arm and laid it on a small side table. She stepped back and completed her inspection.

She touched the chevrons. "*Corporal* Quinsam. How very dashing!"

"Thank you, ma'am," Quinsam said. He took in the royal blue Jersey wool skirt and sweater, the single strand of pearls and the discreet diamond-studded brooch in the shape of a rose.

"You look pretty good yourself."

She laughed, as did the Duke of Edinburgh who just then stepped into the room from the Royal Corridor.

He shook Quinsam's hand firmly. "Good to see you again, young fellow." He caught a look from the Queen. "I'll see you later. A noggin, I should think. Things to do." He turned and left.

The Queen rang a tiny, engraved silver bell. A Royal Marine steward entered with a tray carrying tea things and a plate of thin egg and water cress sandwiches. He put the tray on a mahogany coffee table and left. The Queen poured the tea and directed Quinsam to the settee, where she joined him.

"Well, Jim."

"Ma'am?"

"Time for a chat."

"Always a pleasure, Ma'am."

"Mrs. Grant."

"Oh, Mrs. Grant. Yes."

"I know you have the very best of intentions."

Quinsam moved to speak but she wagged a stern and regal finger. Miss Piggy.

"But it is not going to be."

"But, Your Majesty-"

"Not in my lifetime, Jim. Put it out of your mind. More tea?"

#

Quinsam nodded. "I've been to the yacht."

Dooley wondered if there was something to be read into the tone.

"Is it right, you have your own apartment aboard?"

"That's not for public information, either," Quinsam advised. Dooley noted that Quinsam's gaze had drifted across from the table they were occupying in the media centre, to the Mexican piece, Maria Sanchez, behind the desk.

"Definitely not," Dooley agreed.

"Good. You got all the information you need for tonight?"

Dooley waved the press itinerary, which listed the reception later at the 20th Century Fox studios.

"See you there, then," Quinsam said.

CHAPTER 12

Galiano Island

At first approach the cottage looked as it always did. Its white-painted cedar siding and age-silvered shake roof made suitable partners of the towering stands of hemlock and yellow cedar, clumps of alder, and the occasional ancient maple.

Maggie exclaimed, "Oh, it's beautiful!" as they reached the top of the rutted driveway behind the cottage. She was looking down over the roof and on into the bay and Cooper's home-built dock, with the Boston whaler bobbing comfortably against the tire buffers.

A black and white RCMP four-by-four was parked alongside the cottage. A young constable walked up the footpath towards them as they climbed out of the car.

"Pierre Dionne," he said, offering Cooper his hand. He pointed a thumb at the cottage.

"They gave you a pretty good going over. I done some dusting for prints." The young Quebecer shrugged. "But I would not 'old my breath."

He checked his wristwatch. "I got another call to make. If you like, I could drop back later and you can give me a list of what's missing?"

Cooper shook his head. "It's okay, Pierre. There wasn't anything really worth stealing. Just give me a case number for the damage insurance."

"You got it." He jotted on a slip of paper. "Well, I'll leave you to it. Good luck, eh?" and he shook hands with Cooper and a minute later waved as he pointed the Jeep down the driveway.

"Oh, Matt!"

Maggie Grant had climbed the four steps to the back porch. She looked down over the two-by-six weathered yellow cedar handrail. Her face was pained.

Cromwell bounded up the steps and darted into the house, where he was heard rushing around and whining fretfully.

The door was propped against the splintered jamb. The window beside the door had been smashed out, including the frame. Cooper had picked up the frame, of clear fir, from the demolition sight of an old family home in Vancouver's West End, when he and Sandi were still building the cottage. The frame was century old or more. It lay in splinters on the deck.

The constable had tacked the plywood back lightly in place after dusting for fingerprints, and the sheet came away easily when Cooper tugged it.

"Sons of bitches," he said, as Maggie took a sharp breath at the mess in front of them.

The strip of all-weather carpeting in the narrow lobby was puddled with ketchup and thick with scattered flour. Smashed beer bottles and two of Ballentine's lay in stains and pools of their contents. Two inexpensive framed prints, frontier pictures by Remington and Russell, had been ripped off the cedar panelling wall and lay in splinters of glass and fractured wood. Cooper had done all of the inside carpentry, finishing the walls in one-by-six tongue and groove yellow and red cedar. On the wall where the prints had hung, an ugly, splintered wound ran from one corner near the ceiling, diagonally to the opposite corner at the floor. Whoever had done it had used a one-inch wood chisel that Cooper remembered leaving out the last time he was here when he'd replaced a pane of window glass.

Cromwell ran around whining and snuffling, stopping occasionally to let go an angry bark. Maggie went down on one knee and the dog came to her and allowed itself to be comforted.

The worst damage was in the entrance lobby and in the kitchen, where every cupboard door was either ripped off and lying on the floor, or hanging from a twisted hinge. The marauders had tried to smash the sink but had succeeded only in chipping a dozen spots out of the maroon enamel finish. The refrigerator door hung by a hinge, and the stove was toppled, its burner rings twisted and scattered. Even the linoleum floor tiles had chunks chopped out of them.

"They're sick," Maggie said. She hugged herself, as though against an attack. Her voice was choked and her eyes brimmed. "How could they do that to somebody's home? What on earth is the matter with them?"

Cooper stepped over the mess and carefully down the three steps into the living room. Maggie followed him.

The vandals had completed their art criticism by slicing repeatedly into Sandi's painting of the otter mother and kitten. Cooper picked up the shredded canvas and touched it to his face. Maggie watched and said nothing. She thought it was as just well that those who had done this were not within Matt Cooper's reach at that moment.

Cooper sighed and put the painting down. He surveyed the room. The drapes were ripped from their rods. The contents of the wood box had been dumped in the middle of the once-beige carpet. Ashes from the wood burner were strewn wall to wall.

"Good job they didn't decide to have a fire," Cooper said. And after another look around, "On the other hand, maybe it would have been as well if they had. Christ, what a mess."

He stepped into the hallway off the living room that led to the two bedrooms. The hallway and the rooms were untouched.

"They didn't get this far. They must have been running late for the ferry," Cooper said, and the bleak humour drew a weak laugh from Maggie Grant.

She said, "It probably looks worse than it is. I think your friend Dale was right; once we get the mess cleaned up."

Cooper studied her.

"The internal optimist."

"What?" She laughed.

"That's Jack's version. Kovich. He has his own way with words." He scanned the damage. "All right, let's see what we need."

The telephone had survived the blitz. Cooper dialled a number and asked for Steve Black.

"Matt Cooper, Steve. Yeah, they sure as hell did. Well, as soon as you can. Right, I'll drop a list off at the lumberyard. See you."

Maggie anticipated him: "You go and do what you have to. I'll get started on this."

Cooper's first impulse was to tell her not to. It was something to do, he knew, with his not needing anyone's help, being perfectly capable, thank you. . . His mind formed the thought, but his tongue held it back as he watched the honest look of concern that shaped her face. She was hurt, for him, and she genuinely wanted to help.

He said, "Thanks, that would be great," and he enjoyed her smile of pleasure at his acceptance.

He went up the three steps from the living room. He turned. "I told you it wouldn't be much fun."

"Go get your stuff." She waved him away.

Cooper returned an hour later. The lobby carpeting was stacked outside by the back porch.

"That won't clean," Maggie said. Cooper agreed.

They worked steadily for two hours, and took a break. She had brought home-made scones and sliced ham. They ate out on the deck and washed the food down with a couple of warm beers the vandals had left in the broken fridge.

"What are you looking at?"

Cooper stared intently down into the bay.

"Otters." He told her of the kitten and the crab trap.

Maggie glanced at the ruined painting of the mother and kitten.

"The otters will come back. They'll give you a second chance. Everybody gets a second chance, Matt."

He glanced at her, then back to the ocean.

"You really believe that?"

"Hey, I'm the internal optimist, remember?"

Cooper laughed out loud and slapped the deck rail, and Cromwell looked up sharply, as at a new sound.

By late afternoon much of the mess was up off the floors. The drapes in the living room were back on the windows, and Cooper had a fire going in the wood burner. The house warmed quickly as he fed the fire with split chunks of dried maple and alder.

Cooper checked his watch. He frowned. The handyman, Steve Black, was supposed to have been here by now.

"What time's the ferry?" Maggie said.

"Ten to six. I've never known Steve work after five o' clock. It offends his principles. And he has a daily appointment with the dart board at the pub, he-"

Cooper stopped what he was saying. He shushed Maggie, and pointed to the picture window across the front wall of the living room. She stepped closer to him and looked out, across the broad sun deck and through the rails. A brindle white-tail doe stood at the top of the driveway. Her wide petal-shaped ears were pricked, her head was up, her damp nostrils flared. One hoof was lifted, suspended in air. She looked like a ballerina poised in mid-step. "Ohhh!" Maggie sighed. The doe turned and looked through the framework of the deck rails and seemed to stare directly at them.

Cromwell sniffed the air and wriggled.

"Look," Cooper said quietly. "Behind her."

He heard Maggie's soft intake of breath as twin dappled fawns on spindle legs followed their mother. They turned their heads, like curious children.

Maggie touched Cooper's arm and her fingers squeezed lightly.

"That's wonderful. That's beautiful."

The fawns' heads moved on their slender necks, the soft brown eyes searching.

Cooper and Maggie barely breathed.

Some distance away on a neighboring property suddenly a car door slammed, and two voices raised in a clatter of laughter.

The doe turned her head sharply toward the sound. She high-stepped up the path alongside the house and trotted under greening willow branches and into the bush. The fawns followed. The three of them melted into the shapes and shadows of cedar and alder saplings and tall ferns and nettles.

Maggie peered after them, straining to keep them in view.

"That's the prettiest thing I've ever seen."

"Isn't it, though? There's been a set of twins every year we've been here. The deer enjoy tulips. I don't know why they don't go for the daffodils, but they don't."

"Another of life's mysteries," Maggie said.

Cooper laughed, and she grinned at him.

Cooper checked his watch. It was after five.

"We're going to have to go. Goddam it anyway. Everything on island time as usual: if it doesn't get done today, there's always tomorrow, or maybe the week after next."

"But you can't just leave the door like that, or the window."

"I'll stick the plywood back up."

"No, for heaven's sake, that's why we came over, isn't it, to fix it?"

"Yes, but we have no choice now. Bloody Steve-"

"No, Matt! Like you said, if we leave it, it's just an invitation to whatever other creeps might come around. We've got it almost cleaned up. I just don't see the sense in leaving it now."

She had folded her arms and was facing him, with a determined face he was beginning to recognize.

"Well, what would you suggest?"

"We'll stay, of course. What else?"

"Stay?"

"Stay. You know, as in don't go back to Vancouver. Let the ferry sail without us. You've got two beds, haven't you?"

"Well, yes."

"Good, that settles that." Without waiting for a reply, she picked up a chair that still lay on its side and placed it firmly down on its feet. She started straightening the rest of the furniture.

"Doesn't it?" she said, while she worked.

Cooper raised his hands in surrender.

It took another three hours to get the cottage as close as it was going to be to normal without serious rehabilitation. Cooper re-hung the door and screwed a three-quarter-inch plywood patch over the window opening.

Maggie answered the phone when Steve Black called to say it was too late to do much today but that he could come up and have a quick look around, if Matt wanted.

Maggie told him that wouldn't be necessary but that Cooper would be happy to see him tomorrow.

"If that's all right with you?" she said, a little anxiously to Cooper, after she'd put the phone down.

Cooper was touched by her apprehension that she might have presumed, in giving the handyman his instructions.

"It's fine. And it'll give him something else to talk about at the pub." He smiled as Maggie blushed.

"In fact we could run down to the pub for supper. They do pretty good fish and chips, burgers. . ."

Maggie said, "I'd just as soon stay here. Do you have a can of anything to go with this?" She waggled a half-full packet of linguine that she had found in the back of a kitchen cupboard.

Cooper frowned. "No-wait a minute." His eyes lit up. "Do you like clams?"

"Only on days ending with a Y." She peered into the cupboards. "But I don't see any."

"Get your parka."

He took a flashlight and found a plastic pail and a garden fork in the outside storage shed. With Cooper taking Maggie's arm on the rough spots, and Cromwell charging about among their legs, they made their way down the driveway and along a narrow twisting path on the far side of the boat dock. They navigated through a black thickness of towering maple and hemlock trees whose interlocking boughs groaned ghostly complaints at unannounced gusts of wind that whipped in off the Strait of Georgia, and were as quickly gone. At each grinding of limbs, Maggie Grant gripped Cooper's arm a little more tightly.

Finally they climbed down a steep grassy bank into a short, narrow bay with strips of smooth pebbles and patches of sandy gravel underfoot.

Cooper picked his spot and Maggie held the flashlight. He dug soft-shell clams, turning the sand and gravel bed over with the garden fork. She pointed and shouted as the clams spurted, "There's one! There's one! God, they're everywhere!" and Cooper laughed aloud at her transparent delight.

They picked enough clams in just a few minutes to fill the pail and Maggie was laughing and out of breath when it was done.

She said, "That was marvelous! Would you believe I've never dug clams before?"

"I'd never have guessed."

She giggled, and punched him on the arm.

"Jack Kovich came digging one day," Cooper said, "He never got a single one."

"But they're everywhere!"

"Not for Jack. He said it was like looking for a needle in a hayfield."

Her laughter soared and was caught in a gust off the ocean and tossed into the night sky.

Cooper turned and climbed a short, steep staircase of rock. He reached back to take her hand as she followed him up on to the tip of the low headland that protected the bay and the clam beach.

They looked across the Strait of Georgia to the glittering night lights of metropolitan Vancouver. Behind the city and its suburbs, lights glowed and lent shape to the North Shore mountain ski runs. Cooper turned and pointed to the south. A British Columbia Ferry Service night-run to Swartz Bay for Victoria, windows ablaze, was sticking its bow into the mouth of Active Pass. A headland gradually erased the moving boat from their view, leaving just the shimmering black ocean under a white moon.

After a moment, she said, "Thank you. That was magic."

At the cottage Cooper dropped the pasta into boiling water. He spread the clams on a tray and placed them in the oven of the crudely righted and reconnected stove. He left them until the shells opened. With butter the wreckers had ignored, a spoonful of flour left in the dented flour canister, and the clam nectar, they improvised a sauce that both agreed was fit for a queen.

Maggie produced a carefully wrapped liter of California burgundy from her tote bag and they found two surviving cups with a cornflower pattern.

"That," said Cooper, washing down the last fat clam, "is about as good as supper gets. And the wine was pure inspiration." He raised his cup. "Thank you."

Maggie Grant's face was lightly flushed. She patted her cheeks.

"Red wine does that to me. And sometimes this." She got up and walked around the table. She leaned down and took his face in her hands and kissed him gently on the cheek. And then on the lips. And Cooper responded. Tentatively at first, and then firmly, and then, fired by the wine and by her warmth and her wanting, and his own, he pulled her to him. He shuddered in anticipation as she slipped a hand inside his shirt and touched his skin. His hands slid under the back of her sweater and under a cotton shirt and he touched the thin straps of her brassier and he undid the clasp and felt the light garment slip away from the weight of her breasts. His fingers discovered her hardening nipples. He slipped first the sweater over her head, then the shirt, while she undid the zipper on her own jeans and the one on his. Cooper flipped the light switch on the wall and they lowered each other gently to the carpet and made love in the flickering light from the wood-burning stove.

CHAPTER 13

Southern California.

The envelope had been left for Dooley at the hotel registration desk. The key inside it opened the Greyhound Bus depot locker that held the box with the Colt and six rounds of ammunition. Six rounds had always been more than enough. The gun was a twin to the one he had left in Vancouver as insurance, in the unlikely event that she got that far.

The crowd was a dozen deep at the entrance to the Twentieth Century Fox Studios. Dooley watched Quinsam step out of a black Cadillac into a clatter and flashing of camera shutters and lights, and an expectant clamor of applause.

"They love you, mate." Dooley was at Quinsam's side, his new press credentials hanging from a cord around his neck. "Oh, except that lot."

A group of four men and two women carrying placards pushed through the crowd. Their appearance drew mixed responses, from cynical cheers to isolated spatters of applause, to suggestions of, "Aw, piss off, why dontcha?"

The group's leader was a burly flame-haired man in his late forties with an untamed beard like a bundle of rusted steel wool. He barged to the front, wielding a sign lettered in bold emerald on a gleaming white background: "British Killers out of Ireland!"

Other signs climbed into the night around him, echoing the demand.

Dooley wondered for a second if those who had provided the weapon for him also had arranged the protest. Likely not, though. No one who knew Dooley would consider the need for outside assistance. No, more likely the group had emerged from one or another Sons of Erin lodge where shortly they would gather on their Patron's Saint's day to swill green beer and wail of the tragedy of Young Roddy McCorley and other hero-martyrs of a land that few of them had ever seen, and from whose conflict they were safely distant.

Nevertheless Dooley appreciated the distraction, which now held the attention of all security personnel. He slipped his right hand into the deep pocket of his jacket and felt the Colt's grip slide easily into his palm, snug against the fleshy pad below his thumb.

The protest's fiery leader aimed a finger at Quinsam.

"Colonial lackey!"

The crowd booed him. A partially full beer can bounced off his placard and showered him with suds.

Beside Dooley, Quinsam murmured, "Prick."

Dooley laughed. "Can I quote you?"

The protesters started a chant: "British Killers out of Ireland! British Killers out of Ireland!"

Dooley saw Quinsam checking his watch.

Quinsam caught Dooley's eye and Dooley winked and grinned at him. Quinsam nodded. Dooley watched the Mountie's hand brush against the leather belt holster that held a standard-issue Smith and Wesson .38 Police Special. The Mountie was focused on the protesters. Dooley was simply another--and trusted--media fly on the wall, as he had intended. Part of the tapestry.

Secret Service and FBI agents filtered into the crowd now, along with plainclothes police officers. They closed in on the placards, moving within reach of each protester as the political rhetoric continued.

The flame-haired leader shoved forward. He raised a battery-powered speaker. "We are here to protest the symbol of an oppressor state!"

"Go fuck yourself!" a tall black man in the middle of the crowd shouted, and his neighbors voiced approval.

"This Queen is the symbol. She is the oppressor! Brits out of Ireland! Brits out of Ireland!" Redhead ducked under the police line ropes with his amplifier.

Don't push it. Just stay there and keep their attention, you dumb fucker.

"She is the symbol! We are here to humiliate that symbol!"

"Not on my turf, asshole." A leather-jacketed sergeant of the Long Beach police department stepped past Dooley and past Quinsam and crossed the stretch of sidewalk between them and the protesters. He didn't stop when he reached the man with the amplifier. He walked into him and over him, as if he wasn't there. He slammed the man backwards over the ropes into three of his comrades, two of whom crashed to the ground under him.

The cop looked down at them. "Stay behind the barrier, please," he said evenly, and applause for his action drowned the fury of the disordered demonstrators.

Dooley removed his right hand from his khaki safari-jacket pocket. He wiped the sweat from his palm against his grey cord pants. He replaced his hand in his pocket and gripped the Colt.

The royal limousine slid to a stop and the crowd pressed closer to the ropes. Quinsam was at the door in two steps and had his body between the Queen and the placard wavers, as she stepped from the car.

Dooley was on the other side of the car, with a view of the top of her head.

"Thank you, Jim," Dooley heard her say. "It seems like a nice welcome."

"It is, Ma'am-for the most part."

She seemed to understood the qualification immediately.

"I see," and she turned deliberately towards the nearest section of cheering American faces.

Dooley had the back of her head in full view from about fifteen feet. He waited.

"Head shots are unreliable." The words of the genial IRA mentor-killer Danny McLaughlan flitted through Dooley's mind. "The head is a small target and it moves fast. You might get lucky and put one into the brain, the cerebellum. If you do, it's instant death. But a cough, a sneeze, a simple turn, and you've missed. Go for the body, for the heart. Hit that blood system, and they're dead within ten to twenty seconds. Especially with that," with a nod to the first Colt that Dooley had carried. That had been twenty five years ago. McLaughlan didn't instruct the lads anymore. Instead he haunted the Dublin working men's pubs, sipping draft Guinness and shots of Bushmills and lecturing fearlessly on how the movement had become nothing but a bunch of self-serving thugs and gangsters, and asking what had happened to the glory boys of the republic. McLaughlan had gone soft.

The Queen smiled broadly at the crowd and raised her hand in greeting, and a thunder of welcome filled the night.

Dooley moved to step around the car. A plainclothes cop put a straight arm up across his throat, suggesting he stay put. Quinsam saw the movement and he signaled to the cop that Dooley should be allowed to pass. He mimed the press pass around Dooley's neck, nodded that Dooley was approved. The cop reluctantly lowered his arm and Dooley advanced on Quinsam and the Queen. Not too quickly, nor too close. Only ten feet separated them now. The remaining security men had followed Quinsam's motions. They allowed Dooley to pass. He wanted one second with her in the open.

He got half of that as Quinsam turned during his ceaseless scanning of the crowd and exposed her momentarily to Dooley's full view.

Dooley's hand with the Colt started the journey up from the pocket, just as the red-haired mouthpiece rose up and bulled his way between two members of the security cordon. He drew his arm back and hurled his picket-mounted placard like a javelin towards the Queen.

The missile had barely left his hand before a Secret Service agent lunged and batted it off course. Dooley ducked instinctively and released his grip on the Colt as the thing flew at his face. The placard handle clipped him above the right eye and lanced the skin. Blood welled and ran down Dooley's nose and cheek and trickled into his thin beard.

"You fucker !" The leather-jacketed sergeant of the Long Beach police department seemed to be seriously regretting not having trespassed more comprehensively on the red-bearded protester's constitutional rights under the First Amendment, to say nothing of having not broken his leg. He grabbed the man, spun him, drove his wrists up by his shoulders, and cranked handcuffs on tight enough to draw blood, and a scream of pain.

"You fucker." He drove the man ahead of him, through avenues that opened speedily to ease their passage.

Ahead of Dooley, the Queen spoke to Quinsam. The Mountie nodded, turned and walked towards Dooley.

"You all right? She wanted me to check on you."

Dooley almost laughed.

"I'm okay." He dabbed his face with surgical gauze a uniformed police constable had handed him. "It's a scratch. Tell her thanks for asking."

Quinsam returned to the Queen. She listened, then she smiled at Dooley. Dooley nodded and returned the smile.

The Queen resumed her approach toward the studio's red-carpeted steps amid an increasingly rousing welcome from the people of southern California.

A security line had sprung up since the incident and no one, press pass or otherwise, was going to intrude into the sector they had cleared between the line and the Queen and Quinsam.

Dooley watched her as she walked, beaming, up the red-carpeted sidewalk. Her tiara sparkled in the lights from television cameras and flash units. She stopped three times to greet people at random in the crowd. She smiled as they offered her hands to shake, which she avoided without ever appearing to do so.

The lanky black man who had earlier corrected the protester called, "Hi, Queen, how you doin'?"

She stopped and peered into the crowd to locate the speaker. "Hello, how nice to see you!"

"You too, girl!" he shouted, and the people erupted in laughter and applause.

"She all right, baby!" the man concluded. "Mrs. Queen is all right!" The Queen smiled and waved then mounted the short flight of steps to the studio entrance and the beginning of the receiving line.

Dooley's moment was gone. Temporarily. Consider it a dress rehearsal for the next chance. There would be another. She made it easy.

Dooley accepted a ride back to his hotel with a reporter from the *Los Angeles Times*. As the car moved away he saw Maria Sanchez leave a cab and hurry up the red carpeted steps to the glass entrance doors, where a smiling Quinsam whisked her inside.

CHAPTER 14

Galiano Island.

Later they made love again in the queen-size bed where once he had loved Sandi, and Cooper felt no guilt.

"Second chance, Cooper," Maggie whispered, before she dropped off to sleep, nestling close to him.

Cooper lay awake for some time afterwards.

In the morning he tried to talk her into dropping the arrangement with Quinsam.

"It's crazy. And it's bloody dangerous."

She shook her head, no, as she walked across the living room to the picture window and looked out and down into the bay.

"It's not just that I've agreed, Matt. Although that itself should be enough. You have to be able to trust people's word, don't you?"

"Maggie- "

"I want to do it. For me. It's a very special thing, and it may sound odd, but also a kind of a debt, if you like."

She appeared to have thought it all through.

"Especially now, you see?"

Cooper didn't see, and didn't want to.

"A debt? I don't understand. You don't owe anybody anything on this. You were persuaded into doing it-"

"No, let me explain."

Cooper sighed. "Give me patience, Lord. But hurry."

She giggled.

"That's on a fridge magnet I bought for Sheena years ago." He opened his hands. "All right, let's hear it."

"Right. First, it was doing the performance, the impersonation, which got me back on my feet, back in the world. That, and Jesse. I was a mess. I was going nowhere but down. Getting involved in the show saved me. It put me back in circulation-" She paused, and stressed "-without doing which I would not have met you. If that counts for anything. I feel that if I walked away from this now, I would be jeopardizing all of that."

She hesitated. "Does that make sense?"

"No-o-o - but it does have a familiar sound to it. Let me see-ah, yes. Blackmail. That's the word."

"Matt!"

"But that part about meeting me-I like that bit. And yes, it does count for something, Maggie. It counts for a great deal."

She stepped close to him and kissed him softly on the mouth.

"Thank you. I'm happy to hear you say that."

Cooper returned the kiss, with interest, and took her hands in his. Her fingers were warm, soft.

"And that's even more reason for me to want you to reconsider."

He released her hands and touched her face.

"I like what you said about a second chance, Maggie. I like it a lot."

He worked through it again as he spoke, retrieving the thoughts that had kept him awake the previous night, distilling them into a single, simple proposal.

"When we get back to the city, there is nothing to stop me from walking in to 312 Main and signing out for the last time. I've got the years in for a decent pension."

He marched two steps to an imaginary desk. "Here's my badge, Inspector Kovich, Jack, sir, and here's my gun. I'm taking up with a woman in show business."

She laughed, a joyous sound.

Cooper didn't laugh.

She said, "You're serious, aren't you?"

"Never more so. I thought about it last night. It's one of those moments in life-you're in a situation and something, instinct, whatever, tells you, this is *it*, this is the thing to do, so grab it now, while you can, and run with it, because it might not be there again. And most times we don't. And the thought of, what if we had done, what if we had acted on that instinct? That thought is always there, always nudging you. *What if?* Lost opportunities. That doesn't have to happen this time, Maggie."

"Oh, Matt!" She reached up and pulled him against her. She kissed him. "I love what you're saying. And we will do it."

Cooper smiled and tilted her face up to him. "Now you're talking."

"After it's over."

"Maggie!"

She placed a finger on his mouth.

"Try to understand."

She kissed him again. "It'll be fine, you'll see."

CHAPTER 15

Vancouver.

Vancouver was wet, cold, and windy when Sheena Cooper arrived off a late flight from London. She stayed to check her schedule, talked nicely to the guy making it up, and came away with three more days to coincide with Paul's time off.

The house was dark when she parked her Toyota. The ancient gas furnace thumped into life as she brought the cold air in through the back door.

She emptied half a dozen miniatures of Scotch into the kitchen cupboard that passed for a liquor cabinet.

"You'll get done for that, you know," Cooper kept telling her. "And the fact that everybody does it will be no excuse." Then, "Still, as long as it's here-cheers."

There was a note on the pine table.

'Gone to Galiano this morning. Little problem at the cottage. See you later. Love. Dad.' And his version of hugs and kisses: XOXOXOX

The note was dated the day before.

Over the furnace sounds she heard a car door slam in the driveway. Footsteps on the back stairs and porch. The door banged open.

"Hi," Cooper said, and hugged her. "You had me worried. I phoned last night and you weren't here, so I phoned Air Canada and they explained you were grounded. London fog?"

"Right." She kissed him. "How was the ferry? We came in on some heavy winds a while back."

"It was rolling pretty good. They closed the cafeteria. Handed out barf bags."

"Nice," Sheena said.

He opened the liquor cupboard. "More loot."

She said, "You want a nightcap?"
"I do, but I'll make it a glass of wine."
"That's a change."
Cooper pulled a bottle of Gallo Burgundy from a fabric tote bag.
"A little variety, you know? You going to join me?"
"Sure. How about a snack? Cheese and tomatoes on toast?"
Cooper laughed as he took another wine glass down and carefully poured it three quarters full.
"Always your piece de resistance, sweetheart. Go for it."
He handed her the wineglass.
"Thanks."
She had studied him as they talked. With a small, quizzical smile, she said, "Ah, Dad?"
"What?"
"You sound like. . ."
"What?"
"Well, sorta-bubbly?"
"Bubbly, eh? Must be the wine."
"You just got off the ferry?"
"Yeah. Had to stay the night. It took longer than I expected. Some low IQs broke in. Beat the place up."
"Oh!"
"Nothing that couldn't be fixed. It'll be good as new. Steve Black's been up all day."
Cooper rolled the wine around his tongue.
"How was London anyway? Get to a show?"
"*The Mousetrap* again. I can't resist it . . .Dad?"
"What?"
"Did Mrs.Grant--Maggie--did she go to Galiano?"
Cooper rocked the glass and the wine lapped up and down the sides.
He looked at Sheena.
"Yes, as a matter of fact she did."
Sheena's smiled brightened the already well-lit kitchen.
"Good! That's *good*, dad."
She hugged him, and he held her tight.

"I think it is, sweetheart. I think it is."
His face was troubled.

CHAPTER 16

March 9 1983.
B.C. Place Stadium.
Vancouver.

Matt Cooper placed his hands flat against the front of the reporter's skinny chest, one broad palm on each side of the scratched-up 35mm Nikon dangling from the man's neck.

"I said, back, outside the barrier with the rest of them." He glanced at the press identification card hanging from a cord around Sean Dooley's neck. "Mr. Patterson."

"But I told you, I'm in the press pool."

The reporter pointed to where a group of reporters and photographers stood in a lightly cordoned area in the centre of the cavernous stadium's floor.

Cooper's strained smile suggested that he was rapidly approaching his tolerance limit for assholes.

"Yes, you did tell me that; several times. Unfortunately, I do not see a pool badge on you." The smile slipped away. "So unless you get back outside that barrier, and do it now, you will be not only *still* not in the pool, but you *will* be in very deep shit with me."

The reporter glared at Cooper, who was in casual plain clothes-black leather jacket, grey slacks, and loafers, with a police ID badge clipped to his open-neck black shirt pocket. In the man's glare, Cooper saw something, a flash, that made his skin tingle, made his inner senses scream a warning; something akin to the electric charge he felt when his Emergency Response Team smashed down a locked and barricaded door and he was first man in.

The reporter smiled. "I'm sorry. But really, if you find Corporal Quinsam, he'll tell you. I'm supposed to be in the reporting pool."

Your nerves are a mess, Cooper. You're seeing bogey-

men. This is just another pain-in-the-ass reporter. And he knows Quinsam.

Cooper acknowledged the reporter's diplomatic retreat. But he shook his head, no.

"Like I said, you don't have a pool badge."

Cooper was sick of reporters, sick of Quinsam, sick of the whole fucking operation. He turned his back on the reporter. He scanned the crowd that waited for the royal motorcade, then on its way to the stadium with the inflated mushroom roof, on the edge of False Creek.

Goddam Quinsam.

It was Quinsam who had suggested Cooper help handle the press at the stadium.

"The press? Fuck the press. I'm with Maggie, just like you said."

Quinsam smiled. "I like your new team attitude, Matt. But we can't put you in the car with her. We have to keep everything looking normal-"

He held up a hand to stem Cooper's protest. "I'm not giving you make-work. This will put you as close to Maggie as you need to be, in fact, right beside her if anything happens. But nothing's going to happen, and you'll have her back right after the ceremony. Okay?" And he pushed right on. "The ones with the blue badges are the reporters and photographers who drew the pool positions for today. They're the ones allowed closest to the guest platform. They share their stuff with the others later. During the ceremony, and until the cars have left, the others stay way back."

Quinsam had talked as if nothing unusual was happening. As if Kovich and Quinsam hadn't phoned Cooper and Maggie just after dawn and an hour later they had all met at Maggie's house, where she had coffee waiting. And fresh muffins. Like a goddam bridge party. And Quinsam had laid it out:

"The Queen's flat out, sick as a dog. Amanda French, the doctor, says its a repeat of whatever the bug was that she picked up in the Caribbean. Bad clam chowder or something. There's no way she's going to do the stadium. She's staggering between the bedroom and the john, hardly knows what day it is, according to French. The bug brings a flaming high fever. She's barely conscious half the time."

Cooper said, "But she has agreed to this? The Queen has actually agreed?"

Quinsam looked hard at him.

"I told you-she hardly knows what day it is."

"What you mean, then, is that she doesn't know about it, you're doing it on your own, you're putting Maggie up in her place-"

"It's all right, Matt." From Maggie.

Cooper started to protest, but she overrode him.

"I can do it. I'm *going* to do it, Matt."

Cooper glared at Quinsam. "You said you wouldn't dress her!"

"I said we wouldn't-unless we had to."

Cooper said, "Cancel the ceremony."

Quinsam said, "Nobody's going to let that happen. This is a live speech in front of thousands and it's going out on television to every damned country in the world."

"A speech about a fucking world's fair! A speech that could be made any time! Tape the fucking thing when she's back on her feet!"

He levelled a finger at Quinsam. "What you mean is, you know this asshole is out there and he has only a couple more days to show himself and you want him to because you want to be a fucking hero, isn't that right?"

Jack Kovich rose partway out of his chair but Quinsam waved him down. "It's okay, Jack."

He turned back to Cooper. "Matt, it's fireproof." He counted the order of events off on his fingers.

"She arrives in a limousine through the air-lock doors and drives across the stadium floor. There'll be thirty thousand people in the stands. Most of them will be school kids, Royal Canadian Legion members, and old ladies from the Monarchist League, waving Union Jacks. And half the Legionnaires will be undercover cops anyway. Anybody who looks like he might be our man will be visible a mile away."

He picked up a copy of that morning's *Express* from a side table.

"Here, read your buddy Dhillon. I don't know where he got it, but for once the press is almost right."

Cooper waved the offer away, so Quinsam read it for him: "'A tightly knit and highly organized security network is smoothing the way for the royal couple through the Vancouver portion of their tour.

" 'More than five hundred RCMP officers from surrounding detachments will bolster the hundreds of city police officers controlling today's motorcade route. Marksmen with binoculars will be on virtually every roof along the route. . .' "

Quinsam dropped the paper onto the table. "And he only knows about half of it. Like I said, It's fireproof."

Quinsam helped himself to more coffee and a muffin from the remainder of the dozen Maggie had prepared.

Cooper was silent for a moment. Then, "Wall to wall cops, right?"

Quinsam nodded, his mouth full.

"And the shooter has to get past just one of them. Shit."

Maggie moved closer to him on the sofa where they were sitting and reached out and held his hand and squeezed it.

Quinsam wiped his mouth, and laid the rest of it out: "So we're inside the stadium. Matt, you're with the media pool people by this time. She'll step out of the limousine, wave to the crowd, wait a few seconds to let them do their cheering thing, walk three paces to the platform steps, walk up them, ahead of Philip, and take a seat. Philip will take a seat beside her. The platform guests are all local politicians and assorted Masons. They have been security-vetted back to the day they were born." He poured more coffee, buttered another muffin. "These are *really* good, Maggie."

"Jesus Christ!" Cooper snapped.

Maggie squeezed his hand tighter and pressed her thigh against his. She had on a light silk housecoat and through it Cooper felt her firm, warm flesh against him. "It's all *right*,

Matt."

Quinsam grinned at them, and continued. "She will read her speech, inviting everybody in the world to Vancouver for the Expo fair in 1986, and that will be it. Into the limo, and back home."

He flicked crumbs from his hands onto a plate and licked his fingers clean. "The only other people who'll be anywhere near her will be those reporters and photographers who have drawn in to the pool. And although they believe they were picked by lottery, they were not. They were picked by me. I picked those that I figured are not quite the assholes that most of them are. They'll behave themselves."

"Bet on it," Cooper provided.

#

Dooley pressed the cop with the sergeant I.D. again, and got the same response: "You don't have a blue badge, you're not in the pool." And, as if to a half-wit: "Blue badge, *in*; no blue badge, *out*."

And that dangerous smile again.

Dooley seethed. He cast around the herd of reporters who hadn't made it into the pool. There was none he knew who could vouch for the fact Quinsam had made him a late entry into the pool after the cock-ups in California.

Cock-ups, in spades.

After the American-Irish rent-a-crowd clowns had fucked things up at the studio, everything had gone to shite. California had birthed hurricanes and gales that had sent everybody running for cover and denied him further chance of getting close. Schedules were cancelled and reporters scrambled for stories. A California policeman died when he walked into a helicopter's blades. A car carrying three Secret Service agents checking the route for a royal visit to Yosemite National Park hit a car from the Mariposa County sheriff's department. The three agents were killed and two sheriff's deputies badly injured. The Queen sent messages and flowers.

The disruptions seemed to sharpen the security people's already apparently advanced state of paranoia. Their net around the royal couple closed and stayed tight until the Queen and Philip finally were ushered aboard the *Britannia* and the yacht sailed for Canadian waters.

But California had served its purpose. Dooley had become part of the pattern, as he knew how to. His cover was accepted, as always. Announce yourself as a reporter, show a square of plastic with a photo, and people roll over.

Only once, after Warrenpoint, had he screwed up. It was the exhilaration of seeing a meticulously planned operation run perfectly right down to the last dead British soldier. There was a Land Rover and two four-tonners carrying Second Battalion paras. The Land Rover and the first lorry went by, and Dooley detonated the first bomb in the horse box in the lay-by. The blast demolished the rear four-tonner, confusing the troops in the first two vehicles, which skidded to a stop. The paras jumped out and ran to their dead and wounded. The first blast had killed about six. Then the British army did exactly what Dooley knew they would do, and which he had prepared for them doing- they blanketed the area with more troops and medics and helicopters. That's when the second bomb was triggered, hidden near the old lodge gates. Eighteen of them. And Mountbatten on the same day. Jackpot.

But Dooley had been too quickly on the death scene, with his notebook and pen, and not appearing nearly shocked enough by the carnage to please a captain of the Parachute Regiment's Second Battalion. The officer took Dooley by the throat and slammed him up against the ancient stone wall and started raging at him and demanding to know what the fuck he was doing there and who had fucking well tipped him and his fucking news organization to what was happening? The chunky nine-millimeter Browning semi-automatic pistol, thirteen rounds including one up the spout, in his white-knuckled fist, was drilled into Dooley's chest and Dooley thought, I'm a dead man. This raging lunatic in the maroon beret is going to dust the right man for the wrong reasons.

Dooley was saved by a reporter who had been riding with the Royal Marines 40 Commando. The reporter grabbed the berserk captain, while telling Dooley to get the hell out of there if he knew what was good for him. Dooley slid away. That night he slipped into a Catholic drinking club in Newry and secretly savored the celebrations that went on as they listened to the details of the killings on television and saw the blanketed corpses. He heard the mutterings about the killing of Mountbatten maybe being a step too many, the taking of an old soldier that some of the boyos had served with in the last war. And Dooley had dismissed them. No rules, no prisoners.

From Los Angeles, Dooley had played a modest role in helping to empty the plane's bar supplies on the trip to Vancouver, where Quinsam had promised him a spot in the pool at the stadium.

"Make up for that knock in the head you took," the Mountie laughed.

So, now what? Dooley thought, and he winced as the pain lanced through his gut. He was pouring sweat again, despite having doubled the Leretine dosage.

The stadium was the second-last public appearance she was scheduled to make. This, and a brief walkabout in downtown tomorrow and then a farewell statement at the Hotel Vancouver before she and Philip took the Queen's Flight back to London, leaving the *Britannia* to dead-head home.

There would be no London for Dooley.

It was Vancouver, or not at all.

He searched around for the Paki reporter, Dhillon. Dooley had got to know him in a session the night before at the Vancouver Press Club. He knew Dooley was supposed to be in the pool and could vouch for him. But Dhillon was in the pool, and he and the others with the blue badges were already established in a roped enclosure near the guest platform, a good thirty yards away.

Dooley could not antagonize the cop any further. The man was clearly pissed off and would be capable of tossing him out of the stadium altogether if Dooley pressed his luck.

He had to do something!

Relief filled him as he saw the tall red-coated figure of Quinsam appear at the far end of the stadium, near the door where the motorcade would enter.

"Quinsam!" His voice was immediately engulfed by the sounds of a cheering-rehearsal that rose from a crowd of school kids waving miniature Maple Leaf flags.

The other cop, Cooper, turned at Dooley's shout, and glared at him.

"Quinsam!" Yelling the name and leaning out over the barrier and waving his arms wildly. And grinning like an ape when the Mountie turned, searching for the source of the cry, then raised a hand in acknowledgment and started in Dooley's direction.

Dooley pointed towards the approaching Quinsam. "He'll tell you!" he yelled to Cooper.

Cooper turned his eyes toward Quinsam-just as Quinsam abruptly changed direction and strode to the side of the football-field area and looked up into the front row of seats above the stadium floor.

Cooper said, "He might-if he ever gets here."

And suddenly Cooper seemed to have more than Dooley on his mind. Cooper was focused on Quinsam, whose attention was turned to a plain-clothes officer up in the seats. The officer had one hand cupped to a receiver in his right ear. He nodded twice, then he leaned over the seat rails and spoke sharply to Quinsam.

Come on!

Quinsam checked a watch on his wrist. He turned and faced the doors where the cars would enter the stadium.

Come on! Jesus!

Quinsam waved a signal to a squad of uniformed city police officers in position by the entrance, then he turned and walked quickly towards Dooley.

Dooley saw Cooper send a sour look Quinsam's way, but the Mountie returned it with a smile and said, "Hey, Matt, lookin' good," before addressing Dooley.

"What're you doing here?"

"I thought you'd never ask. I didn't get the pool badge."

"You were supposed to. Who screwed that up?"

"I don't know. It couldn't have been Maria, though."

Quinsam laughed at the Irishman. It was hardly a secret that Maria Sanchez had continued to Vancouver with the royal tour, although her official duties had ended in southern California.

Quinsam briefly introduced Cooper to Dooley. "He's okay, Matt. He took a knock on the head down in California that might have turned him a bit funny, but he's harmless."

Cooper shrugged. "You're the boss." He turned away.

Quinsam hurried Dooley across the stadium floor to the press-pool enclosure and cleared him with the two male and two female plainclothes cops stationed there.

"Owe you one, Jim," Dooley told him, and Quinsam waved as he strode away.

Dooley worked his way to the front of the group, where he stationed himself between a television cameraman and a plump woman writer from the London tabloid *Daily Mirror*.

The Colt sat comfortably in his right hand pocket.

#

"As Queen of Canada, I would now like to extend to all peoples of the world an invitation from the people of Canada to visit the world exposition that will take place in Vancouver in 1986."

Squads of joyous classroom fugitives created waves with Maple Leaf flags, while islands of expatriate Brits flew billowing Union Jacks. The cheers from the crowd of more than thirty thousand crackled and echoed around the stadium.

When she'd arrived, the media bunch had remarked on how chipper the Queen looked today, smiling brilliantly and distributing the royal wave without the usual restraint. She'd been actually *waving*, waggling her wrists, as opposed to bending the white-gloved hand from side to side like a metronome. And the reporters noted a difference in Philip. He seemed unusually concerned. He hovered about her, watching, bending over her and whispering frequently.

"Usually gets on her wick, that does," the *Daily Mirror* woman noted. "He keeps that up, she'll be giving him a right earful."

But she didn't, Dooley noted. Instead, she seemed to listen closely to the Duke, and her response to the crowd lost some of its vigour.

"Not like her at all, that," the Londoner observed.

The Expo message was repeated in French and the media pool chuckled as Canada's other official language was greeted with a few boos but mostly a resounding indifference in the country's third largest city.

Dooley glanced at Quinsam, who stood nearby. The Mountie's eyes never stopped moving; shifting, roaming the crowd, recording.

Dooley's plan was set, and simple. On the side of the limousine facing the press pool, there were only two officers, one at each end of the vehicle. They ignored the two dozen reporters and photographers. Their attention was on the crowd opposite. The cop, Cooper, also was there. When the limousine had stopped, the Queen had acknowledged the news group with a smile that seemed to broaden as her eyes caught Cooper, who, Dooley noted, responded with the slightest inclination of his head. "Hello, hello," the *Mirror* woman murmured. "Maybe that's what's pissed the Duke off, eh? She's always liked the coppers."

Cooper turned his head and stared at the reporter, and she grinned broadly at him.

"Well, never know your luck, do you?" she said.

Dooley knew the arrival routine would be repeated in reverse after the ceremony. She and Philip would descend the steps from the platform, a cop would open the car door. Philip would step in and sit down, and she would wave to the crowd before joining him in the car. The city cop, Cooper, was on the far side of the limousine. The two officers closest to Dooley would concentrate on the crowd. Even when Dooley stepped forward across the low rope they were not going to be alarmed. They had all seen him being personally escorted by Quinsam. They would see him just as another journalist pushing his luck, his left hand busy with the camera around his neck. Dooley guessed that each one would wait at a moment for the other to act. And that would be all he would need.

Dooley calculated three quick steps, raising the Colt on the third step with the right foot slightly forward, into the stance, and shoot her as she stepped into the car, fully exposed. Two seconds, at most.

"Hey, you okay?"

It was Dhillon, the *Express* reporter.

"What?"

"I said are you okay? You were-you sounded a bit shaky."

Dooley realized his breathing had accelerated while he rehearsed his moves.

"No, I'm okay. Thanks. I think I'm getting the flu or something. Or I'm hung over again." He forced a knowing smile.

Dhillon nodded understandingly. "It was a piss-up all right. I thought I was gonna die when I woke up this morning."

"And then for a bit you were worried you might not, right?" Dooley finished for him, and Dhillon laughed.

Dhillons said, "You heading out right after the tour?"

Dooley shook his head. "No, I'll be staying around."

Dhillon said, "Here we go." He nodded to the platform where the speeches were over and the Royals were on their feet. He moved away from Dooley, seeking more shoulder room at the front of the crowd.

Dooley stepped with his left foot across the low rope containing the reporting pool. All eyes were on the platform. The glaring TV camera lights and the erratic chattering of the Nikon choir of the press photographers were at work on Dooley's behalf.

She was at the edge of the platform, smiling and waving enthusiastically at the sea of cheering faces.

The Duke bent down and whispered in her ear. She nodded and brought her hand down, but she kept the smile in place as the applause reached thunderous levels under the domed roof.

Dooley stepped completely over the rope and he was in position, and being ignored.

The Duke stepped down first from the edge of the platform to the first step. He turned with a hand held out, ready to assist her. She brushed his hand away and stepped down jauntily. A ripple of laughter joined the applause from the crowd.

Dooley clenched and unclenched his right hand around the grip on the Colt. His grip was relaxed but firm.

She looked down and lifted her skirt slightly as she stepped down to the second tread. The Duke stayed one step behind her and waited, somewhat stiffly, while she went ahead.

Dooley noted that Quinsam had moved in beside Cooper at the bottom of the steps. Quinsam spoke a few words to the cop, and they both smiled.

She stepped down onto the last stair and grinned at the pair of them.

"Sergeant Cooper," she said. "And Corporal Quinsam. How nice."

Dooley was close enough to hear the pleasantries. He saw Cooper suddenly glance over his shoulder and frown as he noticed Dooley outside of the cordoned area. His expression seemed to say, there's always one, and it would be you.

Dooley gave him an easy smile and a shrug, and watched as the cop shook his head and returned his attention to the Queen, who was now off the last stair and just three or four paces from the car.

A low buzzing sound rose from the audience above and slightly to Dooley's left. He ignored it and focused on her approach to the limousine.

He fastened his fingers snugly onto the Colt. It fit his grip like the handshake of an old friend.

She was one pace from the car. Dooley watched Quinsam and the city cop, Cooper, step apart from each other just far enough to let her slide through. She placed one foot on the running board.

Dooley's index finger slipped inside the guard and onto the trigger.

The buzzing in the crowd had increased and was joined by crackles of laughter and clatters of applause.

Dooley shut the sounds out. Sweat beaded on his scalp and trickled down onto his neck.

She stepped up onto the running board and turned to give one more wave. Her body was side-on to Dooley.

She began the shoulder turn that would bring her face on to him, and he braced to begin the step-off.

She turned, and the crowd noise burst from a buzz to a great shout of laughter and more applause, and Dooley took his first step forward.

His foot had barely touched the ground when a flash of colours, pinks and yellows, burst between him and the limousine. He stopped in his stride as a young girl whose dress was the flurry of pink, carrying an armful of daffodils, flashed past him and slipped between the two cops who had seen her shinnying down from the front row of stadium seats and had tried to head her off.

The girl jumped up and over the side of the limousine between Dooley and his target, and with a great flourish presented the flowers.

The security details fell over themselves like actors in a bad movie as they scrambled toward the limousine and the young intruder.

Cooper was the first into the car, and he stuck himself between the girl and the Queen.

Dooley weighed the situation. He could still get to the car. Everyone close to the vehicle was concentrating on the girl.

He took one more step towards the car, and from nowhere, Quinsam was in his face.

"What the *fuck* do you think you're doing?" the Mountie yelled at Dooley and the rest of the pool reporters, who were pushing after Dooley, following his lead.

Dooley raised his hands. "Hey, I just wanted a better shot." He tapped the Nikon round his neck.

The *Mirror* woman backed him up: "Course he did, didn't he? 'S what we all want, isn't it? I mean, this is *news*, Quinsam!"

Cooper was in control in the car, although the girl hadn't left the vehicle. In fact, Dooley saw, she was sitting beside the Queen, who had an arm wrapped around the kid and was talking quietly to her. The Duke of Edinburgh stood outside the car, shaking his head.

The *Mirror* woman laughed, "Ooo, look at the mug on old Phil. Now who's pissed off, eh?"

"All right, people, back to your pen, please. Thanks." Quinsam shooed them backwards, nodding and "yeah-yeah"-ing at their grumbles as they went. He glanced back to where the Duke was obeying Maggie's imperious hand signals and climbing into the limousine.

Dooley wondered why Quinsam suddenly was laughing.

The limousine was moving. The kid was parked on the seat between the royal couple. The Queen had kept an arm around the youngster and was talking to her. The delighted audience was in uproar. The Duke looked sternly ahead. The limousine's running boards now bore the weight of three hefty plainclothes RCMP security officers on each side.

The limousine stopped at the air-lock entrance. The Queen gave the young girl a hug and a kiss and a last few words as she guided her out of the car. The stadium door slid open and the child waved at the Queen as the car rolled away and headed back out onto the city streets.

Dooley's face was grim.

"And that, thank Christ, is just about that," Dhillon said beside him.

Dooley said, "There's still one more day."

Dhillon glanced up at the odd tone in the other's words. Then Dhillon took a crumpled copy of the tour itinerary from his pocket and examined it.

"Not much to that, though. The morning off, a quick stop at the aquarium, then the final farewell thing at the Hotel Vancouver."

He offered the paper to Dooley. It was titled "Activities for March 10."

Dooley smiled. Maybe that had been it all along. An anniversary to remember.

Dhillon said, "You on for the *Britannia?*"

Dooley said, "I'll be there."

CHAPTER 17

"The Duke was not amused," Maggie said.

They were in Maggie's living room, where a complete set of bookshelves was devoted to books about the Royal family, and pictures of the Queen in various poses covered the upper half of one wall. The fragrance of fresh-brewed coffee wafted from the kitchen. Cooper sat next to Maggie on a smooth-tweed covered sofa. Quinsam occupied an armchair opposite them.

Quinsam said. "I think the wave got to him. It was not a very queenly wave. It was all over the place."

"I was *excited*, I couldn't help it."

"Like you couldn't help letting the kid stay in the car." Quinsam laughed. "She would never have done that."

Maggie said, "No, I think you're wrong. I think she would have seen that little girl just the way I did. The kid had done something that she just couldn't resist, an impulse, and suddenly she realized she could be in a whole load of trouble. You didn't see the look on her face; I did. No, I think the Queen would have done exactly what I did." And with a grin, "Anyway, she did."

Cooper squeezed her hand. He was beginning to relax. They had run with Quinsam's lunatic plan and emerged from it intact, and now it was over, finished.

He had quizzed Quinsam on the Queen's health, after Maggie was spirited back home from the stadium.

"She's a lot better," Quinsam answered.

"How much better is a lot, Jim? Is she conscious? Is she walking? And talking? Does she have a pulse?"

"All of those things."

"And what did she say about today, the stadium?"

Quinsam frowned and wagged his slowly head from side to side. Then he described the one-sided conversation, the intense dressing-down the Queen had given him, and her conclusion.

"*'Don't even **think** of doing that again, Corporal. Remember-I must be seen to be believed. I **will** be seen!'*"

"The very ugliest drill sergeant I ever had was like a fucking dance teacher compared with her."

"Good," Cooper laughed. "You deserved it. And what did *you* say?"

"*I said, 'Yes, Ma'am, yes, Ma'am, three bags full Ma'am.'*"

"I wish I'd been there. That mean she's doing the *Britannia* thing tonight?"

"No question. And I can still get you an invite."

"No thanks. We'll be having an evening at home."

Maggie smiled and squeezed his hand.

Cooper said, "So this still leaves our man with a chance either tonight or tomorrow. Are they leaving on schedule?"

"Right after the deal at the Hotel Vancouver."

"He's leaving it late then, isn't he?"

"I wish I knew, Matt."

Cooper said, "At least Maggie's out of it now. That part's over."

Maggie discovered a stray thread on a cushion and she worried it loose and patted the cushion back into shape.

Quinsam got to his feet, tapping Cooper's arm as he passed him.

"You done good, Matt, thanks."

Cooper grunted.

"Thanks again," Quinsam said to Maggie, and he left.

Cooper waited until the door closed behind Quinsam's broad back.

He kissed Maggie on the lips.

"I really am glad that it's all over."

Maggie touched his cheek with her fingertips.

"Let's not talk about it now." She got up from the sofa. "I'm going to take a shower."

Cooper stood. "Let's conserve water."

CHAPTER 18

The *Britannia.*

The *Britannia's* expansive dining room writhed to the babble and body language of claques of politicians and their executive assistants, clutches of social pretenders, and the media feeders.

David Llewellyn, the British High Commissioner, stood in one corner talking to Dhillon's publisher, a squat, bearded man in his forties with a mesh of broken veins under the skin of his cheekbones, and restless eyes.

Dhillon said, "How did he get in? This is supposed to be for the working press. He wouldn't know a story if it bit him in the ass."

Beside him, Dooley laughed. "They're all alike when they reach t' big office, aren't they? Born to be pricks." Dhillon raised his glass to the thought.

Quinsam, prowling nearby, nodded a greeting.

The reporters predictably had staked a claim on one of the room's half dozen bartenders and were ensuring that the man earned his night's pay. Donald Parker, the reporter who had helped Dooley establish his bona fides in California, was doing his party-piece joke:

"Two southern ladies talking. Rich-bitch Mary Lou gloating about her husband's money to little Jenny-Lee:

"'Why fo' mah first anniversary, he bought me mah very first Mercedes.'

"And Jenny Lee says, 'Tha's naice, Mary Lou, tha's real naice.'

"'Fo' mah second anniversary, that old Billy Joe took me on a three-month cruise around the whole world."

"'Tha's naice, Mary Lou, tha's real naice,'" says Jenny Lee."

Parker gulped down half a glass of what the *Express*

food writer had said would be a Chancellor from a small winery in British Columbia's Okanagan Valley.

"'On mah fifth anniversay, that ol' boy bought me mah mansion on the he-yill!'

"And Jenny Lee goes, 'Oh, that is naice, Mary Lou, that is *so naiice!*'

"And then Mary Lou says to Jenny Lee, 'Jenny Lee, what that ol' Bobby Jim bah fo' you?'

"And Jenny Lee says, 'Why fo' *mah* first anniversary, Bobby Jim sent me to charm school.'

"'Charm school? What y'all go to charm school foah?' says Mary Lou.

"And Jenny Lee says, 'Well, befo' Ah went to charm school, I used t' always say, 'Ah, fuck you.' Now Ah say, 'Tha's naice, that is so *naiice.*'"

Laughter exploded from the group and continued, finally falling away as they realized the rest of the room had gone quiet.

The Queen was standing five feet from them.

They managed to look sheepish, a gang of naughty boys caught in the act.

"Don't worry, I'm married to a sailor; there's nothing I haven't heard before." She was smiling.

Smiling, though appearing very pale, Dooley thought. Looking ill, in fact. She seemed altogether frail, nothing like the woman who had tossed royal decorum to the winds earlier that day and given a young girl with her armful of flowers a moment she would never forget.

Dooley's guts tightened fractionally at the thought that she might be sickening for something. He almost laughed as, in a bizarre flash, he remembered the story of the three IRA volunteers who were waiting for Ian Paisley, the chief Protestant pig in Ulster. They were on an embankment above the road between Belfast and Carrickfergus, where Paisley was scheduled to deliver another Catholic-hating harangue. They carried Armalites, a Kalashnikov, assorted grenades, and five anti-tank rockets, and the road below was mined in three separate spots with a total of 600 pounds of fertilizer-based high explosives attached to a remote control device.

As the time for Paisley's scheduled arrival came and went, one of the lads looked at his watch and fretted, "Sure, an' I hope nothin's happened to the fucken' man."

Dooley harbored a similar sentiment as the Queen stepped up to them. She wore a gown of royal-blue velvet, with a sapphire chain and a sparkling diamond tiara.

She said, "Nice to see you having a good time. May I join you for a moment?" She walked into their centre. "You know I can't resist meeting my press people." She nodded to Dooley. "I remember you from California, of course. That nasty bump on the head. Did you come straight up from Los Angeles?"

Dooley said, "Yes, I did, Your Majesty." And he asked, "How was your weekend with President and Mrs. Reagan?"

"Very pleasant, though wet," she said. "I had to wear my Wellingtons the whole time."

If a tux could have comfortably hidden a Colt revolver, she would have been dead on her own grey carpet. It wouldn't. Dooley was attending the reception because to have not done so would have invited questions. Stay part of the tapestry. Don't change the pattern.

She looked even rougher this close up, beneath the artfully applied makeup.

She said to Dhillon, "I enjoyed the piece you wrote on our Corporal Quinsam. 'Her Majesty's Shadow' indeed," she chided, her eyes sparkling. "He's a very dear man, actually. We're very fond of him." She sighed. "Now I must go and say hello to the minister," nodding to the far side of the room where a glum-looking Canadian External Affairs Minister Charles Garrett nodded repeatedly and insincerely at a torrent of rhetoric pouring from the Premier of British Columbia.

She said, "What a pity Mr. Therrien suddenly had to remain in Ottawa." She sounded anything but sorry over the prime minister's last-minute change in schedule.

"Affairs of state, I understand. We'll just have to soldier

on without him," and she swept across the floor towards Garrett.

The reception lasted just less than an hour.

The Queen left the room hurriedly at one time, seeming a touch anxious, but returned within a few minutes. Twice during the reception she returned to the tight group and enjoyed some light chatter and each time, a half-glass of wine. By the end of the reception Dooley noted a natural colour was back in her cheeks and her eyes had brightened considerably.

Before they left the brilliantly-lit *Britannia*, the guests assembled on the Verandah Deck at the stern. In the chill night air, with the downtown lights of Vancouver to the right, and the competing display across the water in the North Shore municipalities, the Royal Marines band played the "Retreat", and the ship's flags were lowered.

Dooley joined his colleagues and the other guests in singing a stirring rendition of "God Save The Queen."

CHAPTER 19

**March 10, 1983
Ottawa.**

The Prime Minister said, "The whole thing has been a wild goose chase. That McGuire creature has made fools of the lot of you, though God knows what his point was. She's going home tomorrow, isn't she?"

Jacques Therrien's pique was aimed at RCMP Deputy Commissioner O'Connell, who said, "That's what the itinerary calls for sir, yes."

"So you can call off our Scarlet Pimpernel--'He seeks him here, he seeks him there.'--the Prime Minister mocked. "What was his name again?"

"You must mean Corporal Quinsam, sir," O'Connell said, striving to keep his tone neutral.

"Yes. Well, get the corporal back to doing some real police work, instead of chasing bloody leprechauns."

"Yes, sir."

And then O'Connell was not able to resist saying, "What a pity it was that you had to cancel the Vancouver trip, sir. It would have been an appropriate way to wrap up the tour. I'm sure the Queen would have-"

"Thank you, Mr. O'Connell. That will be all."

"Yes, sir." O'Connell turned and left the Prime Minister's office.

O'Connell was firmly of the opinion that the "critical state business" that had caused the Prime Minister to call off his long-planned trip to Vancouver to meet the Queen was inseparably linked to the Prime Minister's concern for his own skin. If there was going to be any shooting, Jacques Therrien was not going to be in the neighborhood. O'Connell walked across Parliament Hill and back to the computer room from where he had been ordered to attend the Prime Minister. He smiled at the transparent sophistry that seemed to come with high office.

At the computer screen, O'Connell frowned as he resumed studying the data that stared back at him. Something was wrong.

He had keyed into the program's options mode because someone had screwed around with the time format. Data was going in under the twelve-hour clock instead of the military and correct twenty-four-hour style. Goddamn civilian clerks who ran things by their wristwatches. He changed it back.

The options screen stared back at him.

Interpol had come up blank, so had the authorities in the U.K. They all now claimed to know *something* about Dooley, but only as the shadow-man McGuire had described. They knew there had been a main man on the Mountbatten assassination and the Warrenpoint paratrooper killings. But they had no suspects.

And that's only what we all know, O'Connell thought. It seemed that all they were doing was sending back to Ottawa, wrapped in their own peculiar jargons, the sketchy information he had sent them, and which initially McGuire had given *him*.

And the connection with the sister and the dead girl had brought nothing more. The sister had been checked into a psychiatric ward the day after the funeral and had walked out a week later. Nobody had heard of her since. The house stood empty. And none of the neighbours knew of anyone named Sean Dooley. Imagine that.

The British Army intelligence people in Belfast had shipped him the little they had connected with the girl's death; blow-ups of pictures taken at the funeral, where six Balaclava-masked IRA riflemen had fired parting shots over the youngster's grave. Perhaps one of them had been Dooley. Or was Dooley the priest who stood with his arm around the mother, her face frozen with grief as she stared at the small white coffin? The priest's face was down, hidden from the lens.

The headstone that would be set in place when the grave was filled, stood to one side. O'Connell squinted and read the inscription again.

Shannon McBride, beloved daughter of Patrick and Siobahn. Lighted our life on 10/3/69; taken from us 5/12/82. At rest with her loving father.

Died on a spring day in May.

No. That wasn't right. It had been December. McGuire had said so, and it was right there in the army reports; at dusk, late afternoon. . .

The options for style of DATE stared at him from the computer screen. MDY, or DMY. He checked the date on the note attached to the British Army intelligence report received three days ago. The date read 7/3/83. Seventh of March, 1983.

They always put the day first in the U.K.

Shannon McBride had died on December 5.

She had been born on March 10.

Today would have been her fourteenth birthday.

O'Connell looked at the clock on the wall. It was 1:30 p.m. In Vancouver it was 10:30. a.m. The Queen was due at the Hotel Vancouver for her farewell speech in about three hours.

O'Connell picked up the telephone receiver and punched a pre-programmed button.

"Get me Quinsam."

CHAPTER 20

March 10, 1983
Vancouver.

Cooper parked behind Maggie's black Honda Civic and chuckled at the ROYAL I vanity license plate. He whistled softly as he walked up the cement path to the white-painted porch railings and the glass-panelled front door.

He pushed the bell button next to the door and he grinned as he heard the first two bars of *Rule Britannia* ringing through the house. Since he had known Maggie the chimes had played *Bless This House*, but she had said yesterday it was sounding a bit pious and she was going to reset it. Cooper wouldn't have cared if it had played *Old MacDonald Had A Farm*.

He glanced about him, enjoying the appearance of Maggie's well-kept yard, and everything else about the day. Two mountain-ash trees displayed fresh green tips, and daffodils and yellow and white narcissus filled the strips of tilled soil bordering the lawn. It was going to be a warm and early spring. It was a time for new beginnings.

Quinsam's nonsense was over, thank God. What Quinsam and Maggie had got away with yesterday was outrageous. But they had got away with it, and the bad guy hadn't shown. With any luck the son of a bitch had crawled into a hole somewhere and died, like he was supposed to be doing. If indeed he had even existed, which Cooper was beginning to doubt.

The house was quiet.

He glanced back at the Toyota. Seeing Maggie's car in its usual place had confirmed his newfound--since yesterday and the stadium aftermath--sense of ease.

He stepped across the porch and peered in through the partly drawn front room drapes. The house was dark inside.

He pushed the bell button again and listened to the chimes ring out, then fade.

On the phone they had agreed on the time he would pick her up, and Cooper had happily reminded her that this was the first full day of the rest of their lives.

"You and me, Maggie. Second chance."

She had said, "You know, Cooper, I'm really getting to like you."

"I would hope so, after all the liberties you've been encouraging me to take with your person."

Maggie laughed. "Right, I recall having to twist your arm."

And she added, softly. "Yes, you and me. Second chance."

The phrase had become their pennant, their promise.

Today they were going to hit Chinatown for lunch before heading for the Hotel Vancouver and the Queen's farewell speech.

He rang the bell again.

Waited.

Silence.

Where the hell was she? They'd said noon. He checked his watch. It was exactly that now.

Maybe she was still in the shower. She sometimes lingered. Often long enough for him to join her.

He left the porch and walked along the cement path that stretched along the side of the house and which passed the frosted-glass bathroom window. He listened for the sound of running water.

Silence.

Maybe she had gone to the corner store.

He walked back down the path and out to the front gate and stared down the block to the Chinese grocery store. He watched three people enter and minutes later leave with small purchases. He turned and walked back to the porch.

She had not taken in the mail yet. An envelope was sticking half out of the oblong tin mailbox. He lifted the lid. There was just the one envelope. It was an obviously quickly scrawled message, to him.

"Matt. Had to see Quinsam. Love. Later." And three kisses.

Cooper's stomach rolled over.

He dropped the envelope and turned and sprinted down the path and was in his car and speeding towards the downtown core, barely aware of his actions. Where would they have taken her? He screeched into the turn on a red light at Alma and Broadway, oblivious to a transit system bus already halfway through the intersection. The bus braked sharply and skidded across the pedestrian crosswalk as he cut in front of it. He was deaf to the shouts of pedestrians and to a chorus of car horns blasted by angry drivers as he cut into the outside lane and rammed his foot down on the gas pedal of the unmarked police car. His mind was swarming, a turmoil of thoughts of what Quinsam was up to, and where Maggie might be. He remembered he was driving a car with equipment. He slapped the cherry onto the dash and hit the switches for the light and the sirens, and the traffic parted for him as he sped west, screaming, on Broadway.

#

Siobahn McBride murmured "Excuse me, thank you," repeatedly as she threaded her way through the crowds packing the Hornby Street sidewalk near the entrance to the Hotel Vancouver. People turned on her as she made her way through and past them, many of them ready with sharp words, only to soften them when they saw her and to allow her passage.

Siobahn affected a warm smile as she approached the two ceremonially-uniformed RCMP constables bracketing the revolving glass door which opened into the hotel lobby.

One of the constables stepped in front of her, also smiling, and planted himself squarely between her and the entrance.

"I'm afraid this is closed, miss. . . ah-" *what the hell do you call them-sisters? Mothers ?-* "Ah, you can't go in here without a pass, I'm afraid."

He indicated with his hand that she might like to carry on through the breezeway and out onto Burrard Street.

Siobahn held his eyes with hers. Her smile became one of girlish pleading.

"Officer, if I don't get to go in there, I will very likely have to *go* right where I'm standing."

The young constable's eyes widened and a blush climbed from the collar of his cherry-red tunic to his smooth polished cheeks.

Siobahn wriggled, visibly moving her legs closer together under her knee-length skirt.

Shit. The Mountie looked to his partner for help. His partner grinned at him.

"Officer?" A statement of dire need.

The Mountie groaned, quietly.

"I have to pee."

"Oh, Jeees. . ."

"Really, I *have* to. Right now. If you don't let me in there within the next very few seconds. . ."

"You'll get me shot." He stepped aside.

His partner pulled the door open for Siobahn and waved her in, laughing at the relief written across her face as she hurried through.

"God bless the both of you," she said.

The Mountie who had given way appealed to his partner. "What was I gonna do, check under her skirt, for Chrissakes?"

"Habits," his partner replied. "They call them habits."

#

Dooley looked up as two more plainclothes Mounties stepped past the glass doors into the lobby of the Hotel

Vancouver. That would make something like fifty police officers in the small area itself, half of them in uniform. His fingers brushed the comforting grip of the Colt in his right pocket.

The searching eyes of one of the two new policemen stopped when they reached Dooley. The cop examined him from across the lobby, taking in the slight frame, the thin, lined face, the wispy, greying beard and mustache. Dooley met the gaze, and casually looked away. The Mountie's eyes stayed on him, appraising, flicking to Dooley's media accreditation badge, and back to his face. Dooley brought his right hand from the coat pocket. He slid his left hand into the other pocket and removed a miniature tape recorder. He played with it, then talked into it. "Testing, one-two-three, testing." The Mountie watched him for a couple of seconds more, then dismissed him and scanned the rest of the media pack.

Dooley had not seen either of the two on the tour up to now, but their identical dapper haircuts and trim, authorized mustaches distinguished them as surely as if they had cantered in on horseback, dressed in red serge and waving bamboo lances at the head of the RCMP's Musical Ride.

A Seattle newspaper reporter had scoffed at Canadian security. "Ah, the Mounties are good enough guys and they mean well, you know, but they're not swift. Most days you could walk a bog-load of Paddies past them if you dressed them up right. They seem to think that if it walks like a duck and quacks like a duck, you can serve the fucker with orange sauce. They'll always check the kid with long hair and ignore the guy in the three-piece suit with the briefcase. Usually the bomb's in the briefcase."

The opinion had been offered across a table in the Vancouver Press Club. The American was drinking with Dooley and the two local reporters, one from the Canadian Press and Dhillon, from the gaudy local morning tabloid, The *Express*, which Dooley thought made an embarrassingly poor job of trying to emulate its Fleet Street models.

The *Express*--specifically, Dhillon--had hammered the

security angle all week, remarking on an unusual twitchiness among the police brass, and speculating on its cause. A story under Dhillon's byline, citing "sources close to Royal Visit security officials," reported the recent clandestine arrival at Vancouver airport of six members of the anti-terrorist squad of the British Army's elite 22nd Regiment of the Special Air Service. There was an official "no comment." The paper had also run colour pictures of what looked like pods of SCUBA divers in the downtown inner harbour of Victoria, the little-England capital city of British Columbia near the south end of Vancouver Island, where the Queen after her arrival from California had toured the provincial legislature. Those pictures were accompanied by other rather hazy ones of what appeared to be armed jump-suited figures on the rooflines of both the venerable Empress Hotel and the sprawling granite parliament buildings across the street. Something obviously was up, The *Express* editorial page noted, as the Queen and Prince Philip aboard the Royal Yacht had headed across the Georgia Strait to Vancouver. "Routine security," was the official response.

Not that it mattered, Dooley thought, as he glanced around the long room. Neither the SAS assassins nor all the Royal Canadian Mounted Police *and* their fucking horses would make any difference when the moment came. And that within minutes now.

The pain touched Dooley then, and his face paled as it flared and flickered, a hot blade deep in his bowels. He stopped breathing as it enclosed him for an excruciating moment, then he exhaled a shallow, ragged gust, as it receded. Sweat beaded and trickled on his scalp, and he wiped a sleeve across his brow. When had he taken the Leritine? Four hours ago? Five. He could do with some more. But forget it. Just hang on. Not long now. Then it wouldn't matter. No more Leritine; no more pain. Dooley had no doubt that he would go down with her.

His vision blurred and he shut his eyes tight. What was that quote from Johnson that the lads used to use before they blew up the next lot of Brits? Something about the knowledge of imminent death concentrating the mind.

He concentrated, made himself see once more the tiny white marker of grief in the lush green churchyard. He opened his eyes. His vision was clear again.

The two new Mounties examined the rest of the crush of reporters and photographers, stiffly acknowledged a couple of familiar faces, and positioned themselves in obliquely opposite corners of the lobby.

The media pool had stirred with their entrance, now its members settled back and resumed the waiting. They'd been given the drill by Quinsam at the daily red-eye news briefing, held in the lobby:

"You'll be able to follow her up to the convention room and you'll be there for the whole farewell speech. He had indicated the double doors that led out to the hotel's taxi and passenger drop-off zone.

"The Queen will come in there, and she'll leave the same way after the ceremony. Prince Philip is going to be staying to open the Amazon exhibit at the aquarium but he should be back in time for the speech."

The *Daily Mirror* writer cracked something about Philip usually finding other fish to fry anyway, and Quinsam waited tolerantly until the laughter stopped.

#

Siobahn took slow, deep breaths to calm her fluttering insides. Her flat black shoes made gentle scuffing sounds on the strip of red centred on the marble-tiled floor. She turned into the women's restroom and washed her hands at the sink until a young woman finished fussing with her makeup in front of one of the mirrors and finally left.

Siobahn checked that the stalls were empty. She entered the cubicle furthest from the door. It took her just seconds to slip out of the nun's habit, bundle the skirts and the rest of the clothing and stuff the bundle into the water tank atop the toilet. Under the habit, she wore the uniform of a hotel chambermaid. From her apron pocket she took a folded "out-of-order" sign, which she hung from the doorknob as she stepped from the cubicle and closed the door.

She started as the washroom door shot open and two young women burst in, laughing.

Siobahn smiled at them and indicated the notice. "That one won't flush," she said.

She walked over to the small broom closet and turned the doorknob. She had entered the hotel in the guise of two entirely different women on each of the past two days. Each time, the bucket had been in its same place just inside the closet door, along with its collection of brushes, dusters, polish and mops.

Siobahn had travelled to Vancouver after the California part of the tour had ended with no result. She had said her good-byes to Sean, sobbing as she did, and brushing away the tears and nodding as he told her, "Be brave, darlin', be strong."

She tugged on the doorknob.

The door stayed shut.

Siobahn's hands suddenly were slick with sweat. The gun in her apron pocket banged against her thigh. The door had a lock with a keyhole, but it had been open both the previous days. It *had* to be open.

She pulled again, and her hand slipped from the knob. Her heart thundered.

Sirens wailed. In the distance, but approaching. *Christ!*

Siobahn sobbed in frustration and near panic as she tried the knob again, and the door remained stubbornly shut.

"Here, lemme try."

The girl's eyes were overly bright and her breath was a light warm breeze scented with alcohol. She grabbed the door handle. She heaved, and the door flew open, sending her yelling back into her companion who shouted, laughing, "Oh, shit, Debbie!"

Siobahn sagged with relief. She reached into the closet and picked up the bucket filled with cleaning equipment.

She forced herself to be calm.

"Thank you. Thank you very much."

"Hey, no problem," the girl laughed. "You gonna see the Queen?"

Siobahn said, "Yes, I believe so."

She left the washroom. She slipped the gun from her apron pocket and placed it under a cluster of dusters at the bottom of her bucket.

A uniformed Vancouver city police sergeant watched Siobahn as she stepped out of the alcove of the washroom door. His alert, dark eyes above a bushy mustache and a sharp nose locked with her eyes. He frowned, and walked towards her.

Siobahn picked a soft cloth from the bucket and began touching up the brass doorknob.

She stepped back and admired her work. She turned and smiled at the sergeant.

"Has to be just right, doesn't it?"

The sergeant's examined her. Gradually his frown disappeared. He smiled. "I'm sure she'll appreciate it." He turned and retraced his route to the lobby.

Siobahn replaced the cloth in the bucket. She slung the bucket across her left forearm and followed the police sergeant.

#

Matt Cooper gripped the phone at the public safety building front desk and yelled into the mouthpiece at Jack Kovich. He listened, and sweat formed where his fist clamped the telephone.

Kovich had not been in the building when Cooper screamed up to the front steps and parked the car in the 'no parking anytime' zone in front of the building and left it with the motor still running.

The busty red-haired corporal had handed him a number

Kovich had left, for a mobile phone, and pointed him to the desk phone. She listened, intrigued, to Cooper's conversation, first with the Inspector, then with someone else. The essence was that both their characters were seriously flawed and they might like to go fuck themselves, and that Cooper was on his way to the Hotel Vancouver.

Cooper banged the phone down hard enough to crack the moulded mouthpiece and strode from the building. He shoved aside two skid-road drunks who were debating the risk level attached to theft of an unmarked police car that was ready to go. He jumped into the car and slammed the door shut. The car exploded away from the curb in a blast of burning, screeching rubber.

#

Maggie Grant said, "She talked to me as if we'd known each other for years." She was still finding it hard to believe that within the last few minutes she had sat and had tea with the Queen, and the Queen had poured.

#

"I've been looking forward to meeting you, Mrs. Grant – Maggie – is it all right if I call you Maggie?"

"Of course, ma-am." Maggie said.

"We live in interesting times."

Maggie nodded. Do we ever. She really was on the Royal Yacht Britannia, with the Queen, chatting over tea. Wait until she got to tell Cooper about this!

"Tell me about your policeman." As though the Queen had read her mind. "He must have been concerned — at the stadium, I mean."

Maggie nodded. 'Concerned' would cover it, she

thought. Pissed-off would really cover it.

"I have had words with Jim Quinsam. He's a dear man and his intentions are always for the best , but . . . let us just say"— and a suddenly severe look was fixed on Maggie — "there will not be a repeat performance."

"No," Maggie managed to say.

"Talking of performances, I've seen a tape of your one-woman show."

Maggie cringed inwardly.

"I liked this one:" The Queen recited: " ' lot of the, ah, boys at Buckingham Palace are, well, they're - ' "and someone in the audience shouts, " 'Pansies!'" – and then you say, "'Thank you.' Then you say, 'My mother phoned down to the kitchen one night--she'd already had a couple-- and said, 'I don't know what you lot of old queens are doing down there, but this old Queen up here would love another gin and tonic.'!"

Maggie said, "Yes, well, I read that - "

"I thought it was quite brilliant," The queen laughed as she spoke. "I would give it full marks."

"Oh . . ."

"And mummy will love it when I show her the tape. She's not at all as stuffy as some would have her be."

"Ah. . ."

"Anyway, as I was saying. There will be no repeat of the stadium antics. I have, once more, drummed into them that fact that *I must be seen to be believed*. No terrorist or threat will ever change that I *will* be seen.."

Maggie said, "Of course."

End of that discussion, she thought.

The Queen smiled. So. . . your policeman. . . Sergeant Cooper . . . and you. . . . tell me about you and him . . ."

Maggie told her.

The Queen nodded when Maggie had finished.

"And you both have come through those darker early days, " she said. "And he is good for you, obviously."

"The best," Maggie agreed.

"I'm given to understand that a good man is hard to

find."

Maggie nodded. "So I'm told."

"Philip actually is a good man." She smiled. "He has his ways, of course. . .but I suppose they all do, don't they?"

Maggie nodded again. This was the Queen, but it might well have been Jesse.

"It's a second chance for you. People deserve second chances."

"Yes! that is exactly how we both see it!. . . . A second chance."

The Queen poured more tea and they continued chatting.

#

"I can't believe she's taking it all so. . .calmly."

"She knows what has to be done, Maggie," Quinsam said. "She's going to do it right. She asked me if I was sure that you--we--are prepared. I assured her we are."

Quinsam had stopped pacing the floor of the suite in the select, small hotel situated halfway between the *Britannia's* moorage in Coal Harbour and the Hotel Vancouver. David Llewellyn and Jack Kovich sat in separate flower-pattern-covered armchairs, listening to Maggie's description of her meeting with Queen Elizabeth II.

"She told me details I'd never have dreamed of. Little things, signals that she has to let Philip or her staff know that she wants something--like go to the john; I hadn't thought of the Queen going to the john--or that she's bored silly with somebody and please get rid of them a.s.a.p.! I really think that I *do* know what it must be like to be her."

Llewellyn said. "She does nothing by halves."

Maggie had noticed a distinct change in the chain of command since the three of them had entered the suite. Llewellyn was in charge. Quinsam and Kovich deferred to him.

"And talking of doing things-" Llewellyn began, but was

interrupted by the muted ringing of the portable phone in Jack Kovich's pocket.

Kovich put the phone to his ear.

"Kovich." And he flinched at the sound of the voice on the other end.

"I want to know exactly where she is, Jack."

Kovich glanced at Maggie.

"I can't tell you that."

"I want to know where she is, Jack. Where *is* she!"

Kovich said nothing.

"You can't tell me, or you *won't* tell me?"

Kovich's mouth tightened. He gripped the phone.

"I can't, Matt-I won't, Jesus!" He waved the phone at Quinsam, looking for help, and the Mountie took the instrument from his hand.

"Matt. Jim Quinsam."

Quinsam listened, his head nodding and bobbing as though riding punches. All of them heard the angry, splintered sounds coming from the phone.

Finally, abruptly, Quinsam said, "No, I can't guarantee anything, Matt. All I can promise is to do everything we can to see that no harm comes to anybody."

He talked over the response, which was Cooper at his best, advising authority of its comprehensive shortcomings.

"Gotta go, Matt. Time's short. Gotta go, now." He pressed the button that muted the phone and he handed the instrument back to Jack Kovich.

Quinsam said, "He's steamed. No surprise there."

"*Damn*," Maggie groaned.

Llewellyn leaned towards her. "Maggie, it's not too late to change your mind. I repeat what I said earlier. If this thing goes to the conclusion that it obviously could-well, the consequences..."

Maggie shook her head.

"I'm not backing out now. I've played the part once, and I can do it again, if I have to. And better, after being with her this morning. And that was the point of the meeting, wasn't it?" She nodded to Quinsam. "Anyway, I'm confident that Jim will prevent anything terrible happening. And if it turns out that he can't, well, then, yes, we do know the consequences, and we'll have to—" she smiled--"live with them, won't we?"

None of the others shared her smile.

She said, "I'm worried about Matt. That's my biggest concern. We had plans."

Quinsam said, "You *have* plans, Maggie. Let's stay positive."

Jack Kovich added, "We'll take care of Cooper, Maggie."

Maggie looked at him.

He said, "We'll do all the right things, exactly as we've discussed them."

"Cross your heart, Jack?"

Kovich smiled. "Bet on it-in the highly unlikely case that it becomes necessary."

"The internal optimist," Maggie said.

David Llewellyn said, "Amen to that, Jack." Then, "The decision is made, then? We're all comfortable with it?"

"Maggie?" Quinsam said.

One last chance to walk away.

She stood up, adjusted her skirt and looked at them, steadily, each in turn.

"I'm ready."

#

Siobahn turned into a short corridor leading to the Hotel's main lobby. The place was thick with security; men and women, uniformed and otherwise. She moved slowly, studying every piece of brass and pane of glass for specks, and polishing as she progressed. She was two paces from the end of the corridor. Her view into the lobby entrance was blocked by several sets of broad shoulders.

Behind her a female voice called out, "You! Hey, with

the bucket!"

Siobahn swung around and her heart climbed into her throat as a lanky RCMP woman constable took three quick steps towards her. The policewoman grabbed her by the arms. Siobahn's bucket fell from her hand and clattered to the floor. A small brush, a yellow chamois duster, and a spray can of polish rolled out onto the tile floor.

At the policewoman's shout, one of the sets of broad shoulders in front of Siobahn had turned faster than the others. The owner of the shoulders, a plainclothes Vancouver city policeman was crouched, facing her in combat stance, a large black-barreled pistol aimed firmly at her mid section.

Siobahn called on every skill she had developed during eight years of repertory at the Abbey Theatre and in smaller houses in and around Dublin, where she had played everything from kitchen sink slut to the Maid of Orleans. She sagged in the policewoman's arms and flung her hands up, terrified of the gun pointed at her.

"What? What are you doing? What have I done?"

The woman Mountie eased her grip.

"All right, okay." She said. She waved off the plainclothes cop pointing the gun, "No problem. She's just a cleaner."

#

In the lobby, Dooley had started as a sudden shout went up and some kind of struggle erupted in a corridor off the far side of the lobby. The press corps surged towards the disruption. A photographer from the *Los Angeles Times* banged the London woman reporter on the chin with his camera and was told in fiery Cockney to fuck off and stay out of her way. She tore past him and then stopped and laughed, "Aw, shit!" as the source of the scuffle was exposed.

An RCMP woman constable had her hand on the arm of

an obviously scared hotel chambermaid. The clattering noise had been the young woman's bucket of utensils falling from her hands.

The pain hammered Dooley again then, savage and deep. The sudden distress on his face as he looked up was mirrored in that of the frightened young woman in the chambermaid's uniform as their eyes met briefly across the room.

#

Siobahn saw the policeman facing her with the gun relax. He shook his head, and grinned. He straightened up, and slid the pistol back into a holster on the back of his belt.

Siobahn saw Sean across the lobby; saw the alarm, and the pain, and the love. Saw him smile.

The cop who had drawn his gun walked up to her, concerned. "Are you all right, dear?"

"Yes." She forced a small laugh. "You just scared me a bit, you know?"

The cop said, "Had to make sure."

The woman Mountie was less forgiving. "That wasn't smart, wandering in here like that." She released her grip on Siobahn. "You could have got yourself hurt there, you know that?"

Siobahn allowed tears to well in her eyes, and she nodded her head, contrite.

"Yes, yes, I'm sorry," she stuttered. She wiped her face. "I'm really very sorry. I didn't mean to cause any trouble. I just wanted to be close enough. . ."

The policewoman finally found a smile. "All right; don't worry about it. Here, let me get your things." She reached down to pick up the bucket.

"I'll get it." Siobahn stepped forward

The policewoman easily kept her back with one hand. "It's okay." She bent down, picked up a hand-brush and a duster that had fallen out, and dropped them back into the bucket. The wooden back of the brush bounced off the small handgun lying beneath a duster, moving a fold of the duster and exposing an inch or so of the gun's barrel and the front sight. Siobahn stared at the weapon, paralyzed, unable to move or even breathe, all her stage skills suddenly abandoning her; an opening-night panic.

The policewoman had started to hand the bucket back to the cleaning woman. She hesitated, puzzled by the look on the maid's face, and followed the woman's stare.

"Constable!"

The policewoman's head jerked upwards at the command-note in the voice of the mustachioed city police sergeant. He was pointing at her, and from her to the lobby.

"Let's go, it's show-time. Forming ranks."

The policewoman frowned, hesitated, stared at Siobahn.

"Constable! Now, please!"

"Yeah, yeah," she muttered. She shoved the bucket to Siobahn. "There you go," she said. "Now stay back out of the way. Down the corridor there. Okay?"

"Yes." Siobahn's heart had re-started and her wits had returned. She took the bucket and retreated a few steps. She indicated a space between a wall and a marble pillar.

"Is it all right if I stand here? Just to see her, like?"

"That's fine. You can watch from there. But keep out of the way." She still seemed to sense that something was not quite right. but had no idea what.

Siobahn nodded timidly, grateful. "Thank you. I will. I promise." Little-girl act. Yes, Mummy. The policewoman rolled her eyes and turned away.

"You'll be a spectator, darlin'," Sean had said. "She's mine. This is going to be just in case the very worst happens. Insurance."

Siobahn slid her right hand into the bucket and under the duster and felt the sculpted wood grips on the Walther PPK.

Siobahn had never touched a handgun until three months ago, never wanted to. The men of her family had always been the republican soldiers, the women always the mourners. Until the British had taken her beloved Shannon. After the funeral, all she wanted to do was satisfy the relentless craving to pay them back.

A queen for her princess.

Sean had schooled her in the use of the .380 semi automatic with the snub 3.3-inch barrel. There was one round of the hollow point Winchester 80-grain Wintertips in the chamber now, seven more in the magazine. Sean said she was the best he'd ever taught, and that because of her need. She had de-cocked the gun after loading. She thought herself through the routine again: first round with a long, strong double action pull. Next fast ones at single action with less than half that pull. From thirty feet she consistently placed her shots inside a four-inch circle.

She leaned against the wall, breathing evenly, the bucket clasped in her left hand.

#

Dooley saw that Siobahn was back in control. His clenched gut relaxed and he took several slow deep breaths. He thought about Quinsam, who would be tight to the Queen. He wondered how fast the big Indian would be with the Smith and Wesson .38 Police Special in the stiff, awkward-looking holster with the fastened-down flap. Not fast enough.

One of the swing doors at the entrance suddenly banged open and Dooley was looking at Cooper, the Vancouver police sergeant from the stadium.

Cooper was in slacks and sports coat and his tie sagged at the neck of his open shirt. He talked earnestly to one of the RCMP VIP Security officers. The Mountie shrugged and Dooley heard, "All I know is that Quinsam's with the Queen."

Cooper turned sharply towards the doors and Dooley registered a spread of deep emotions on the sergeant's face. Rage, for sure.

What was happening now?

A uniformed Mountie constable stepped through the swing doors, searched around, and crooked a finger at two of the plainclothes men who had stayed in the middle of the news pack since they had gathered there an hour before. The royal party had arrived.

Dooley straightened as Quinsam's massive frame in its red serge tunic appeared at the doorway. Around Dooley a dozen camera motor-drives snickered and clicked, television lights flared, and elbows collided amid a soft jostling rush of protests and curses.

The double doors swung open and she entered.

#

Siobahn came upright against the wall as she heard the stirring in the lobby and the snickering of what Sean had told her the press mob called the Nikon choir. She squinted as the television lights bathed the walls and floor.

She saw the red serge uniform at the main doors, and watched as Queen Elizabeth II entered. The Queen was followed immediately by the Red Indian Mountie and a trail of plainclothes cops. Siobahn moved closer to the broad back of the policewoman. The woman constable turned. She warned Siobahn off with a look, then she returned her attention on the Queen's entrance.

#

The glow from the fluorescent ceiling lights caught the Queen's jaunty straw boater with the oversized blue velvet bow on the band and reflected its colours back at the television cameras.

Dooley thought the Queen's smile looked strained,

somehow distracted. She glanced over her shoulder at Quinsam, who nodded, as if reassuring her, Dooley thought.

"Something's bugging her," the *Mirror* reporter said. "Probably pissed off 'cos Philip's late again."

The Queen was very close now. For a fleeting moment, Dooley saw Shannon's shining black hair and radiant young face, and the cold white satin around it. He turned the picture off, and focused on the target. His eyes registered the three-strand necklace of smoky grey pearls and the matching ear rings, the diamond-studded spray brooch on her left lapel, and a vagrant speck of lipstick on an otherwise perfect smile. He automatically took in, and dismissed, the three plainclothes cops tucked in several paces behind her and to the side, as close as she'd permit them to be. Quinsam had inserted himself between them and her.

She smiled as she approached, nodding to the reporters who'd been on the royal tour for almost a month now. She smiled at Dooley, and an errant part of his mind reflected again how surprisingly small she was when you were this close up, and that she seemed to have lost the pallor she had worn the evening before. Probably had a good night's sleep. And he wondered at his mind entertaining the string of commonplace thoughts while he waited to kill her.

#

Siobahn watched Sean, watched his eyes balancing every move as the Queen walked towards him.

#

Her skin was flawless, and his mind started wondering how she kept it so smooth at her age. Like a young girl. A young girl with a gentle, laughing face. Dooley returned her smile, and his fingers curled around the neoprene grip.

#

Siobahn saw the Queen's smile of recognition. She saw the Indian Mountie scanning, scanning, everywhere, saw his eyes rest on Sean, saw the Mountie's eyes begin to widen, caught her breath as she watched his eyes suddenly flare with a realization, and blaze in disbelief.

#

Quinsam was three steps behind the Queen. In the moment that Dooley's finger closed on the Colt, the Mountie's head turned, tracking, in the way of his warrior ancestors. The smouldering eyes settled on the Irishman, cutting the distance between them to nothing, and suddenly blazed as they read the intent in Dooley's face.

Quinsam shouted, "You!"

The deep pain lanced Dooley at the same second, and the Indian was faster than Dooley had ever dreamed he could be. The .38 was out of the shiny brown police holster and its muzzle rising. Dooley brought the Colt up and squeezed the trigger once, twice. Quinsam sprang, shouting to distract. He threw himself past the suddenly still and terribly vulnerable royal figure. He smashed a hand upward against the Colt's five-inch barrel as it erupted in flame and thunder. Dooley muttered a quick prayer for Siobahn.

Quinsam fired as he moved and the shots from his .38 came between the two blasts from Dooley's Colt. The Mountie's slugs shattered bone and ripped through glistening tissue. Soft, pulsing organs exploded into a cataract of blood and a pink fog of flecks of matter. One of the deflected slugs from Dooley's Colt blasted a television camera lens into a storm of shimmering splinters. The other raised an agonized scream from one of the plainclothes Mounties as it took away half of his right ear and a scallop of bone from his temple.

Dooley crashed back against the wall. His revolver flew towards the now erupting media crowd. He toppled, sliding, sketching a ragged crimson trail down the wall's fresh semi-gloss latex cream finish. A pink froth bubbled from his mouth and he folded inelegantly and finally crumpled where the wall joined the fitted edges of the grey wool carpet.

#

In the flash-frozen instant that followed the shots, Quinsam registered Matt Cooper over by the swing door. Fear and rage were etched on Cooper's face as he crouched, his gun extended. And then relief, as he saw her standing unharmed.

Relief washed over Quinsam also as she turned to him. She was pale, but she was untouched.

He missed! Quinsam exulted. *The bastard missed!*

Quinsam stared at Dooley, who lay still against the blood-spattered grey carpet. The Irishman's remaining eye flickered and opened, and focused on the Mountie. Something hot and liquid squirmed deep in Quinsam's gut, because Dooley's dying Irish eye was smiling and his mostly shattered head was turning. . .

#

Siobahn saw the guns drawn and heard the thunder-blast of their detonations in the closed space. She saw a TV camera explode into a storm of particles. She saw parts of Sean's face and head fly away and she watched as he sagged against the wall and saw his blood leaving a ragged crimson brushstroke on the new paint.

She saw the Queen, unharmed, turn towards the Mountie. And she saw, for the last time, Sean's face; ghastly, dying and--incredibly--smiling. In one movement she dropped the bucket, brought the Walther up and fired, three times, past the RCMP woman constable. The policewoman spun around. Rage and belated comprehension twisted her features as she clawed her own weapon from its holster.

The last things that Siobahn McBride saw before her life ended was the policewoman's gun barrel aimed at her heart, and the Queen moving in a lurching turn towards Quinsam.

#

Quinsam saw sad surprise in the soft blue eyes, below the flat rim of the basket-weave boater, as the impact of the three slugs knocked her through the rest of her turn towards him.

A small red flower had appeared on the left breast of the primrose-yellow two-piece suit. As Quinsam reached out to her, one of the petals surprisingly drooped, slipping down her bosom and lengthening as it fell. Then it bloomed, a glistening scarlet blossom advancing across the sunshine-yellow jacket, towards her armpit, and down.

He saw her smile then, a small smile of resignation, before the pain hit her. She folded and slipped gently to the strip of new-laid royal red over the grey wool carpet, kneeling first as though briefly in prayer, then toppling over.

#

Matt Cooper was in Bedlam. Reporters and photographers battled to reach the crumpled form on the carpet.

Some police fought them back; others ran to the source of the shots.

Cooper exploded through the tangling mob.

"Maggie! Jesus! Maggie!"

He smashed a television cameraman out of the way, drove an elbow into a print reporter's ribs.

"Maggie!"

He saw blood pooling under the shoulders.

"Oh, God! Get out of my way! Get out of my fucking way!"

#

Quinsam saw Cooper hit the crowd, thrashing and hammering his way through, felling a TV cameraman, shouting Maggie's name.

He snapped at two plainclothes officers who had stayed tight beside him.

"Get Cooper. Get him out of here *now*!"

He swept a hand at security police ringing the lobby.

"Hold those reporters! Nobody leaves!"

The police closed ranks, a wall of blue uniforms and dark suits. A radio reporter barged through and was dropped by a vicious, fast chop to the neck. Other reporters who saw it yelled a protest, but none tried to follow his example.

Quinsam's two men slammed into Cooper, one on each side.

He fought them. "Get off! You sonsabitches, get off me!"

They forced him back, jamming one arm up his back until his fingers touched his collar.

They said nothing, just marched him, his feet barely touching the floor, past the surging media ranks and through a space that opened for them in the wall of security and as quickly closed behind them. Cooper managed to raise his head before they forced him out the doors. He stared over the yelling, surging mob, straight into Quinsam's eyes.

He had no need to shout. Quinsam could read the words.

"You bastard. You fucking bastard."

The two cops tightened their grip and walked him through the lobby and out of the hotel.

#

Dr. Amelia French kneeled by the still form, working desperately, as ambulance sirens wailed in the streets of Vancouver. The Queen's physician had been one of the first to reach her when she went down. Quinsam stood over the doctor. Blood had soaked into the red carpet, darkening it to a shade of Merlot.

The doctor straightened the arm that had bent under her as she fell. She turned and looked up at Quinsam, shaking her head, her face stricken.

"It's no use. She's dead."

CHAPTER 21

Quinsam stood at the top of a three-step rise in a lounge off the hotel lobby and repeated: "It's not the Queen."

The heat from TV camera lights bore in, raising sweat on his forehead and upper lip. He had removed his dress-uniform Stetson, which sat on the mahogany and brass bar next to him.

Yelled responses flew from an animated media crowd that had been corralled and directed into the lounge by an uncompromising body of police who were taking their orders exclusively from the Mountie corporal.

Darshan Dhillon flashed back to a night at the small theatre on Marine Drive, and muttered quietly, "Cooper, you asshole."

"Not the Queen? Not the *Queen*? How can it not be the Queen?" The *Mirror* woman. Angry, utterly disbelieving.

A *Los Angeles Times* writer called, "Who in hell is it then? What do you mean, it's not the Queen, for Chrissakes!"

And the rest joined in, screaming for answers.

Quinsam stared them down and waited. Eventually, grumbling, they subsided.

Quinsam said, "It's a woman who entertained people by impersonating the Queen." He shook his head and folded his arms as the shouting resumed. Again he waited until they stopped.

They had tasted blood and the only way to get the rest of the course was to shut up and let Quinsam talk. A few of them had covered Kennedy in Dallas. For the rest, it was the biggest story of their careers.

"I said she was acting queer, didn't I?" the *Mirror* woman said, with the true journalist's grasp of sudden and incisive hindsight. "I said she didn't look right. Remember?" This would be the lead on her sidebar column to go with the main news story. The *Mirror* would trumpet: "Our woman knew the truth!"

Quinsam said, "You'll get your chance in a minute. Right now, just let me have the floor. Can we agree on that?"

Their consent was a restless silence.

"The lady who was shot to death next door is. . .was. . ." Quinsam faltered, recovered, and continued. . .is named Margaret Grant. Maggie Grant. She is a stage actress who did a show in which she portrayed Queen Elizabeth."

"I saw the show! I saw her! Holy shit!"

"I don't fucking believe this-this is insane. . ."

"Why?" The call came from the middle of the pack, a San Francisco reporter. "What was she doing here?"

Dhillon muttered, "Cooper, you fucker."

Quinsam waited for quiet again.

"We knew since before the tour started that there was a high risk of an assassination attempt. We knew it was being planned by a member of the Irish Republican Army. It was a personal vendetta, apparently not sanctioned by the IRA itself."

Murmurs again, "Son of a bitch. . ."

"We had every reason to believe it would be a lone attacker, and that we could contain him."

"Well, you screwed that up!"

Quinsam glared at the speaker.

"We had no reason to suspect an accomplice." And he stressed, "The fact that the man lived among you for weeks, masquerading successfully as one of your number, is an indication of what we faced."

A few muttered a grudging assent.

"Did anyone here suspect him? Did anyone here have the faintest idea that he was not what he presented himself as-a working reporter?"

Heads shook, negative, around the room.

"It could have been any one of you."

Quinsam wiped sweat from his brow with the sleeve of his red serge tunic while they considered his last statement.

After a moment, Quinsam said, "I'll take questions, now."

He kept his replies brief.

"The Queen is on the *Britannia*."

"Yes, of course she has been advised. She is devastated, naturally."

"Yes, Mrs. Grant stood in for the Queen once before, at the stadium ceremony. The Queen was ill, and we took advantage of the situation."

"No, she did not stand in at the *Britannia* reception. That *was* the Queen."

Dhillon decided that would explain why the Queen had looked so vibrant and energetic at the stadium, and so pale on the yacht.

Dhillon asked how much they knew about the gunman and woman.

"We believe his real name is Sean Dooley, that he has a lengthy history as an IRA killer." Pens raced over the pages of notebooks. "We know that a woman accomplice fired the fatal shots. We suspect it could be Dooley's sister, but that will have to be confirmed."

He added, "As far as we know, it was a revenge killing for the accidental shooting death of Dooley's niece, the woman's daughter, in Ireland last year."

The Los Angeles reporter waved a hand, and Quinsam nodded to him.

"It seems to me that what you're saying is that you deliberately set this woman up?"

"I think that has been explained."

"Bullshit it has. You used her as bait and got her killed, right?"

Quinsam stared at him, said nothing.

The American said, "Remind me never to get you people pissed off at me. You make the CIA look like Mormons."

Quinsam answered questions for another three minutes, and ended the news conference.

"That's it for now." To the security cordon he said, "They can go."

Police officers moved aside as reporters raced to call their desk editors.

CHAPTER 22

The two Mountie hard men hustled Cooper out of the hotel and stuffed him into an unmarked car. The taller of the two sat in the back seat with Cooper, keeping Cooper's head forced down below window-level. His partner drove swiftly through back lanes and then the streets of Chinatown to a rear entrance of the Public Safety Building. An open elevator was manned by another expressionless suit with the standard bulge under the jacket and radio earplug in place. This one stood face to face with Cooper and blank as a statue as they rode up four floors. He put a quick and painful thumb-lock on Cooper and marched him to an empty office.

Two of the Mounties stayed with him. One occupied a chair by the locked door, the other flicked on a television set. Every channel was re-playing and updating the morning's events.

Cooper raged. "The bastards! I can't believe they did it. I can't believe it! Oh, God, the bastards!"

The two guards concentrated on the television. It showed her stopping, turning, then folding almost gracefully, and slipping to the carpet. The camera went to a close-up of the blood spreading across her primrose-coloured suit. The station ran the clips again, and again, with a reporter's voice over. He might as well have been doing hockey play-by-play:

"This is where Quinsam blasted the gunman. Watch as she turns. Who would guess that wasn't really the Queen? Huh? I mean, who would have *guessed* it? Now watch this; Quinsam sees something. His head starts turning. There! Boom! There it goes!"

Three sharp gunshots, followed by screams and shouts from the sound track.

Cooper closed his eye and tried to shut out the sounds,

and failed, and was drawn irresistibly back to the screen
"See there, now!"
The reporter's voice soared with the thrill of it all.
Cooper would have killed him without a qualm.
"First a kind of puff as the first shot hits her in the chest, then two more, bang! Bang! And right away the blood starts spreading across her chest almost to the armpit, and there she go-o-o-es, around, and dowwwwwn!"

Cooper put his head in his hands and tried to shut out the sound. The two cops' eyes stayed fixed on the screen.

The station went live to a news conference that combined the Prime Minister of Canada in Ottawa, and Quinsam and the British High Commissioner to Canada, David Llewellyn, in Vancouver.

The Prime Minister read from notes.

"The tragic events in Vancouver today are a reminder to all of us that in a decent world there are always decent people who will sacrifice themselves to preserve those things we hold most precious."

Cooper wanted to vomit.

"One of these people was Margaret Grant."

Margaret. Cooper had never thought of Maggie as a Margaret. It made her sound like someone else.

"Her selfless act cost her her life," the Prime Minister continued. "But it saved the life of another, a woman who is more than a head of state, more than just Queen Elizabeth the Second. A woman who is the embodiment of the Commonwealth of Nations, a body that stands for the highest ideals that the world's peoples can aspire to, and of which Canada is a proud and loyal member."

David Llewellyn studied his shoes.

"We would not see that struck down," the Prime Minister continued. "Margaret Grant would not see that struck down."

He said that both the Canadian and British governments fully supported the decisions and actions that had led to Maggie Grant's tragic, and heroic, death. He spoke solemnly and cryptically of dark forces that were abroad, forces that went far beyond the vicious, vengeance-driven goals of two terrorists who had met their just ends. He did not elaborate on who or where the dark forces might be, despite grumblings and repeated questions from the crush of reporters.

The Prime Minister endorsed Quinsam's actions.

"In making the decisions that he did, Corporal James Quinsam of the Royal Canadian Mounted Police lived up to the highest traditions and standards of our national force."

The *Los Angeles Times* reporter had had enough of the droning platitudes. He ignored the televised figure of the Prime Minister and addressed his question to David Llewellyn, who had now become the official British spokesman.

"Mr. Llewellyn, how does the Queen feel about this? What does she have to say about it? Is she going to talk to us."

The Queen, Llewellyn said, was distraught. And with this tragedy coming on the heels of a recent severe illness, on firm orders of the royal physician she was resting under strong sedation. And, by the way, the Queen does not give interviews.

Llewellyn then asked Quinsam if there was anything he would like to add to what had been said, and Quinsam stepped up to the microphone.

He said, "The Queen was persuaded by me, and very much against her will, that this was the correct choice of action. She accepted that the threat was against much more than her own person. It was always my responsibility, my clear mandate, as personal bodyguard to Her Majesty, to make the decisions, on a minute-to-minute basis, that would ensure her safety. I made the decision because I was convinced that the assassination attempt would be made today. We were confident that we could prevent what happened.

"Our confidence was misplaced, and the result has been the tragic death of a courageous woman."

He anticipated and answered the obvious next question before it could be asked.

"I would make the same decision again."

Cooper watched the news conference as though it were taking place on another planet, as words like duty and sacrifice and courage spilled out from Quinsam and the Prime Minister and Llewellyn. Platitudes, rationalizations. Why didn't they call it what it was? A travesty.

And the end of a brief, sweet, dream.

The news conference ended with the Prime Minister's statement that the Queen and the Duke of Edinburgh would attend the funeral planned for Margaret Grant in two days time, and that he, the Prime Minister, would drop all other matters and fly to Vancouver for the service.

The Mounties released Cooper in the early evening. The two who had taken him from the hotel escorted him to Kovich's office door.

"The corporal and the inspector would like to talk to you before you go."

They left him and marched away. As they rounded the end of the corridor and went from his sight, Cooper heard one of them say, "The poor fucker, though, eh?"

Cooper opened the door and stepped into Kovich's office. An image flashed in his mind, of six glossy photographs laid out on Jack Kovich's desk. He shook it away. His eyes went to the picture of the Queen high on the wall behind Jack's desk, then he was looking into Kovich's face.

Kovich sat behind the desk, seeming deliberately to have placed the piece of furniture between himself and Cooper. A defence. But there was no defence, never would be, for what these two had done.

Kovich's face was a study in apprehension and, Cooper recognized, sympathy. But it was too late for the old friend act.

He turned his look to Quinsam, who sat in a rail-backed wooden chair to the right of Kovich's desk.

Quinsam was out of his ceremonial dress, now slumped in jeans and a plaid sports shirt under a plain black blazer.

"Matt," Kovich began, and choked on the word.

Cooper remained silent. His hands made tight fists at his

sides.

"Matt, it was-" Kovich started again and Cooper cut him off..

"Murder."

"Matt-" Quinsam now, starting to rise from his chair.

Cooper stopped him with a raised hand, his shaking forefinger pointing like a wavering gun.

"You'll continue to call it what you want to, the pair of you. What it was, was murder. And you two," he covered them both in turn with the finger, "are as guilty as that bitch that pulled the trigger." Cooper's voice cracked and he wiped tears from his face.

Kovich had expected rage. This was worse.

"You murdered her."

Quinsam climbed to his feet. "You can't say that, Matt!"

Cooper took in a shuddering breath, let it go, struggled for control.

"You said you would keep her on the bench, you wouldn't dress her, she wouldn't be a player."

Cooper's tone now was almost a plea, Jack Kovich thought. Like a kid who'd caught his father in a lie for the first time. Kovich had never seen Cooper like this. He'd seen him in bad shape. He'd never seen him whipped.

Hang in, Matt, he silently begged.

Quinsam said, "I said we would keep her on the bench unless we had to use her. That's what I said. And we had to use her. She wasn't forced to do this, Matt. She wanted to. She was *going* to. You know that."

Cooper said, "We were going to have a second chance. 'Everybody should have a second chance, Cooper,' she said. Did you know that, Jack?"

Kovich dropped his gaze, stared at the top of his desk.

Cooper walked across to the window and looked down through the drizzle that fell on Main Street and the people hurrying along on the sidewalk.

"Everybody should get a second chance," he murmured.

Cooper turned from the window. He took a thin black leather case from his inside pocket and withdrew his chrome sergeant's badge with the Vancouver city coat of arms. He took out his city police force identification card. He crossed the room and placed the badge and the card on Kovich's desk.

Kovich said, "Matt, take some time, give it a chance."

Cooper said, "You already got my gun."

The two Mounties had disarmed him at the start and had not returned his weapon when they let him go.

Kovich nodded, his attention on the badge in front of him. For Christ's sake! He glared at Quinsam, who gave a brief shake of the head and stared him down.

"Yeah, we got that, Matt. But look-"

"'But' nothing, Jack. Nothing."

He turned and walked to the door. He opened it and left, closing the door quietly behind him.

Jack Kovich started up out of his chair. "Jim-"

"No. Leave it. Let him be."

"Jesus, man!"

"I said, *leave* it, Jack." Quinsam stared hard at Kovich.

Kovich subsided. "Right. You're right. Jesus, that was the toughest thing I have ever done, ever had to do. Honest to Christ. I mean who in hell would have thought that Matt and her would get together like that? I mean, we sure as hell didn't count on that, did we?"

"No, we didn't. But it wouldn't have made any difference, would it? What was going to happen was going to happen. Nothing could have stopped it. The Queen herself made the decision. That's all there is to it. Now we just have to go forward. Life goes on. We have no choice."

Kovich nodded a slow concurrence.

"And there was no other way to handle it with Matt, Jack. You played a blinder. I know it was tough, I know it has to be brutal for him. But the worst of it's over now."

He walked over and placed a hand on Kovich's bulky shoulder.

"He'll handle it, Jack. Matt Cooper always handles things in the crunch. You know that. He'll come through it."

Kovich sighed. "I hope you're right."

Don Hunter

CHAPTER 23

The report and pictures of the funeral covered The *Express* front page and the centre-spread, under Darshan Dhillon's by-line.

"Matt Cooper was among those who filed solemnly into the Church of the Holy Spirit for the service to pay respect to Margaret Grant. The former city police sergeant appeared still to be shaken by the three-day-old murder of the woman he had been assigned to protect during the Royal Visit."

Cooper ignored Kovich and Quinsam at the funeral. He stood, grey-faced and dour, with Jesse Lee, who gripped his arm throughout the service at the stone-built Anglican church two blocks from Maggie's house.

"Margaret Grant's daughter, flown in from England with her children in a Royal Air Force special flight, appeared to be overwhelmed as she watched six members of the Royal Canadian Mounted Police in ceremonial dress uniform carry the coffin up the flagstone path and into the church.
"At one point the Queen, veiled, and dressed in black, moved as if to go to comfort the young mother of two, but appeared to be dissuaded by Prince Philip, who placed an arm around her."

Cooper met Maggie's daughter briefly after the service, and had no idea what to say to her. Jesse Lee looked after her.

"The Duke of Edinburgh laid a tribute of rosebuds and daffodils among the small mountain of wreaths that

climbed up and around the simple coffin. Reporters noted that he was visibly touched by the moment, tears apparent in his eyes as he lingered by the coffin, speaking a few soft words. He wiped his eyes and returned with head bowed to his heavily guarded pew. It is not known whether the Duke ever met the dead woman.

"As the royal couple left the church, the Queen, closely attended by Prince Philip and the British High Commissioner to Canada, David Llewellyn, stopped beside Matt Cooper, and placed a consoling hand on his. It was a brief, touching moment amid a deeply moving event."

Cooper had felt her hand, warm on his, and vaguely had registered a glint of tears in the eyes behind the heavy veil. He had had to turn his face away.

"The royal party flew out of Vancouver yesterday afternoon and landed in London under the tightest security reporters there could recall.

"The *Britannia* left on the morning tide, its flags at half mast."

Cooper stopped at the liquor store on his way home.

CHAPTER 24

Galiano Island.

Cooper slumped on the bench seat, his elbows resting on the warped two-by-four surface of the rickety picnic table on the sun deck.

The noon sun warmed his arms where he had rolled up the paint-stained sleeves of an old grey denim work shirt. His jeans were unwashed, the laces on his work boots were untied. Somewhere was the list he had made of chores to be done.

Below the cottage the Boston whaler bobbed and rubbed against the dock as the tide slipped into the bay. On the other side of the dock the waves crept across the strip of sand beach and broke against the pebbles behind it.

The Strait of Georgia stretched flat and gray-green to the Lower Mainland of British Columbia. A tugboat plowed northward, followed dutifully by a blood-red barge loaded with a small mountain of wood chips.

A movement cut the surface of the bay about twenty feet out from the dock. Cooper watched the v-shaped ripple all the way in to the beach, where the otter touched bottom and scampered up the rocks to the dozen clams that Cooper had set out on the sandstone. Cooper had felt a peculiar sense of gratitude when he realized the otters were back in the bay; a sense of something regained. He picked up the coffee mug close to his hand and sipped.

He should finish sanding and filling the gouges on the interior wall panelling. That was on the list. And take the boat out of the water and scrape it. And paint the boat. He had been compiling the list since he got here two weeks ago.

Dale Mitchell had come by twice in that time. Cooper's former colleague on the force had stood in the kitchen doorway, taking in the condition of the table, the counters, and the sink piled high with pots and dishes.

"How about grabbing your clubs, Matt, play a few holes?"

"Not today, Dale," Cooper said.

His friend had tried again the two following days, with the same result.

On the third day, he shrugged and said, "Okay, Matt, you let me know when you're ready."

He had turned to leave, then spun back and pointed at one end of the counter.

"That's a lot of dead fucking soldiers, pal," he said, indicating the parade of empty bottles. He marched out and slammed the door of his pickup hard and roared down the driveway and out onto the bottom road.

For a second Cooper was tempted to get into the Plymouth and follow him, but the urge didn't last. Cooper was not interested in golf. He was not interested in much, except sitting, and sipping.

The deck rail needed re-staining, marked up as it was from last summer's wasps stripping it for shavings for their nests. He would put it on the list.

Once, the day he had arrived, he had turned on the ancient fourteen-inch television set for the news. The report was from a somber correspondent in London.

"The Queen arrived back in London today and was whisked immediately to Buckingham Palace. Royal physician Dr. Amelia French said it will be some time before Her Majesty is fully recovered from the shock of events in Vancouver.

"Meanwhile, Sinn Fein, the Political Wing of the IRA, issued a statement divorcing the IRA from the events in Vancouver and from any connection with Sean Dooley and the actual killer, the woman believed to have been Dooley's sister.

" 'The man Dooley acted on his own. He had no association with and no authority from the Irish Republican Army,' the statement said. 'It was a personal vendetta; the IRA does not countenance personal vendettas.' "

The correspondent talked over film that showed a glimpse of her in the back seat of a Rolls Royce. Cooper's throat had jammed as scenes from the last few weeks raced through his mind, tearing at him, driving him down. He switched the set off and turned away from the blank screen. He hadn't turned it on since.

Cooper sipped from the half-full mug. It was lukewarm. He screwed the top off the Ballentine's bottle and filled the mug almost to the brim.

He was aware that it was taking a little longer each day to get his head cleared and his system functioning, as it recovered from the previous day's booze. He drank to go to sleep at night, and woke far too early, parched and hurting, and each new day arrived before he was ready to meet it. He had tried, once, to do without the booze and had lain through the night with every nerve taut and humming, every thought a re-run of memories that thronged like wild things. He spent the next day in a haze of exhaustion, and booze.

He lifted the mug, swallowed, welcomed the familiar feeling of false well-being. The to-do list could wait. Fuck it, for now.

And fuck you, too, whoever you are, as a car turned into the driveway and made its way up the steep, rutted incline.

An old, well-kept Chevrolet that Cooper recognized, bounced into view and stopped. The driver's door swung open and Jack Kovich climbed out. Cooper turned his head away.

Kovich walked over and stopped and examined Cooper through the space between the sun deck rails that were above his face. He shook his head.

"You look like shit, Cooper."

Kovich climbed the steps up to the deck.

Jesus, the guy looks like a corpse. Dead eyes with rings around them like a fuckin' raccoon, pasty cheeks, and up closer, breath like an abandoned distillery. This whole thing was in danger of fucking Cooper up for good. Kovich worried that Quinsam's confidence might have been too optimistic when he said, "He'll handle it. . .he'll come through it."

The newspapers only had it half right. Somebody had tipped the media to the fact that Matt Cooper and Maggie Grant had been much more than protector and protected. They had splashed dramatic stories about the city cop who now seemed to have become a recluse. Not just the local press, either. The Americans and, especially, the British tabloids, had all sent reporters looking for Cooper, the tragic hero. One of the more adventurous sheets, using "sources who wished to remain anonymous," speculated that Cooper had considered suicide. Another said he had been admitted to a monastery.

A fuckin' de-tox centre would have been a better bet, Kovich thought now.

Cooper turned away from Kovich's pained scrutiny.

Kovich said, "You growin' a beard or what? You look like some kinda fuckin' hippie or somethin'. You look like shit."

Cooper turned his head. His dull eyes held a pinpoint of life.

"I heard you. Now fuck off."

Kovich grinned. "That's more like it. I thought for a minute there I'd have to check your pulse." He lifted a hand and showed Cooper a white envelope. "I brought somethin' for you."

Cooper looked at him dully. "I don't want anything from you, Jack. I don't need you here. I don't want you here."

"Matt-"

"Get in your car and go, Jack. Just fucking go, will you?"

Kovich swallowed. He wanted to grab Cooper, wanted desperately to comfort him. But Quinsam had said, "Just give him the letter and leave it."

"Right," Kovich said into Cooper's flat stare. "This," he tapped the envelope, "came from the Brits for you to the department. By government courier, personal, by hand. I think it's-I think the Brits want to help out, you know? Offer the olive tree, kinda?"

Cooper's snort of laughter was involuntary, and short-lived.

"The Brits. Yeah, they've brought me nothing but good times so far." He shook his head. "Tell them I don't need their help." He turned his face away again from Kovich.

Kovich sighed. "Right. I'll just leave it, then."

He placed the envelope on the table beside the coffee mug. The envelope was of thick cream-colored paper and on it embossed in maroon lettering the inscription, 'Buckingham Palace.'

"I think they wanna thank you, kinda," Kovich said, and he thought, right, asshole, that's all she wrote in your script. Now go, before your mouth takes over from your brain.

He touched Cooper on the shoulder, then he walked back across the deck to the top of the steps.

"So long, Matt. Hang in, eh?"

He thumped down the steps. He climbed into the Chevrolet and slammed the door shut. He started the motor, looked back once at his former partner, raised his hand, and turned the car down the driveway.

Cooper listened as the car turned out of the driveway onto the blacktop. The sound of the motor diminished and faded as Kovich found the main road back to the ferry terminal. He'd have a long wait for the next boat.

Cooper glanced at the envelope. He pushed it aside and pulled the liquor bottle closer.

CHAPTER 25

Galiano Island.

"What's in it?" Sheena Cooper asked.

Cooper said, "I don't know. And I don't care."

"That seems fairly clear."

She fought the mix of emotions--anger, pity, she wasn't sure which--that threatened to engulf her.

She looked around the cottage, at the mess in the kitchen; clothing, undershirts and socks left wherever Cooper had dropped them on the floor after he last changed them. The washing machine in the small basement had seen little recent service, she guessed.

This was no time for soft and sweet.

"The place stinks." She stopped short of adding that so did Cooper.

It was two days after Kovich's visit. Sheena had returned from a London and Paris trip that had lasted more than a week. Kovich had called her and warned her about Cooper, had told her of the envelope from Buckingham Palace.

"Get him to read it, if he hasn't."

Cooper had not read the letter. He hadn't opened it. Sheena found it under a scattering of magazines on a low coffee table. She opened it and read it.

"Dad, listen!"

"Sheena-"

"Just *listen*, will you?"

The letter was signed by Simon Shaw-Guilliard, private secretary to the Queen.

Sheena read, " '. . .deepest condolences on your personal grief in this terrible affair, and in acknowledgment of both your selfless behavior-' "

"For Christ's sake, Sheena!"

" '-and your outstanding career record as an officer of

the Vancouver City Police Department--' just hold on, will you, and listen--'it has long been a tradition to have a significant Commonwealth representation on the security and communications staff of the Royal Household. Her Majesty and Prince Philip would be most happy if you would accept. . .' "

She read the remaining paragraphs and said, "Dad, take it. Take their offer. Jack Kovich was right; it's exactly what you need."

Cooper had sagged back in the chair while she read, his eyes closed. Now when she finished, he sat up. He leaned forward and reached for the one-third full bottle of Scotch and said, "No."

Sheena grabbed the bottle and Cooper almost toppled out of the chair trying to retrieve it. She yanked it away from him and slammed it down on the table, out of his reach.

Cooper moved to get to his feet and Sheena pushed him back heavily into the chair, both hands against his chest. The move surprised her as much, it seemed, as it did Cooper.

"Look at you!" she cried. "Look at this place, for God's sake. It's a pig sty!"

Cooper followed her hand as she swept it around the room.

Filthy, crusted dishes on the table; clothing in crumpled small heaps; a cup on the carpet, upturned in a black ragged stain, cigarettes crushed in a saucer doing time as an ashtray. He had bought a pack, drunk, at the pub one night when plans to eat dinner there had dissolved in a river of draft lager and whisky chasers. He had come back and smoked three cigarettes in succession and then had vomited, mostly down his shirt and pants. He had not smoked another.

"My mother would never have put up with this."

"That's a low one, Sheena." He struggled to his feet, stumbled, almost fell.

"It's the truth! Christ, look at you! You're disgusting!"

Cooper's eyes widened. "Don't you dare talk to me like that! You can't-"

"Oh, yes I can! Oh yes, I *can*! Remember what you always told me, 'If you got something to say, sweetheart, stand up and say it'? Well, that's what I'm doing. Don't try to change the damn rules on me now just because it doesn't suit you!"

She clung to the anger. She fought off the urge to fold him into her arms and hug away the hurt, as he had so often done for her.

"Look at you-you're pathetic!"

The words hit Cooper like a flurry of sharp jabs and crosses. She held his gaze. Gradually his fighting stance wavered, then collapsed. He turned away.

Sheena yearned to throw her arms around him. And she knew that would be the worst thing she could do. He was already carrying enough self-pity to put him on his knees, if it were allowed to.

"My mother would have been sick at the sight of this. . . .this. . . garbage dump, is what it is. And so would Maggie Grant have been, dammit! They would both have been just disgusted!"

Cooper glared at her, started to protest, but she cut him off again.

"You know what-you know what? Two good women loved you. That's how lucky you were. Two very good women. And they would have been revolted to see you like this! Revolted! You hear me?"

Cooper stared at her. His lips trembled.

"They wouldn't have put up with this, Dad. Neither one of them."

Cooper turned his head, took in the room; the clutter, the mess. He swallowed. He moved his tongue across dried and cracked lips, and he shuddered.

"Dad?"

He nodded his head, slowly. His eyes turned to her. She saw tears, and shame.

"Jesus, sweetheart."

She went to him. She placed her arms around him and pulled him to her. She smelled the sourness of his unwashed body and the reek of the whisky. And she knew that none of that mattered now. She punched him in the shoulder.

"Hey, you always said they couldn't knock a Cooper down with a shotgun. We come from good stock. Quality folks. Remember?"

He nodded and the tears transferred from his cheek to hers and trickled down her face.

She pushed gently away from him.

"I love you, Dad."

Cooper's eyes brimmed. "I know. I know, sweetheart."

He hugged her. "Thanks. You know, you can be a real witch when you try-when you were a little kid your grandmother used to say you could start a fight in an empty room. You remind me of somebody."

They started cleaning up the cottage. Sheena began calling him the Commonwealth Rep, and by the end of the day they were back to where they had always been-father and daughter; friends.

Cooper would face his ghosts; would give the Buckingham Palace offer a try. Sheena would live in the Kitsilano house and rent out part of it. She knew plenty of girls at the airline who would jump at the chance to share the place and who would be glad to help look after Cromwell. And they would keep the Galiano cottage for now at least.

Two weeks later Cooper flew to London aboard an Air Canada flight where his daughter served him champagne in the first-class section. He was met at Heathrow by Simon Shaw-Guilliard and two days later he started his duties as a member of the communications and security staff at Buckingham Palace.

For the first month that he was in London, Cooper was pestered by reporters from the tabloids about his connection with the late Maggie Grant. When their baiting and speculations in print were ignored, and as other, more titillating business concerning the Royal Family began to surface, their interest in Cooper died.

Epilogue

Today

Vancouver International Airport.

"Just a coupla minutes," Quinsam said to the tall young man at his side who fidgeted in a white shirt and tie, black blazer and grey slacks in the flat heat of a British Columbia summer. He glanced up at Quinsam, a larger copy of himself.
"She invited me special, eh?"
"She sure did."
Beside them Quinsam's wife smiled at the pair.
Next to her Jack Kovich raised a hand, pointing.
"There. Right on schedule."
They followed his pointing finger and saw the approaching plane in the east against the mid-morning sun and the clear deep blue sky.
They were on a specially roped off area on the tarmac at Vancouver International Airport.
The *Express* had splashed a banner headline when the visit was announced by Buckingham Palace:
"Welcome Home Your Majesty!"
Dhillon had penned the headline, happily buying into the *Daily Mirror* claims of the pending abdication and Canada as her likely retirement place. Buckingham Palace had vaguely poo-poohed the reports, but there had been no firm denial. If it turned out there was nothing to it, Dhillon would run a righteous editorial trashing irresponsible British tabloid journalism.
The royal visit was to be for a week, on the heels of a state visit to Washington, D.C. The first two days would be spent "resting at the home of unidentified close personal friends." The media would as usual respect the request for privacy on that part of the visit.
Dhillon stood further along the receiving line. His invitation had been personally signed by Matt Cooper of the Buckingham Palace communications staff.

Jack Kovich had crooked a finger at Dhillon as they assembled for the receiving line a few minutes earlier. "Don't go asking her about that abdication stuff," he warned. "You're here as a guest, not as a fucken' journalist."

"Elegant, and eloquent, Jack," Dhillon had laughed.

Smoke puffed from the tires of the Air Canada Airbus 343 as the Queen's Flight touched down. The plane taxied to a stop. A crew wheeled a set of steps up to the door. Television and press cameras whirred and clicked in the media pen.

Quinsam looked over and winked at the familiar face he'd spotted earlier. Donald Parker.

"Same old, then, Jim?" Parker had said, after they'd shared a brief reunion, the first since 1983.

"More or less," Quinsam agreed. "Little quieter this time, we hope." And he asked, "How'd the book do?"

"Made a killing," Parker said, and immediately winced, and added, "Sorry."

Parker had been first on the bookshelves with a quick paperback after the Hotel Vancouver killings. He had collaborated with Dhillon, who was able to pack the pages with local detail and color. They had padded it mercilessly with background on the Haida Indian Mountie hero who had been given the official credit for saving the Queen's life. Parker had been the only one of the 1983 press crowd who had known Dooley. In the book he recounted how he had saved Dooley's life on the day that he, Parker, had been travelling with the Royal Marines when the two bombs went off at Warrenpoint, and that mad captain from the paras had looked like he was going to rip Dooley's heart out. He remarked on the two other times they'd met up at the scene of IRA bombings, and speculated on the coincidences. He did not dwell on his role in assisting Dooley in acquiring accreditation in 1983 in Long Beach. His book explained how World News Features was traced to a flat in the Worsley, area of Manchester, where Joseph Sheehy maintained that by providing accreditation he had simply been doing a favour for an old school friend who he understood was free-lance reporting, and he had no knowledge of Dooley's real activities. There was no evidence to the contrary.

The plane door opened. Jack Kovich said, "Huh?" as three teenagers wearing ripped jeans and stained tee shirts and with respectively neon-pink, purple and orange hair, stood on the top step and waved and bowed to the reception committee. Jack then recalled reading that a rock group named Duckheads was the high bidder for the block of twenty of the thirty-two seats in Executive Class not occupied by the Buckingham Palace contingent. A Buckingham Palace news release had described the seat auction as an economy move that would cover the full cost of flying the Royal Party to Vancouver, one of many austerity moves taken at the express order of the Queen in recent years.

The rockers and their herd of scruffy roadies were followed by the plane's 252 economy section passengers, all of whom had paid a premium for the privilege of sitting next door to the Royals. Many of the economy crowd turned and waved at the open Airbus door before boarding shuttle buses for the terminal.

Finally there was a glimpse of a tanned but clearly aging Duke of Edinburgh, dressed in a double-breasted grey three-piece suit. Then she was there, in a simple royal blue cotton suit with a diamond brooch and a single strand of pearls, and a typical floppy hat with the brim deliberately well back off the face as always to accommodate the photographers.

Quinsam said, "She looks marvelous."

"Stunning," said Sir David Llewellyn. Sir David had timed perfectly his calling of the annual general meeting in Vancouver of the British-controlled property development company that he served as chairman of the board. "Especially after what the family has put her through over the years. She held it all together. Remarkable woman."

A puff of wind lifted her hat as she reached the bottom step and she laughed as she grabbed it. The Duke of Edinburgh smiled down at her, and then they were at the head of the receiving line.

Cooper followed behind the Duke, acknowledging faces along the line of VIP guests.

Kovich grinned happily back at Cooper.

He'd never seen Matt look so good. Impeccable summer-weight tan suit with a blue cotton shirt and a subdued maroon and grey-striped tie, perfectly trimmed hair, for God's sake! And deeply tanned. That would be the week they'd had in the Caribbean before the Washington trip.

Dirty job, but somebody had to do it. Way to go, Matt.

She shook hands with the British Columbia premier. Then the mayor of Vancouver was introducing them.

"Former Chief Constable Jack Kovich."

Well done, Jack. Cooper was laughing to himself, remembering:

'*I can be the chief constable, Matt. Some of them could suck the shine off a brass door knob.*'

When she passed Kovich, Cooper grabbed Jack's hand and the two men hugged.

Cooper stepped past Kovich and ushered forward his daughter, Sheena Grainger, with her husband Rob and their late-teens twins, Sandra and Jack. The girl curtsied elegantly and her brother almost brought off a perfect bow before she reached out and embraced them.

Then it was Quinsam's turn.

"*Assistant Commissioner.* That's wonderful, Jim! We're so pleased." She turned to the Duke. "Aren't we Philip?"

"That calls for a noggin, later, Jim," the Duke said.

Quinsam said, "I'm very happy to introduce my wife, Maria, and my son, Matthew Sanchez Quinsam."

It had taken three years of bureaucratic obstacle-jumping to convince Canadian authorities that the then Maria Sanchez was unlikely to pose a terrorist threat and should be allowed into the country on a spousal sponsorship, whereupon she and Quinsam had tied the knot. Matt Quinsam had come along six years later.

Young Matt bowed to Her Royal Highness, who hugged him until he could barely breathe.

"Ma'am," Cooper said, moving on, "I would like to introduce one of the city's most prominent journalists, Darshan Dhillon. And his wife, Rajinder."

She shook both their hands and said how pleased she was to see them. "I've heard so much about you."

Cooper said, "Darshan has recently been appointed Executive Editor of the Vancouver *Express*."

Cooper waited until the entourage moved on.

"And how did that happen?"

Rajinder Dhillon said, "Both shoes dry," and the three of them shared a burst of laughter that caused the Duke of Edinburgh to glance back over his shoulder.

Dhillon said, "You're looking great, Matt. You thinking of coming home?"

"Thinking of it." Cooper moved to catch up with the others.

#

"But understand me now," she said. "I am finished with it. I have been on the throne long enough. We will return to London to put things in place, and then when the time is right, we will formally announce the abdication..."

She smiled across at Dhillon. "Rather we will confirm the decision, after it has been reported by Darshan, who has heard it from a Palace source." The Duke glared at Cooper.

On the porch glider the lumber billionaires puffed up like a pair of pouter pigeons as their mansion's walls recorded history in the making.

She sipped from her freshly filled glass. Jesse continued doing a sturdy bar service, Cooper acknowledged uneasily, keeping both the contestants well supplied. And still no white flag from Philip, who said, "But what about me? What will that look like, with you here, and-"

"That won't be a problem," she said. Just carry on with your Awards and wildlife missions. You're hardly ever at home any more anyway, so no one will notice the difference. And Jesse likes to travel."

The three women at the table shot collective looks at Jesse Lee and at the Duke, then stared at each other across the table with an unspoken, "Huh?" before returning their attention to the main speaker.

"The rest of it," she mused. "I can't help but wonder if the Irish situation would have worked out differently if we had made a different decision. Would David Llewellyn's predictions have come true? Ireland destroyed? American intervention? Or would the north and south have tried coming to terms sooner? If indeed they really have done. I suppose we'll never know, will we?"

Prince Philip said, "No, we never will know. But we made a decision at the time and we had to live with it. He nodded towards Quinsam. "Jim did the right thing."

Dhillon said, "What?" Quinsam just shook his head. *Jim didn't have much choice, he thought.*

The Spaniel wandered over to her. It wagged its stubby tail, brushing against her tanned legs. She leaned down and rubbed its ears, then she stretched out an open hand and said, "Give me four, Oliver."

The Spaniel dropped in front of her, head flat on its extended front feet, soft brown eyes fixed on her face.

"Good boy, Oliver." The dog wriggled with pleasure.

The Duke snorted. "Another bloody republican." He chuckled at his own wit.

She smiled to acknowledge the apparent cease-fire.

He said, "At least he's a damned sight more amenable than the corgis."

She agreed. "Vicious little sods." She held up a white-scarred thumb where one of the royal corgis in 1992 had almost removed part of the digit and the reports of it had provided three days of headlines.

"Yes, they were hard to handle for anyone else." The Duke's gazed drifted somewhere off to sea. He murmured, ". . . have to be . . . *will* be seen. . . "

Dhillon turned his head and stared at Quinsam.

"What?" Quinsam said.

Dhillon said, quietly, "What the hell is he talking about?"

"He's under the influence," Quinsam said. "In vino, you know?"

Now Cooper was wishing that *she* would let things die, but she emptied her wine glass and now turned the conversation to the young Royals.

"Apart from the Irish thing –I often wonder if the young people might not have worked out better, if we'd just left the situation to look after itself. Before Diana died, I always tried to help them, tried to give them what I thought was a good mother's advice. But they never listened. They didn't care a damn about the bigger picture; just out for themselves, all of them. The Royal Me generation. Very disappointing. People - I - had expected so much more from them." Her face was slightly flushed.

The Duke looked glum as he stared down into his glass, and she continued.

"I forget whether it was Sarah Ferguson or Diana who told me to, well, to 'just fuck off' over one or other of their rows or divorces. 'Just fuck off, *mother-in-law,*' she said. Can you believe that?"

The mansion couple's eyes glazed.

Rajinder Dhillon's bright eyes widened. She turned and stared at her husband and mouthed, incredulously, " 'Fuck off?' The Queen?"

A bemused Dhillon lifted his shoulders and spread his palms. What can I tell you?

The Duke laughed - a little too loudly for Cooper's comfort.

She sipped from her glass.

"But at least Sarah had the gumption to go out and find work when she needed to, and started to pay off her debts."

Oh, Christ, Cooper thought, this one.

"Which is more than I can say for a long list of other hangers-on I could mention."

The Duke said, "You *have* mentioned them. Often."

She ignored him, and continued.

"That's when Charles and Diana started going off the rails, too. And whatever I said, it was suggested that I just keep the palace going smoothly, as though I were some kind of housekeeper. Damned arrogance."

She said, "You know, I did try to mend fences with Diana. Paul Burrell was quite correct on that, about the letters I wrote her. I'm sure he still has them. I still wonder. . .I never found out what else Diana had told him-I mean, I couldn't come right out and ask him . . ." and she drifted into momentary thought.

And that's why you did what you did, Cooper thought, and he turned as he heard the timber wife say to her husband, "Oh, Paul Burrell! Wasn't that the butler. . .?" and left the rest unsaid as her husband shook his head and touched a cautionary finger to his lips.

#

The Paul Burrell situation had surfaced on their return from the Jubilee tour of Canada. Burrell, former butler to Princess Diana, and before that a footman for ten years at Buckingham Palace, was in the dock at the Old Bailey charged with stealing letters and other items belonging to Diana after her death.

She had told no-one what she intended to do, not even Cooper, with whom she always consulted-a practice which still infuriated the Duke of Edinburgh. She had told Prince Charles that she had remembered a meeting five years ago with Burrell in which Burrell had told her he had taken many items of Diana's for safekeeping after the young princess's death.

The announcement of the recollection came the day before Burrell was to have taken the stand for what would have been several days of detailed questioning under oath about his life in Diana's employ, "and God only knows what else," she had said to Cooper.

The announcement from the Palace destroyed the prosecution's case. All charges against Burrell were dropped, and all hell broke loose as the British press unsheathed its knives.

The *Daily Mirror* said, "Thanks, ma'am, But what took you so long?" (Within a couple of days the *Mirror* would experience an epic conversion of its attitude when Burrell accepted the paper's large cash offer to tell his version of life with Di.)

The Independent said, "This case could do more damage to the monarchy than any amount of adultery or tawdry tape recordings, not least because it reflects so poorly on the character of the monarch herself."

The *Guardian* believed "It is hard not to sense something wider and darker at work . . .The collapse of the case stinks of something worse than incompetence."

A Labour MP, Paul Flynn, accused the Queen of self-interest in overcoming a five-year memory lapse: "The most likely reason is that when Paul Burrell came to give evidence he was going to provide new information which would be extremely damaging to the Royal Family. This was the reason the trial was halted prematurely on this entirely unconvincing pretext."

Everywhere was the suspicion, the suggestion, that she had lied, that there was much more to be found skulking under the royal rugs.

The *Mirror* quoted her as having told Burrell during their meeting that there were "powers at work in this country about which we have no knowledge."

"I said nothing of the kind," she told Cooper and a sceptical Duke of Edinburgh. "Why on earth would I? Paul Burrell made it up, or the paper did, which would hardly be unusual if they did. They just came up with a catchy idea that happens to be closer to the facts than we'd like it to be. But they don't *know* anything."

The *Mirror* continued to like the conspiracy notion, speculating--now that the paper apparently was bent on sanctifying Burrell and thus justifying its outlay of what

Cooper had calculated was about $1 million Canadian for his story--"Was it the dark forces she spoke of who pressed on with Paul Burrell's case, ignoring the hugely damaging effect it might have on the monarchy?"

The palace was forced to announce an internal inquiry into her role in the Burrell case, to be conducted by Prince Charles' private secretary, Sir Michael Peat, who vowed there would be no whitewash. The Queen, he said, would not be one of those questioned. Everything that she had to say had already been said.

"Amen to that," she said.

The Burrell case was what had tipped the scales towards thoughts of abdication, Cooper knew.

He had asked her about her sudden recollection of the Burrell meeting after five years, and, uncharacteristically, she had dissembled.

"If I said it happened, and Paul Burrell confirmed that, why would anyone doubt it?"

"I just find it odd that *I* don't remember it," Cooper said.

"Matt, you forgot my last birthday," she said. He laughed and started to speak. She raised a hand.

"Matt, let it be. I will say only that I was--and am--never going to let her down, not after what she did, what she gave. We could not let that sad little man destroy what we have built.

Philip had just entered the room. He said, "But how much does he really know? He's telling his silly stories about her tripping to the door with no knickers on to greet her fancy men, but how much of the rest does he really know? We could just continue-"

"Good God, Philip!" She turned on him. "The whole point is that we don't *know* how much he knows-how much Diana told him of the situation before he came to work for us." She included both of them in a look. "But whatever he knows, I'm sure he won't be telling."

Philip's brow creased. His eyes narrowed. Philip in thought. A few seconds, and a light came on. "You say you're *sure*. My God, you paid him!"

She said nothing.

"You did have a meeting. But it wasn't five years before. It was right after we returned. The night before he was due on the stand. You met him, you arranged your stories, and you paid him--a damned sight more than that bloody *Daily Mirror* is giving him to "bare his soul"--as if the little swine had one. Didn't you?" Philip was smiling now.

Cooper cast his mind back to the days after they had landed from Canada, when Burrell, and what might be forthcoming from him, was dominating the news. For two consecutive evenings Cooper had been away from the Palace, earning his pay by entertaining--by way of extensive pub crawls--visiting officials from New Zealand and Australia respectively-Christ, but they could shift the beer. He had been back too late--and in no condition--to see her on both evenings. Anything could have happened.

If the Duke was right, he was enjoying it. He beamed, "Jolly well done, old girl! Good Lord, what an inspired thought. That should fix things, yes? We *can* carry on."

No thought of right or wrong there, Cooper thought. Any conspiracy that managed to keep Philip's job intact was a damn good conspiracy.

She shook her head as Philip rattled on. She looked tired, Cooper thought, more so than he had ever seen her to be. No wonder, the load she had carried.

"Philip," she said. "Let us suppose that in the Burrell fiasco, someone, somewhere, has been, shall we say, economical with the truth-"

"Ah-hah!"

She glanced at Cooper and murmured, "Give me patience, Lord. But hurry."

She continued, "If there has been some dissembling, it was necessary. I believe in what we did in the beginning, I believe in what we have done since."

"Yes, but -"

She waved him down. She turned to a coffee table and picked up a newspaper clipping.

"The Daily Mirror. Read it, please." She pushed it at the

Duke.

Philip said, "That rag, I -"

"Read it...please."

"For Christ's-"

"Read it!" She glared.

"Oh, hell." He took it and read it, aloud.

"'Without the Queen, the monarchy would be collapsing like a pack of cards. Her Majesty is the only member of the house of Windsor with a genuine claim to the love and loyalty of the people of Britain ...'hmmph." He glowered at her over the clipping, but he continued. "'Singlehandedly she has steered the Royal Family through a decade of scandal, intrigue, debauchery, moral bankruptcy and political chicanery.'"

He tossed the newsprint, which fluttered back onto the table. "Well? Your point is?"

"'Without the Queen', it says, Philip. I know that, you know that. *I* prevented that pack of cards from collapsing."

"Yes, but-"

"No 'buts', Philip."

He scowled.

"Philip!"

"All right, dammit!"

"Good. Now, I believe that having done all that, I have fully honoured the commitment I made. I have kept my promise to a good woman who paid the ultimate sacrifice for what she loved and believed in. I know she would understand and approve of my decision."

The Burrell meeting was history, along with everything else.

Philip had glared, turned, and marched away.

#

Philip had walked away then, but he still was not quitting at this stage, Cooper realised, when she tapped her refilled glass and continued. "I must say that I think we made some positive changes in recent years, things that will stand the test of time."

The Duke turned back, sputtering. "Like destroying the House of Lords? You and Mr. bloody Blair? No more hereditary peers? The end of titles that go back to the Middle Ages-"

"And some of those people on the red benches act as if they've been sitting there since then."

She looked over and smiled as Rajinder Dhillon smacked the table in front of her and bent over laughing.

"Now they can look for a job, if the concept doesn't kill them. Adapt, or die, Philip."

"And the income tax matter," Philip said, abandoning the old aristocracy to their alarmingly new and uncertain future. "You're decision that we should pay income tax! My God, do you know how much that's going to cost us?"

She smiled. "Well, I do now, since we agreed to open the books as well."

Philip bristled, but she held a hand up, and he subsided, grumbling to himself.

She continued, "I sincerely believe that those were the type of democratic gestures whose time had come. I think they have retrieved a lot of public support that was in danger of being lost. And The Firm can easily afford it."

The Duke sniffed. "And if it happens that we can't, then your other democratic gesture of turning the palace into a public spectacle should help, shouldn't it? Entrance fees, for heaven's sake!"

"Philip, the place was sitting empty half the year. Except for the staff, that is, and all they do is sit around filling their fat faces, and one half of them prodding the other half in the bum-"

Rajinder Dhillon lost it. She coughed up half the wine she had just taken in and spat it onto the tabletop in front of her. She let loose a shout of laugher that sent two bald eagles wickering and circling away from their nest in the top of a towering balsam behind the mansion. She smothered the sound as quickly as it had escaped, and the dialogue on the other side of the deck continued.

"-when they're not scavenging through waste paper baskets and listening at keyholes for whatever bits of gossip and lies they can sell to those pathetic press vultures - no offence, Darshan."

"None taken, Your Majesty," Dhillon replied.

She returned her attention to the Duke.

"My goodness, I would think you would be more grateful for a little show of Canadian free enterprise." She pointed a finger at Cooper. "It was actually Cooper's idea."

"I will be eternally grateful," the Duke said, lancing Cooper with a look.

Cooper wished she wouldn't, but Jesse Lee took Philip's glass and splashed in more gin. Some of it washed over the sides. Jesse ran a finger up the glass and licked off the surplus. She gave Cooper a sloppy smile.

Jesse had been interviewed some years back by Dhillon, after receiving her third of what would be many invitations, to spend time at Buckingham Palace.

"Obviously, she knew that I was close to Maggie," Jesse had told Dhillon.

"And what is the Queen really like as a person?" he'd asked.

"She's a good woman. She's the kind of woman anybody would want as a close friend. Very warm, very caring."

She told him how Maggie Grant's grandchildren and their mother, Maggie's daughter Michelle, had also become regular visitors from Chester to the palace and to Balmoral, where the Royal Family usually spent the summers.

Cooper watched Jesse hand the glass to Philip, saw her fingers linger on the back of his hand. Cooper had some time ago decided that Philip and Jesse had become more than just Commonwealth cousins during Jesse's frequent visits to London.

It seemed finally that the Duke had concluded that discreet withdrawal was his best move. He got to his feet, mustering dignity while a little unsteady, and walked, step by carefully measured step, to the edge of the terrace, where a flight of steps led down to the beach.

"Good job he ain't drivin'," Jack Kovich said in his best aside, which raised two ruffed grouse from salal bushes at the side of the terrace, and a threatening look from his much better half, Helen.

Clasping the wrought-iron support railing with one hand, his drink in the other, the Duke descended and on reaching the sand, stared out across the water.

He sipped on his drink, then turned and raised the glass toward Dhillon. "Thank you again, Mr. Dhillon. That was a nice thing that you did."

Dhillon said, "You're welcome, sir."

The *Express* had run an editorial applauding the actions of the Duke of Edinburgh after the Royal party's arrival in Vancouver. The Duke had gone, on his own and hours after a public ceremony had been held there, to the cemetery beside the old stone church, and placed a simple bunch of roses at the foot of the gravestone. The inscription on the stone said, "Margaret Grant. Always Remembered. Always Loved." The card with the roses was signed, simply, "Philip."

Dhillon had written the editorial, which described the Duke's actions as "those of a true gentleman."

The Duke was followed by Jesse, who carried the gin bottle and a small bucket of ice.

The Duke turned and peered up at them on the terrace.

. "She was quite an actress, wasn't she?"

She smiled. "As good as they come. She was a remarkable woman. An example to us all."

Philip nodded, and recited, "'All the world's a stage, and all the men and women merely players: They have their exits and their entrances. . . .'"

He raised his glass, then turned and headed along the beach.

Dhillon said, "What the hell does all that mean?" He appealed to Kovich, who gave the matter several seconds of brow-furrowing concentration before popping the top on another beer can. He said, "Guy reads a lot. Could be something outta Hamlet." He tipped the can skyward and poured half the contents down his throat. "Or maybe Shakespeare."

Dhillon looked to Quinsam, who shrugged.

Quinsam recalled that last morning of the tour, aboard the *Britannia*..

"Are we ready to leave for the hotel, Jim?"

"We're ready, Ma'am."

"And Mrs. Grant-is she prepared?"

"Fully, Ma'am."

"Of course she is. It's a role. A part. She knows about roles. Every day another performance." A brief pause. *"We have never avoided situations of this kind, Jim. We will never permit people such as this man to dissuade us from our duty, no matter the cost."*

"Yes, Ma'am."

"Wish us both luck, young man."

"I'll wish us all luck, Ma'am."

The Duke was right. Some performance.

On the deck, Cooper said, "So that's it. It's over."

"It is," she replied. It was time."

"And things worked out."

She nodded. "Of course. It was always going to work out. That day, when she and I talked, we agreed that people deserve a second chance. Everyone deserves a second chance."

Cooper's reply was lost in the rush of a wave over the sand below.

Jack Kovich nodded to Dhillon and Quinsam. "Let's hit the pub," he said. "They'll want to talk."

#

VANCOUVER(CP) - It was confirmed today that the Queen will abdicate and that her grandson Prince William will succeed her and become King William V.

In an unprecedented move, following earlier press reports, the Queen herself gave a brief personal interview to Darshan Dhillon, Executive Editor of the Vancouver *Express*. "My role is over," the Queen told Dhillon. "I have done my duty, as I know William will do his."

The Queen confirmed earlier speculation that her stay in Canada, the country she has visited more than any other, will be an extended one. Repeating what she has said on many previous Canadian visits, she declared, "It is very good to be home."

The Queen will be accompanied on a private tour of British Columbia's Gulf Islands by the Palace's Commonwealth Representative and former Vancouver police sergeant, Matt Cooper. Cooper, who has announced his retirement from the Palace post, has been a fixture at the Queen's side at home and abroad since he arrived at the Palace in 1983.

CPSIA information can be obtained at www.ICGtesting.com
Printed in the USA
241782LV00001B/4/P